DEATH OF THE DAWN

AMANDA V. KING

This book is a work of fiction. Names, characters, places,
and events are a work of the author's overwrought imagination or are used fictitiously. Any resemblance to actual persons, living or dead or undead, is entirely incidental and not intended by the author.

Cover Artwork by Grace Zhu

ISBN (hardback): 978-0-6453512-2-4

ISBN (paperback): 978-0-6453512-1-7

ISBN (ebook): 978-0-6453512-0-0

To all my sisters.

CHAPTER ONE

The evening sun shone through the chapel's crumbled roof, painting pictures of orange and gold on the trapdoor. I knelt and placed my ear to the wood, steeling myself for the scuffling of rats, but I need not have worried. The silence was nearly oppressive.

Curiosity pounded through me, a steady rhythm to my heartbeat. I'd pushed the veiled altar out of the way to reach a prayer book on the pulpit. I did not expect to find a hidden passageway beneath, nor for the Dawn Lord's statue atop the altar to tumble to the ground and shatter.

I was probably going to hell for that.

The trapdoor's latch was stiff, but the wood was brittle, and all it took was a couple of well-placed hits with the broken statue to cave in a hole at its base. An awful squeal rose from the hinges as I opened it, but what had me wincing was the stench—mildew and stagnancy. I covered my nose, trying not to gag.

Narrow stairs descended into darkness. I took them slowly, one by one, raising my candle in front of me. Perhaps I would find a torture chamber—or, if not a torture chamber, then at least a pile of bones and a blood-washed floor. That was what all the villagers' stories, hushed in nature and hesitant in kind, promised I'd find in the bowels of this long-abandoned, decrepit castle.

A perverse thrill ran through me as I reached the final step.

Before me were a dozen gravestones, each shrouded with varying degrees of moss and dirt. Shadows writhed against the stone fixtures as though in protest of having to share their domain with the light once more. Filmy webs threaded up the walls, linking across to several large pillars.

If the rumours were true, then this castle and all within it had remained untouched for nigh on a century.

Well. Untouched, until I'd broken in a year ago.

And here I'd thought the spoils of the day would consist of the usual antiquated trinket or semi-valuable set of spoons. A burial ground was a refreshing change.

I made my way past the gravestones to the very back of the crypt, where a looming structure waited.

The mausoleum stood tall and proud, the unfamiliar symbols engraved on its walls daring me to enter, to uncover its secrets. I hesitated at the door. The arch would have once been beautiful, but the wood had long since started to rot, and fissures of mould crept from the corners like black veins of disease.

Unease gnawed at me, the type unable to be explained and therefore easy to ignore.

I hope nobody's home, I thought and pushed open the door.

The air was stale. The room disappointingly sparse.

I frowned.

Wine bottles littered the ground, and a large wooden chest was nestled in the corner. Yards of velvet hung from the ceiling, moth-eaten drapes for windows that did not exist. My mood soured. If the material had been cared for—hadn't been exposed to humidity, hadn't been hung with decades of tension to pull it thin—then it would be worth fifty gold coins at least. Enough money to buy any ticket for any boat to any destination.

What a waste.

I turned, abandoning the velvet for the real curiosity. Raised on a dais in the centre of the room was a sarcophagus. Gruesome carvings were etched across its side—thick, gouging lines creating a picture of carnage: a woman hung from a tree by her neck while a boy at her feet was ravaged by some great beast. The forest surrounding them was on fire. A tale of this corpse's violent conquests, no doubt. Perhaps a touting nobleman, the once-lord of this castle, who wanted to revel in the pain of others even after death.

I stepped onto the dais to wipe the stone lid free of dust and said, "I bet you were the paranoid, eccentric type who bathed in the tears of small children and thought evil spirits lived in asparagus."

The dust flew up and tickled my nose, lodging itself in my sinuses. I coughed, hard and dry, the sound echoing through the chamber.

"Sorry," I said out of habit and leaned my hand on the edge of the sarcophagus. Pain bit into me, and I yelped, pulling away so fast I almost dropped the candle. A cut angled across my palm, deep enough for blood to well and ooze down my fingers.

I cursed.

This would take days to heal. Weeks, if I wasn't careful.

Blood ran down the sarcophagus, narrow trails blackening the stone. I knelt, turning my head this way and that. There was a thin blade of silver beneath the lip of the lid, spanning its four sides.

This nobleman. He'd made a trap against graverobbers.

"Just how important did you think you were?" I asked, the pain turning me irritable. I felt like fetching a mallet and chisel to crack the lid open, just to spite him.

My blue dress was worn, no stranger to a bit of blood, and I consoled myself with the fact as I ripped the hem, wrapping the fabric around my hand. The blood soaked through immediately, and I made a noise of annoyance.

Stepping off the dais so I wouldn't be tempted to kick the sarcophagus—it would hurt me far more than whoever was inside—I bent over to inspect a wine bottle.

A muffled scratching came from behind me.

Please, please, don't be rats.

I'd once opened a closet in one of the castle bedchambers, and a stampede of them had rushed over my feet, between my legs. Now I wanted to retch every time I so much as heard the scuffling of tiny claws. A moment passed, and the sound petered out.

I sighed in relief.

But then an almighty *bang* echoed through the room, and I shrieked, holding up the wine bottle in my injured hand, ready to smash it over anything that moved.

I swallowed and tried to sound brave. "Is someone there?"

Silence.

I didn't believe in ghosts, not the literal kind. Perhaps the mushrooms I'd eaten for lunch had been hallucinogenic? Hugo had been the one to forage for them, so it would hardly be a surprise. The hairs on the back of my neck prickled, and for a second, I seriously considered it. But too much time had elapsed, and I would have noticed the effects much sooner than now.

The scratching started again. I dropped the bottle and ran.

Out of that death house, past the gravestones, up the stairs—I didn't stop moving until the trapdoor was shut and hidden once more beneath the altar. One eye of the Dawn Lord stared up at me as I panted. Even laid out in pieces, he looked like he was smiling.

Laughing at me.

I stumbled to the only serviceable pew, tangles of ivy crunching beneath my feet. "If that was payback for breaking you," I said, leaning back against the wood, "let's call it even."

The wind filtered through the chapel's collapsed wall, soft as a lullaby, and I breathed in the clean air, the freshness of it. The last dregs of sunlight lit the shards of a broken stained-glass window, the bright and colourful pieces glinting throughout the ivy.

I looked at the darkening sky and squawked like a chicken before rushing out the chapel door and through the east wing to the servants' quarters.

I was running very late.

The Festival of Providence had only just begun as I stepped onto the main street—almost the only street—of the village of Myrtle Gully. The cloak of night had fallen across the land in the thirty-minute walk it took to wend through the ancient, seemingly endless forest that surrounded the castle. If I had looked over my shoulder an inordinate amount, I would never admit it.

The scratching, I'd decided, had been the rotten mausoleum door waving back and forth on its hinges. The bang had been said door hitting the outside wall. There was nothing else my imagination conjured that it could have been.

As I entered the village and saw the garlands of marigold and garlic on the eaves of each building, saw the Dawn Lord's cross nailed atop every humble wooden doorway, I relaxed. The anxiety squirming in my chest calmed.

Even if the villagers enjoyed telling tales of otherwise, it was a fact: nothing bad ever really happened in Myrtle

Gully.

I passed traders from Haycock, the northern town, who were putting the finishing touches on their wagons, smoothing out their dyed fabrics, straightening their displays of farming tools. I smiled discreetly, recognising most of them, and they smiled back. The village was small enough that everyone knew each other's business but large enough that, if cautious, one could keep a secret.

And I'd always been very cautious in my dealings with the traders.

Children played games of horseshoes and hopscotch, waving when they called out to me. Their excited squeals faded as I stepped inside the clinic, inside home.

Markus was there, hobbling from room to room, agitated without any patients to tend. He swore at me when I showed him my bloodied palm and ushered me into a chair before bringing out the plate of honeycomb he saved for his favourite patients.

He cleaned the wound quickly, meaning he poured what felt like a gallon of whiskey over my hand and then smothered it in honey. By the time he'd bandaged it, the tips of my fingers were numb, and I regretted asking for help. I could have done it myself, more gently at that, and I said as much.

He ushered me out the front door with a grumble. "Don't come back," he said, "until you learn some manners."

The door slammed shut, and I laughed. "You have a nice night, too."

I'd never really known my grandparents, but with a mentor like Markus, I didn't feel the need.

Happiness was everywhere as I walked towards the main square. I could see it in the buoyant steps of the elderly and hear it in the warm conversation of married couples. A row of apple-bobbers plucked the fruit from their water pails with varying levels of success. The wagon parked opposite the game was overflowing with effigies of the Dawn Lord—statues, paintings, mosaics. Each one depicted him with his arms raised, the sun following at his back, heeding his call.

I winced, not only at the reminder of the statue I'd broken but at the cost of all the effigies. If anyone needed an explanation of why we poor folk used simple crosses to represent the Dawn Lord, it would be that he was an expensive man to buy.

The puppet show had started in front of the church. I joined the small crowd, watching as the marionettes came to life within the theatre box. Their grotesque, caricatured bodies told the same story they told every year—of a creature that would terrorise the village, stealing men and women from their beds. These men and women would later be found in the depths of the forest, bloodless and withered. One of the marionettes screamed as it made the discovery.

In front of me, a child clutched her father's hand.

Not everyone in the crowd looked on in horror. There were faces like mine, pensive and sceptical, watching only for entertainment's sake. But then there were the eyes that followed the tale a little too closely, with gazes that were old and wise and sharp, as though they knew the truth of the matter. Those were the gazes that believed in the stories. But even if they did believe, they did not readily voice it.

Vampires, whether fact or fiction, did not make for polite conversation in any setting.

Still, it was tradition, and so we would all go along with it regardless of belief. We would decorate the village and cheer for our bumbling priest as he returned to the church at midnight, having warded our home from evil.

The show finished, and I clapped politely, my feet already taking me towards the smell of roasting meat and freshly baked goods. I bought a plate of food piled so high it could have been mistaken for a mountain, then left the main street, making myself comfortable in the grassy area behind the church.

A light sheen of sweat clung to me, as did the scent of mildew. My hair had curled in the humidity, the blonde strands tickling my shoulders. Summer had been kind so far this year, bringing the occasional night shower when needed and reserving the days for an encompassing warmth.

A lizard lay in the remnants of that warmth, not ten feet from me, so still that I wouldn't have noticed him if not for the paleness beneath his chin. He blended in with the earth as easily as I wished to blend in with the villagers.

I bit the end of a strawberry and threw him the other half. He didn't even look at it.

"I'll share with you if it doesn't want to."

I flinched, nearly dropping my plate.

"Sorry," Trudi said as she plonked down at my side. "I didn't mean to startle you." She was in her prettiest dress, a yellow gown that matched the dahlias pinned into her braids. A clove of garlic had been sewn on her collar.

"Yes, you did," I said, breaking a cinnamon bun in half and passing her the bigger piece. "But I forgive you for it. Are you enjoying the festival?"

Trudi raised a dark eyebrow. "Almost as much as you, it seems. Why are you hiding back here by yourself?"

"Just enjoying the peace. It's been a busy day." I took a bite, the sugar melting in my mouth.

I found a hidden underground mausoleum-lair, I wanted to say, so I could tell the bizarre, hair-raising story to someone. But it couldn't be Trudi. Even if she could keep a secret, she worried enough about me already.

"Busy? But I thought Hugo was the one working to—oh." She picked at the glaze on her bun. "You went back? Again?"

I sighed and drew my knees to my chest. The sugar turned sour on my tongue. "Yes."

"Well, I'm glad you were safe," was all she said.

"Actually"—I raised my bandaged hand—"I probably should have listened to you this time."

Trudi grimaced. "I was going to ask what happened."

"I cut it on a stray bit of metal."

"Ouch."

I nodded. "Ouch is correct."

"Maybe you could get it blessed at this week's service?" Her voice was hesitant. She placed the bun down. "I'd save you a seat next to me if you wanted?"

"That's a nice idea," I forced out. "I'll ask Father Snow about it later."

Trudi flushed, her features glowing with happy surprise. "Really? I'll, um, make sure to get a seat at the front, then."

There was a moment of quiet between us as I tried not to take back the words. She meant well, inviting me. She always meant well.

Abruptly, she asked, "What happened to your dress?"

I smiled sheepishly, fingering the ripped hem. "I had to improvise."

"You used your *dress* on that cut?"

"It's not like it complained," I said, laughing.

She shook her head. "And you didn't even bother to change out of it. I wish I had that kind of confidence."

A drumbeat started at our backs, and Trudi turned to me as the pipes joined in. She held out her hand. "Ruined dress or not, will you dance with me?"

I laughed again, louder this time, and clasped her palm with my good one. "I imagine I'll be fighting Hugo for the honour, but yes. Let's dance."

Anything to shake my sense of foreboding.

CHAPTER TWO

Everyone congregated in the church at midnight to await Father Snow.

A chill curled in the air, and the sky had started a slow, mournful drizzle. The cool droplets were refreshing after the night we'd had. Hugo had joined Trudi and me as we danced in the village square. When it grew late enough for the musicians to call it a night, we retired to the inn and drank ourselves to pieces. By the time we made it to the church, the pews were already bursting, and we had to content ourselves with standing at the back.

My eyes were shutting of their own accord as I leaned against the open doorway. Hugo was holding on to Trudi in what could almost pass as an embrace, but what was, I suspected, an attempt to keep himself upright. He'd drunk more than Trudi and me combined.

Despite our heady exhaustion, we waited.

And waited.

And waited.

"Where is he?" Trudi muttered, rubbing her eyes. It was well past midnight, and the villagers were growing restless.

Myrtle Gully's cobbler, Ernst, took care of village matters when Father Snow was absent. He stood near the pulpit, wringing his hands.

Hugo shuffled on his feet, his ungainly limbs draping over Trudi's back. He sighed and nuzzled his face into her neck. "Lost?"

I frowned at the thought. The route Father Snow took was not a difficult one; it skirted around the forest, circling the village, then doubled back to follow the river. I would think someone who had done it annually for the past three decades would be familiar enough to not lose their way.

But then, this *was* Father Snow.

We continued to wait, albeit impatiently, Trudi and I passing Hugo back and forth between our shoulders when his slouching grew too heavy. Many of the villagers were muttering, some of them even breaking from the crowd to pass by us and make the short walk to their beds. We were deciding whether to follow their example when Ernst finally spoke up, asking for volunteers to make a search party.

There was a collective groan amongst those who had waited too long.

"He could be drunk and passed out somewhere," Trudi said, and we shared a look. It wouldn't be the first time.

"Let's just go home," I said, cupping my hands together to breathe some warmth into them. My injured palm was starting to ache.

Hugo sniffed loudly and stood upright, nearly hitting his auburn head on the doorway. "You both go. I'll stay and"—he yawned—"help with the search party."

"No, come on," Trudi said. "You're about to fall over as it is."

"But I should stay," he mumbled, and I gave a mental groan. He was right. One of us needed to help.

"I'll stay," I said, already resigned to the fact.

Trudi's gaze shot to me. "Lena," she began.

"I don't mind. If Father Snow's fallen or passed out, they'll need someone there to look at him, anyway." And Hugo was far too out of it for that. Markus could do it, but I'd imagine he was already asleep. He never did like to join in the festivities.

Trudi looked me up and down. "Are you sure? It's not going to be too much?"

I'd just spent the night dancing. If that didn't hurt me, another walk through the forest wouldn't either.

"I'll be fine, thanks," I said and patted Hugo's arm. "Now go and make sure this one gets to bed without hurting himself."

"If you're sure." Trudi wrapped an arm around Hugo's back. "Be safe, Lena."

I watched them leave. "I will."

I was paired with Angela, the innkeeper's daughter, and we wandered into the forest, lanterns in hand. The rain had stopped just in time for our search, but the mud squelched beneath our feet and stuck to the soles of our shoes.

"I hope he's okay," Angela said quietly as we headed towards the river.

"He's probably fine, fast asleep somewhere." I laughed. "Though I almost hope we're not the ones to find him. Which half of him do you want to carry?"

She shuddered. "That makes it sound like we'll find him cut in two."

I cringed at my thoughtlessness. I hadn't taken into account how young she was—only fourteen to my twenty.

"I'm sure the Dawn Lord will keep him safe," I commented lamely.

We drew deeper into the forest, deep enough that the myrtle trees pushed against each other to veil the sky, deep enough that the knots in their trunks blinked and strained against the lanterns' light. But we did not go so deep as to be unsafe.

"This isn't working," I said as we circled a hollowed stump we'd passed before. "He could have wandered off anywhere."

"Should we go back?" She was gnawing at her lip, fidgeting with her braid. Her gaze caught on something behind me, and I glanced over my shoulder.

The castle.

"It's just a building," I said gently. "It won't grow feet and stomp on us."

Her answering smile was a valiant effort. "I know."

“We should keep—” I cut myself off. She was obviously nervous. “Actually, I think you’re right. You go ahead, and I’ll let the others know.”

“Really? You don’t mind?”

I nodded. “Yeah, off you go.”

“Thank you, Lena!” Angela hitched up her muddied skirts and ran.

“Don’t get lost,” I called, but I wasn’t worried. We hadn’t strayed too far from the path.

I waited until her figure disappeared between the gaps in the trees before setting my course further east, closer to the castle. Regardless of my words to Angela, it was still the way I would go if I were drunk and warding against evil.

The further I walked, the tighter the shadows wrapped around the forest. Moss covered the rocks and roots, made them slippery, and I had to keep an eye on my feet to scale the uneven terrain. I was about to turn back, find an easier route, when a shape moved in the distance.

I paused.

Was that—

It was. It was a person.

I spurred into action, climbing around the trees.

“Father! Father Snow, are you—” I stopped dead, mere yards away.

That wasn’t Father Snow.

Before me, standing at the base of an ancient elm, was a man I’d never seen—for, if I had seen him, I would never have been able to forget him. His hair was long, reaching his waist, and shone the deep, dark blue of a raven feather. Next to his pale skin, the contrast was that of wet soil against bone.

His clothes were beautiful, made of rich, heavy fabrics. But the waistcoat was outdated, the sleeves too frilled for convenience, and the cape belonged in a family portrait, one that, although worthy of a king, was long forgotten.

The black hair and angular features ... A northerner, perhaps?

I'm staring, I thought with a jolt and shook away the haze that had settled over me. It cleared enough for me to realise that, without meaning to, I'd moved closer to him.

Close enough to touch. Panic lanced through me.

A violent tremor wracked my hand, and I dropped the lantern. It hit the ground with a dull thud. "Um," I started to stutter, but my throat closed up.

What's wrong with me?

The man hadn't moved, hadn't even blinked in acknowledgement.

I tried again. "Have you, uh, seen a priest around? Portly and smelling like a brewery ..."

He rested his palm against the elm. His fingers were long and slender, but his nails were overgrown, grey and sharp. The creases in his skin held the splotched remnants of blood.

"Are you okay?" I asked, knowing this was the point I should leave but unable to make my body cooperate. It was as though the words were coming of their own accord. "The village isn't far if you need help. I work at the clinic. You're welcome to come back with me." I snapped my mouth shut, teeth clicking together.

Pick up the lantern, Lena. Pick up the lantern and leave.

Right. The lantern. I'd dropped it.

I knelt to scoop it up—the flame had not gone out, thankfully—and the softest of touches caressed my knuckles. His cape, swinging in the wind. But there was no wind, not this deep in the forest. No small breeze.

Which meant he had moved.

I stumbled backwards, clutching the lantern. The man watched me coldly, indifferently, from beneath heavy eyelids. He parted his lips to run a serpentine tongue across blackened fangs. No, not blackened.

Bloodied.

My heartbeat stopped before picking up at a gallop.

This couldn't be real.

This was impossible.

Years ago, a professor from a prestigious school had come to the village searching for undiscovered wildlife throughout the continent. He was a little man with a moustache that ate the bottom half of his face and a smile that lit up the room. He'd told us of his and his late partner's most impressive findings, a wolf species in the Carmahine Desert, and how it was because of said wolves his partner had become 'late'.

"It's dangerous to run from wolves," he'd explained, not telling us anything new, but weaving his words in such a way that they were a pleasure to relearn. *"The chase is what excites them, turns their curiosity into a hunt."*

I had the sudden overwhelming impression that the same rule applied to vampires.

Fear pulsed through me, flooding my veins with the urge to run and run until I was out of that forest and as far away as possible. Without meaning to, I stepped back.

The man—he couldn't be what he appeared to be, he *couldn't*—snapped his chin up and followed my movements with buzzard-like acuity.

I took a step back.

He took one forward.

I took another, and he smiled widely, wickedly. He mirrored my footing.

I threw the lantern at him, and the sound as it struck his chest was the thud of an axe on the executioner's block. His figure blurred, and then he was right in front of me, icy fingers wrapping around my neck and squeezing. I scratched at his hands, tried to push my fingers beneath his, but he was immovable. He didn't flinch as I managed to lift my leg in a solid kick to his shin.

There was no mercy in his eyes. No hesitation in their flat, stony depths.

Black splotches passed over my vision.

My limbs turned numb.

The pounding of my heart became a clock toll inside my temples, counting down the seconds until Death would chime his bell and come for me.

No. *No.*

I had been through too much, had survived too long to let it end like this. To let my last breath be so sudden. This was not how I was to die.

I refused.

He must have seen the shift in my face, because the man's brow quirked. He licked his bloodstained lips, cocking his head. Summoning every last vestige of willpower I possessed, I unlatched my fingers from his devastating grip.

And then I stabbed my finger through his eye.

He roared, dropping me to clutch his face, and I landed heavily on my knees. Agony clawed its way up my throat as I coughed wetly, until I was doubled over, stomach spasming. The mud soaked into my shins, slickened my palms, aggravated my wounded hand. Footsteps crunched behind me.

Get away, get away, get away.

The world tilted as he slammed me onto my back, knocking the wind from me. I groped blindly at the ground, searching for a rock, a twig—anything. My fingers closed over something thin and jagged—a stick, I realised—as he stretched open his mouth, fangs growing impossibly longer.

I thrust the stick through his chest.

He exhaled, a whining, raspy sound. His grip slackened.

I fled, crawling out from beneath him and through the trees. My throat burned, my lungs burned, everything burned, and when I tried to scream, nothing came out.

A vampire. A *vampire.*

I had never considered that the villagers' tales, told in hushed whispers to rooms of children and rebellious youths, had any truth to them. I'd thought it was a way to keep them in line and ensure gullible travellers would return for more.

How wrong I had been.

It was too soon before I had to slow my stumbling pace, and I clutched my side, listening. The trees sheltered me, limbs creeping closer, wanting to smother me in their burls.

I waited for a sign I had been followed. The forest was silent, like the moment before a breath. Like it, too, was waiting.

I needed to keep running, I needed to get away, I needed to live.

Someone called out in the distance, and I gasped.

One of the villagers.

Hope twisted my gut as I stumbled towards the voice.

"*Hello?*" I tried to scream. "*There's a—*" My foot caught on something, and I fell, my head smacking against the ground. White stars exploded beneath my eyelids. I groaned and blinked, once, twice. Rising to my elbows, I froze.

My legs were elevated, cushioned by something softer than the forest floor.

I shut my eyes. Tried to calm myself at the shudder that worked through me. When I turned, I still wasn't prepared for the sight.

Father Snow's head was attached to his body by a mere thread of skin. Hundreds of tiny flies dug into the fatty flesh of his neck, flew into his gaping mouth and up his nostrils. Blood saturated his gold collar and turned it a festering red.

I covered my mouth as bile touched the back of my tongue.

The vampire had done this. Had gouged out a chunk of the Father's neck and nearly ripped his head off in the process. I reached a shaking hand out to shut his eyes, and the flies jolted away before swarming back in.

A sob welled in my chest.

His eyelids were stiff and—they didn't stay shut. I tried again, but his skin was too cold, biting at my fingertips.

I had seen death. Had watched my mother die peacefully, had seen villagers pass on the healer's bed. But I understood now that the calm and forgiving kind of death I had witnessed was only the beginning. This meat sack, with its sunken cheeks and bruising skin, was no longer a person. It was a broken, empty husk. This man I had known for almost a decade was now nothing.

Less than nothing.

He was just ... gone.

Voices rang out in the distance and passed through me unacknowledged as the night's shadows teased the edges of my sight. My skin prickled with awareness. The air thickened.

The vampire was behind me.

I was suddenly very, very dizzy.

That's, uh—that's not good, I thought as the shadows grew bolder. My temple started throbbing. *Must have ... hit my head ... harder than I thought.*

I tried to crawl, but my fingers slipped, and the dead weight of my legs scraped across the mud.

I don't want to die.

Something tugged at the heel of my boot.

"*No,*" I rasped as my eyes fluttered shut, and I collapsed beside Father Snow. Two corpses, he and I, like the pair of crooked marionettes, this forest the theatre box of our final show.

I don't want to die.

This wasn't how I was supposed to die. It wasn't supposed to be like this.

And I couldn't help but wonder, as the nothingness forced itself upon me, if Father Snow had had the very same thought.

CHAPTER THREE

Someone was pounding a nail into my skull. Harder and harder it dug, scraping across the bone, trying to find purchase. Trepanning? Were they trying to cure me?

But it wouldn't work. I didn't have a head injury.

I tried to tell them to stop but didn't recognise the sound that came from my lips. Didn't understand why my neck ached so intensely.

I opened my eyes a sliver, and the nail dug deeper for my efforts. It was dark, but not so dark that I couldn't make out the wooden ceiling above me or the window opposite where I lay, its ledge spilling with pot plants and worthless baubles.

I was in my bedroom, lying on my bed. Not the surgical table. My relieved exhale was short-lived, because in the next moment, my chest cinched and I began a vicious, hacking cough.

"Oh dear," said someone from beside me. His voice was deep, with the precise inflection of the upper class. "You sound like you're dying."

Any breath I had left caught in my throat as my joints locked together. My skin flushed hot and cold as memories I'd rather have forgotten rushed to the forefront of my mind.

He continued, reasonable, unhurried, "It's my fault, I know. I do apologise for that, but you caught me at a bad time."

Father Snow. Eyes that wouldn't shut. Putrid smells, gaping mouth.

I turned on my side, all hurts momentarily forgotten.

The vampire was draped across my wooden armchair, flicking through a book with one hand and rubbing his temple with the other.

It felt like insects were scuttling beneath my skin, burrowing around my arms and between my shoulder blades, trying to burst free.

But I'm alive, a small part of me celebrated. *I'm alive, in pain and mortal danger, but alive.*

Which, along with the ache in my chest, reminded me I needed to breathe if I wanted to stay in said state. I gulped down a mouthful of air.

"Do not scream," he said, clearly misinterpreting my priorities. "I have a terrible headache, courtesy of you, and it would very much inconvenience me to kill you right now."

I stared at him, speechless.

He was beautiful. Straight nosed, with thin lips and high cheekbones. But looking at him, he felt ... unnatural. Like a flower that had been pressed, still intact but without fragrance or vibrancy of colour.

Silver earrings swung to his shoulders; inlaid with black gems, they matched the ring on his finger, the pin at his collar. There was a hole in his waistcoat, but other than a small amount of dried, flaking blood, there was no evidence of any injury.

From where I'd stabbed him, there was no wound.

He snapped the book shut and smiled at me, but it was fake—condescending and nasty. His fangs pushed his top lip up when he smiled like that. They were still a little bloody, dark red staining the crevices between his teeth. I had the urge to scrub my body free of his attention with boiling water, maybe use a potato peeler for good measure.

A soft thump came from the far side of my bedroom, and I whipped my head around, heart stuttering. Hugo was slumped in the corner of the room, chin to his chest, as if he'd been played with like a doll and then discarded.

"Hugo?" I whispered, fire raking down my throat.

The vampire unfolded himself from the chair, his black cape trailing behind him. "Now, now, let's stay calm. He's just sleeping, you see?" He lifted Hugo by the top of his hair, exposing his throat.

"Wait," I said, throwing the blankets off and pushing through the pain in my limbs. "Let go of him. Please," I added when the vampire pursed his lips.

He narrowed his eyes, thinking about it, and smoothed Hugo's hair into place. "All I'm here for is a little chat, yes? Can we manage that?"

His tone was patronising, and it spoke volumes as to how he saw me. Weak little mortal, begging for her friend, unable to defend herself. Determination seeped into my fear, clearing my mind.

This needed to end. Right now.

I kept a cross in my bedside table, more for expectation's sake than anything else. I rushed for it, flinging the drawer open and holding it in front of me.

He blinked slowly, then cocked his head. "What's this?" Dropping Hugo, he leaned forward to pluck the wood from my hands.

My jaw fell slack, and I breathed out a word so foul that even the vampire glanced at me with disapproval.

The Dawn Lord and I would be having serious words later.

If there is a later.

"A pathetic effort, that's what. All this is," he said, waggling the cross, "is two pieces of wood nailed together. The one on the door is much lovelier."

Indeed, there on the door was a cross made of myrtle, carved with sunbursts. Hugo must have put it up when he was decorating.

I blanched at the revelation, sitting back on the bed before my knees could give out. The clinic was in the middle of the village—on the main street of the village. The vampire would have passed every ward, every protection we had from the festival, to get here. The crosses, the garlic, maybe even the church and its hallowed ground.

And yet here he was, at my bedside, watching me as cruel amusement bracketed his wide mouth.

He raised his eyebrows as if in question. *Well? What will you do now?*

I felt nauseous. "What do you want?"

"Hmm, that's a very broad question." He walked back to the chair, each purposeful footstep a blow to my ears. "But I suppose we could start with the date. Tell me, what year is it?"

More than a little confused, I told him.

He went very still.

"Is that so?" he whispered, then fell back in the chair as though shocked. "Well, that changes nothing, I suppose. But no wonder you look as though you're in your undergarments. Has fashion really regressed to such an extent? I'm glad I was not awake to see that. Who's the current reigning monarch—*is* there still a reigning monarch? I hope we have not fallen so low as to consider democracy. Is fox tossing still a popular sport?"

The onslaught of questions had me so muddled I could barely keep up. "Uh," I started, but he spoke over me.

"Do not interrupt me, please. I'm not finished. Do you know a man named Quincey Rinehart?" His shoulders slumped. "No, he'd be long dead. And is this building new? I like it, although whoever put those candle fixtures in did an appalling job. Most importantly, is the existence of vampires common knowledge yet, or do you all still prefer to cower in ignorance?"

"What do you want?" I repeated, much louder and sharper than I meant to, nerves forming cracks in my voice.

He smiled as if he knew a secret I did not. "I already told you, I'm here to apologise. I am *very* sorry for earlier."

He couldn't have sounded any less sincere.

I said, "And—Father Snow? Are you sorry about him?"

"Who?" There was a beat of silence as puzzlement overtook his features. Then he laughed, light and unrestrained. "Oh, him. Not particularly. Why? Does he have some poor mistress weeping over him at home?"

Well. That answered that question.

"No, no mistress. But still plenty of loved ones."

"Of course, of course. Ah well, that's life for you. But let us forget about all that, for I'd like to propose a deal."

That's life for you? His words were horrific. If he had that little remorse after committing such a heinous act, it was sickening to think what else he was capable of.

"You're disgusting," I whispered, then realised what I'd done and smacked a hand over my mouth.

He only shrugged. "And you are close-minded, I see it already. But moving on—I seem to have a vague memory of you claiming to be a healer." It didn't sound like a question, but he appeared to expect an answer.

I nodded. He copied the action, eyebrows raised.

"Which means," he continued, as if we were two friends conspiring, "that we can use each other, you and I."

The room was warm, but I rearranged the blankets back over my legs, stalling. "If you're going to ask me for a weekly sacrifice, my answer is no."

He clicked his tongue. "A weekly sacrifice would be impractical. Use your head, girl."

A vampire wanting the service of a healer ...

It took me another breath to understand. "You want blood."

He stared, waiting. Expectant, unimpressed.

"Without drawing any attention," I finished.

"Very good," he said, voice low.

I met his gaze. His eyes—dark, solid blue—were empty. Abysses, devoid of life or feeling. They were a dead man's eyes, a murderer's eyes, a lost man's eyes, all at once.

"Why?" I asked, truly not understanding. He could feast on me now, could save Hugo for later, could have anyone he wanted in the village.

He curled his hand in the air as if trying to pluck out an appropriate answer. "Because I am undecided as to how long I shall remain here and am in no way interested in alerting the village savages to my presence so they can come and bother me in my home with their ineffectual pitchforks. The drapes in the vestibule do not take kindly to bloodstains, a lesson I've learnt too many times over."

Everything clicked into place, and dread tore through my being. I had already begun to suspect, but I dearly didn't want to be right.

"The vestibule?" I said, tears welling in my eyes.

"Yes, the vestibule." He peered at me as though I was some strange creature. "Do you have a problem with the word? Ah, perhaps you do not know what it means?"

"You live in the castle?" My voice broke as I pushed the tears back. Now was not the time.

And I did not have the right.

"I live in my castle, yes." He patted the bed gingerly. "There, there."

Don't panic, I told myself. *Don't panic, you're okay. It's going to be okay.*

But it wouldn't be okay, because he was asparagus man, the dead noble who revelled in riches and hurt and suffering. But not dead, after all. Not in the truest sense of the word. He implied he'd been sleeping, which meant I was the stupid, unsuspecting girl who'd gone and woken him. That was what the sounds had been.

I stared at my injured hand. The silver lining made sense now. Somehow, my blood had woken a vampire, and that vampire had brutally murdered the village priest.

I really was going to hell.

"How much blood?" I asked, barely hearing the words over the sudden ringing in my ears. This was all my fault.

"A few bottles each week will do."

I nearly choked. "A few bottles? That's impossible. No one will think that's normal."

He rested his cheek on his hand and drawled, "Then I suggest you get creative."

My mind went blank. And then I laughed, just quietly, a nervous giggle. It was the kind of sound children made when their mother told them the stray cat outside had died or when their best friend developed the palsy and walked funny because of it.

Not even bothering to hide the twisted mirth, I asked, "I take it that if I do this, you'll leave the village—and me—alone?"

"Well, those terms seem uninspired to me, but if that's what you want." He shrugged, inspecting his nails. They were more like claws.

I laughed again. "Deal." I'd almost lost my mind enough to offer him my hand to shake. Instead, I fiddled with my bandage, pulling at the knot. It had been redressed while I was unconscious.

"Good." He clapped his hands together and stood. "Oh, and I'll be taking these back." The bag he tossed over his shoulder was bulging with—

"No!" I was instantly sober, scurrying off the bed. The sudden movement sent the room spinning again. "Don't take those. Please, I need them."

A sceptical look. "You need an embroidered cushion, a string of pearls and several candelabra?" He glanced about my room, at the bare walls, the chipped wooden floors. "Now I think you're just being greedy."

Hatred started a slow simmer in my heart.

Greedy. He, with his fine clothes, his ridiculous jewels, his *immortality*, had the gall to call me greedy.

I took a deep breath.

It did not matter what this devil's spawn thought, nor what he called me. He had slaughtered Father Snow, tried to kill me, used the villagers—my family—against me. No matter what deal we had made, his opinion was worthless.

I clasped my hands, not showing even the slightest grimace of pain. And I smiled at him, this creature who thought he was worth the endless amount of years he had undoubtedly lived.

"You should probably go now." I jerked my chin to the window. "See? It's getting awfully pale out there."

There was a knowing glint in his eyes, a vicious spark that set my resentment ablaze all over again. "Such kind words you give, little thief." He walked to the door and tapped his knuckles on the myrtle cross. "You have a few days to collect the blood. Bring it to the castle when you have it. And don't forget," he said over his shoulder, smile coiling, "to come at night."

I was staring at the door long after he'd shut it behind him.

I couldn't be sure of how much time had passed—everything was slow like I was underwater—when footsteps in the hall tore me from my thoughts.

I rushed to Hugo and was shaking him, muttering his name, when Markus came in.

"Lena?" Markus was at my side in a moment, pulling my hands from Hugo's shoulders and cupping them in his own weathered ones. I wrenched away.

Hugo's breathing was shallow, his temples sweaty, and he smelled of ... alcohol.

I shut my eyes and resisted smacking him upside the head. Panic had made me forgetful. Our night of happiness and festivity seemed a lifetime away.

I turned to Markus. Words, hundreds of them, were on the tip of my tongue, but the second I met his gaze was the second I couldn't keep it in anymore. I started to cry.

Markus gripped my shoulders and guided me back to the bed. "No need to cry," he said gruffly. "Stupid boy's drunk is all." He patted me on the back, and I buried my face in his chest.

Why now? Why did this have to happen, and why *now?*

I sobbed, clutching Markus, until the pain it caused wasn't worth the tears and I had a headache even worse than when I awoke.

Judging by the imminent sunrise, I must have been unconscious for quite a while. If I had the option, I'd stay in bed, hide under the covers for as long as I could, or maybe run to the furthest corners of the world to escape the fear and guilt. But I didn't have time. It wouldn't be fair to the villagers. I needed to be strong. I was going to make it through this alive and so was everyone else.

I would make sure of it.

Pushing away from Markus, I gestured to the soggy mess I'd left on his tunic. "Sorry."

He shook his head, gifting me with a rare smile that hinted at crooked teeth—but then his eyes narrowed, and the sun-spotted skin of his forehead sagged.

"Who did that to you?" he asked, sweeping loose hair away from my shoulder. I frowned and reached for the small mirror on my bedside table.

Bruises adorned my neck, the deep blues and purples accentuating the sickly sheen of my skin.

The mirror shook in my hand. I should have thought of this when I felt the burn of my throat. These weren't bruises one could get by accident.

"I don't want to talk about it," I said. Speaking hurt even more, now that I'd seen the physical damage.

His gnarled mouth bunched at the side. “Do I know them?”

“No. And it won’t happen again.”

A pause. “The villagers found you passed out beside the dead Father. Was it him?”

It felt like he’d slapped me. I could say it was Father Snow. I could say it was him, and then Markus would stop asking questions.

For one dirty moment, I considered it.

But even as I thought of the idea, callous and practical, I knew I wouldn’t give in to the temptation. It would be too hard, breathing such a lie against the dead. I couldn’t do that to Father Snow, not after I’d seen him mangled yet innocent of anything other than wandering too far into the forest.

It could have been anyone. It was nearly me.

I shook my head and rasped, “No. Really, you don’t know him, and this happened ... before I found Father Snow.”

It’s all true, I tried to justify. *Everything I said was true*.

Markus would be suspicious of every man in the village now. I clenched my good fist around my blankets, annoyed I couldn’t have come up with a better story. If only I had seen the bruises earlier. Another thing to hate the vampire for. My list was growing by the minute.

“It’s stupid of you, tryin’ to protect anyone right now,” Markus grumbled. “The villagers will be fair suspicious of you if they think you’re keepin’ any secrets.”

I couldn’t answer. There was no good way to reply.

It was then that Hugo snorted loudly, flinched at the sound, and slumped back over.

I chuckled, and Markus let out an exasperated sigh. "If he wasn't my sister's boy," he muttered, "he'd be sleepin' in the chicken coop." He turned back to me. "I'll get you some tea. How much brandy do you want in it?"

I smiled, my dry lips cracking. "Just a little. And a bowl of mint leaves, please. I'll be chewing until midday if I want to be rid of this headache."

"Och," Markus said but clapped me on the shoulder. "Fine."

I waited until he'd turned away to wince. My body was tender all over.

"Lena," he said, stopping at the door, and for the space of a breath, I saw the vampire again. I blinked, and he disappeared.

"Yes?" I asked.

"It's been a damned bad night, but we need to talk about what happened. If not about your neck, then about the priest."

He was right. I would bet my life savings there was a room of people downstairs waiting for me. They needed to know if there was something dangerous in the woods to hunt. It worried me how effortlessly the vampire had managed to get in and out without being discovered by them, but it didn't surprise me. His steps had been silent.

If the villagers knew of him, they would fight him, and if they fought him, they would lose. They would die more painful deaths than Father Snow.

Hoping desperately that I was making the correct choice, I said, "Bring me that tea and you can ask whatever you need. I'll do my best to help."

CHAPTER FOUR

I had been right in that a gaggle of villagers—those in the search party—had been waiting for me to emerge. I'd gone downstairs and talked with them as the sun rose, its bright rays deceptively cheerful.

The villagers had ranged from concerned, to impatient, to plain suspicious. Markus had obviously warned them against prodding too deeply, for they did not harangue me with questions as I thought they would. I made myself comfortable at the kitchen table, quilt wrapped around me as though I could hide the physical evidence of a struggle. I spoke softly, so they couldn't hear it in my voice.

I told them the truth where I could—that I had stumbled over Father Snow, already dead, and had passed out soon after. A general consensus formed that it must have been some kind of beast that attacked Father Snow. I almost pitied them for their wilful ignorance. They were fooling themselves, and they all knew it. No beast lived in the forest.

But it was better than thinking one of the villagers had done it. It was better than knowing the truth.

They left late that morning after agreeing upon a nightly guard for the following days, and a couple of them made their way to the village square as bearers of the unhappy news. It wasn't long before wailing could be heard from every house in every alley.

I stood at my bedroom window for most of the afternoon, nursing tea I couldn't taste. The castle loomed two miles to the east like a bottomless, craggy mountain, its towers and turrets rising well above the tree line. The wing that faced the village was in ruins, ivy having long crawled through the gaping chasms of blackened stone and lichen-spattered rubble. It was only yesterday I'd been there, curious and hopeful. I'd never considered it a cursed place as the villagers had.

I should have taken their tales more seriously when I had the chance.

Trudi came when she heard the news, and I held her as she cried. She lay in bed with me, and it was a relief to be with someone who didn't look at me as though I were about to brandish the murder weapon. I fell asleep beside her, and when I next opened my eyes, she was gone.

It was only when I started coughing a few hours later and was rummaging through my basket for the vials I kept within that Markus reappeared, an infusion hot in his hands. I downed it as Hugo shuffled in behind him.

Markus left when my coughing calmed, but Hugo stayed to apply a poultice to my injured palm and various other aching parts of my body. He did his best to speak with me, his words trivial and meant to distract, but I stayed wary, fearful of saying the wrong thing. My inability to give Markus a reasonable explanation about the bruises on my neck made it clear I didn't only need to be strong—I also needed to be clever.

Only a day had passed, and I'd already made a mistake. I couldn't afford to make another.

Sleep that night was plagued with nightmares, and I rose early, as exhausted as when I'd gone to bed. But the new day had snapped me out of my stupor, and it was like being plunged into the river in the middle of winter.

What was I doing, wasting away in my bedroom while precious hours passed?

I needed blood. Lots of it.

Markus may have been taken aback to see me in the clinic that morning, but the patients weren't. The exact details of what had happened weren't common knowledge yet. I'd give it a week until Myrtle Gully's rumour mill let everyone know I'd been found in the forest next to a mangled Father Snow, bruises on my neck.

Hugo, who I suspected was blaming himself for not joining the search party, gave me a curious look when I started bloodletting people who so obviously didn't need it. He soon shrugged it off because what was there to suspect me of?

That made me feel guilty.

It was worth it, though. So the vampire wouldn't touch the villagers, it was worth it.

So they wouldn't find out it was I who damned them.

I'd been wearing denial like a pair of comfortable socks for months already. It was not difficult to push my feet in a little further.

Father Snow was buried that afternoon, the blackbirds singing him into the frigid earth as sunshine beat down upon our backs. A priest from Haycock undertook the service. He was a soft-spoken man with pretty almond skin and eyes turned hazel by the gold paint on his eyelids and cheekbones. That he dressed in full priest regalia for a mere funeral warmed me to him immediately.

He introduced himself as Father Pentaghast with a throaty accent that hinted at lands beyond our region's borders. I suspected that if it were any other occasion, many of the village girls would have been giving him eyes. As it was, not even the most enthusiastic of us were able to conjure a smile.

Father Snow's coffin was a plain wooden box adorned with wildflowers. He would have liked it—particularly the bottle of whiskey that had been placed between the stems. Trudi stood with me as Father Pentaghast committed Father Snow's soul to the Dawn Lord, and I wrapped my arms around her when she started sobbing.

My gaze strayed to a corner of the graveyard, one that was isolated, where a single grave marker stood unadorned but for a name that had been roughly scratched into the wood. I cast my head down, sighing. There were enough ghosts lurking in my mind this day without needing to add another.

The villagers watched in silence as two men filled the grave until Father Snow's final resting place was no different to a patch of earth freshly turned in preparation for a new harvest. Father Pentaghast finished his final prayer, and the crowd started to disperse.

The stonemason's mother shuffled past Trudi, Hugo, and me, clenching her grandson's hand so tightly his fingers were turning purple. I had never seen the woman in anything but soft, muted colours, and the coarse grey she wore now aged her. I stepped back to let her through, but she paused in front of me.

"Swine," she hissed and spat at my feet. She glared at me, gaze burning on the high collar I wore, before pulling the little boy away with her.

Shocked, I moved to follow. "What did you just say?"

"Lena, wait." Hugo wrapped his arms around me.

"Did you just hear that?" Why would she say something like that, *do* something like that? We were at a funeral. I had treated her once for sore joints, and she'd been perfectly courteous then.

Hurt bubbled.

Hugo made a noise in the back of his throat. "You know she didn't mean it. It's the grief, it makes people act out."

But Trudi sniffled and said, "That old cow. You think she'd have better manners than to pick fights at a funeral!" The last word was a shout, and Hugo moved to cover her mouth. She slapped him away.

People were staring at us now, their gazes heavy on my face. I turned my back to them. "Does everyone know already? That I found him?" The words were like freshly ripped scabs.

They glanced at each other, then at me.

Trudi said, "Not everyone. But they will soon."

I breathed in the scents of summer—freshly cut grass, honeysuckle, and peach blossoms—trying to curb my wounded feelings. It almost worked.

Swine.

I shook my head. It was just the grief.

Markus, who was speaking with Father Pentaghast, beckoned me over. I stood rooted to the spot, knowing what he was trying to do and not appreciating it.

"I think Markus wants a word," Hugo said hesitantly.

"I can see that."

Markus's face scrunched up when he realised I was ignoring him. Next to him, Father Pentaghast smiled politely. They obviously hadn't seen what'd happened.

Hugo pushed me. "Just go over, Lena. He'll be testy all afternoon if you don't."

"He'll be testy anyway," I muttered but started walking.

Markus raised a bushy eyebrow as I neared. "Nice of you to join us," he said, and I sighed, not having the emotional capacity for a response.

I held my hand out for the priest to clasp. His white vestment fluttered in the breeze as he wrapped his calloused fingers around mine.

"Well met," he murmured.

I managed a smile. "I'm Lena. Thank you for the service, it was lovely." As lovely as any death could be.

"Thank you." He adjusted the rows of wooden beads curled about his wrist, fiddling with the cross at their centre. "Markus here has been explaining the ... situation."

Annoyance tightened my chest, and I glowered at Markus. His mouth was a hard line.

"Oh?" I said. "Markus, I didn't know you were one for gossiping."

"I do not mean to pry," the Father cut in before Markus could reply, "and upsetting you is not my intention. I'd only like to offer you the opportunity to talk if you should need it."

I chewed the inside of my cheek. Trudi and Hugo loitered at the edge of the graveyard, watching us with concern. I said to Father Pentaghast, "Thank you for the offer, but I don't think I'm ready to revisit those memories yet."

That was a lie. I'd been revisiting them every second since I'd fallen over Father Snow's corpse.

"I understand." He linked his fingers. "If you ever feel ready, you are welcome to come speak with me."

I glanced between them.

Markus grunted. "He's the new priest 'ere."

"A temporary calling." Father Pentaghast smiled, lowering his eyes. "Until a new priest comes from the Holy City."

"The Holy City?" My heart pulled with longing.

"Yes. A newly ordained fellow, most likely, at the beginning of his service. Still, until then, I am blessed to be in your company."

Blessed to be in our company?

I almost scoffed. This priest didn't want to be here at all.

I could empathise.

I said goodbye after that, walking home with Markus and Hugo in silence as Trudi headed the opposite way with her father. My stomach turned with hunger, and I tried to come up with ways I could distract myself until sundown when the funeral fast would come to an end. But instead of distracting myself, I pondered.

I pondered as I returned home and changed into my gardening clothes, on the disgust in the woman's voice as she called me swine. I pondered as I weeded the herb garden, on the way the villagers' eyes followed me when they thought I wasn't looking. I pondered as I scrubbed the dirt from beneath my fingernails, on Father Pentaghast, who was ignorant of the evil lurking at the doorstep of his new parish. And I pondered as I slipped into bed that night, too tired to have eaten, on how I'd been proved wrong.

The Myrtle Gully rumour mill was far more effective than I'd given credit.

CHAPTER FIVE

I snuck out of the house the next evening before the sun had fully set. The memories were fresh and oozing, and I didn't want to be out in the forest any later than necessary.

I took a different path than usual, avoiding the strip of trees Father Snow had been in, as well as the villagers who were keeping watch—even if the term 'keeping watch' was generous. Old Man Kenny's loopy cackle echoed throughout the village, letting anyone foolish enough to venture out know that he was more than halfway to rip-roaring drunk.

Once, he'd gotten so inebriated he'd freed his neighbour's geese from their yard and chased them to the river. A smile worked its way onto my mouth, the first one that day.

The forest quickly forced that smile away.

Every black crevice resembled the Father's broken body. Reaching for me from the corner of my eyes. Crawling to me from beneath the underbrush.

I stared straight ahead as I walked, fists clenched. The pain in my palm helped me differentiate between what was real and what was an imaginary spectre haunting my steps.

The castle's front gates were rusted shut as they'd always been. What remained of the garden was a tangle of overgrown shrubs and blackberry bushes that crept out to scratch at my ankles. I circled around the back to the east wing, where part of the iron fence had collapsed, forming a small opening. The door to the servants' quarters was still open. A faint light capered across the hallway as I ascended the stairs into the heart of the castle.

I almost didn't recognise it.

The vampire had obviously been hard at work, for the entrance hall had undergone a transformation. Gone were the frayed tapestries, beady-eyed portraits, and the broken pieces of chandelier. Instead, the walls and floor were bare, blank. It made the hall seem larger than it already was, the castle even more desolate.

I made my way through the stony corridors, almost expecting to find the vampire scuttling through the lengthening shadows and hissing at rats. Minutes passed, with no sign of him.

"Hello?" I called out eventually, tightening my grip on my basket. I passed by the library, catching sight of the sky through the window. The stars were beginning to make an appearance, bearing down on a sea of endless forest and the jagged mountain peaks that bordered the land far to the north.

Did vampires sleep? I wracked my brain, thinking back to the villagers' legends, and decided they must. He had mentioned something about waking up, so that would mean ...

I stopped at the turn that led to the chapel.

Had I wasted a week despairing when the answer was so simple? I barely deliberated before coming to a decision.

The chapel was chilly, open to the air as it was, and I convinced myself that was why I shivered.

The Dawn Lord's altar had been moved, and the broken statue sat upon it once more. The trapdoor was open. My palm pulsed with pain, reminding me of the last time I'd done something rash and how abysmally it had turned out. Fragments of wood—remnants of pews—rested on the bed of ivy that tangled over the floor. I picked one up. It was the size of my forearm, thick at the base and tapering to a point.

I opened the trapdoor and descended the stairs, squinting into the gloom. The door to the crypt was shut, a flickering light emanating from beneath. I kept my eyes on it as I moved past the nameless gravestones and deeper into the darkness.

One push was all it took for the mausoleum door to creak open.

The crypt was unchanged from last I'd seen it but for two things. First, a candle was lit and nearing the end of its wick, about to drown in the seeping wax. Second, the lid of the sarcophagus had been pushed to the ground.

The vampire lay sleeping, eyelashes casting shadows down his cheeks. His hair flowed over his shoulders like a river of ink, the smooth strands pooling to the red velvet lining either side of him. Both hands rested on his stomach, fingers curled, moving with the minuscule rise and fall of his breaths. His lips were tilted up at the sides like he was dreaming happy dreams.

I hesitated.

I couldn't see his fangs, not even an outline of them. Without them, he could pass as a human. Not a normal man—even now, my instincts screamed there was something far too dark lurking within him for that—but a mortal man, nonetheless. And I had only ever tried to help mortal men, with their frailties and ailments. I had only ever tried to heal them. That I was about to kill a breathing, sentient being ...

Maybe I was just as bad as him.

I gritted my teeth. I couldn't think like that. A moment of hesitation didn't change anything. He was evil. I wanted him to disappear.

I clenched my fingers around the wood, its uneven length digging into my skin. It was heavy in my grip, growing heavier by the second. This was not taking a life. It was saving the villagers, saving myself, because one day I would disappear, and I had no doubt he would follow through with his threats.

I nodded to myself. This had to work. He may not shy away from the Dawn Lord's symbol, but a stake through his heart should do the trick. It was too late to go back now. I'd found a glimmer of hope and couldn't turn away from it.

Do it, Lena, I thought. *Just like you're coring an apple.*

I raised the stake, readying to put as much strength into it as I could. I blinked away the wetness gathering in my eyes.

And I plunged the stake down.

Before it hit, before it even connected with fabric and flesh, it was pulled from my grip and thrown across the room with such force that it snapped in two. The vampire's hand encircled my wrist, his fingers overlapping and tightening. His eyes fluttered open.

"Good evening," he said, voice thick with sleep.

My pulse jolted. I tried to jerk my hand away, but his grip was cast iron. His little finger tapped against my skin, the nail poking and prodding.

"Let me go," I said, panicking. What had I just done? I'd gone and ruined everything, that's what. A layer of sweat gathered at my temple, on the back of my neck. All of me was cold.

He let go, and I stumbled off the dais.

Don't run, I had to remind myself. *Run and you're dead. Run and you can't salvage the situation.*

He sat up, rubbing the bridge of his nose with his thumb and forefinger. Waving vaguely towards the back of the crypt, he said, "Pass me that candle."

I reached for it, not daring to give him my back.

Perhaps if I throw this at him, he'll catch on fire?

I promised myself I'd find out one day.

He took the candle from me. I tried not to cringe away when his skin grazed mine.

He massaged two fingers against his temple. "That's better," he murmured. His gaze was lazy, heavy-lidded. "What time is it?"

"Just after sunset," I squeaked.

He yawned, mouth splitting open. His fangs were elongated, as sharp as a viper's, and I didn't take my eyes off them as he leaned back in his sarcophagus.

"Come here, please," he said after a pause.

"Why?" I rocked back on my feet. *Don't run, don't run.*

He looked at me like I was a child talking back. "Come. Here."

I stepped forward. I didn't want to, but just like in the forest, my body had a mind of its own. Like this vampire was the piper whose tune I couldn't help but dance to.

"Closer," he purred when I only just cleared the dais. I bit into my cheeks, keeping my shoulders straight, chin high, and moved to where he lounged.

"Now," he said, "hold out your arm."

I shook my head wildly. "I need that arm."

He waited. Fist clenched, I raised my arm.

"Naughty girl." He smacked me on the wrist lightly, and I yelped. He lifted out of the sarcophagus, fluid as quicksilver. "Don't do it again."

My jaw swung open, and I cradled my wrist. I wasn't in pain—I was just stunned.

"Um," was all I could manage. My state of mind was such that I'd probably agree with him if he donned a crown and pronounced himself king of the world.

The vampire ran his fingers through his hair, neatening it. "I'm famished. Did you bring my blood, or was that little exchange indicative that you didn't bother?"

It took me a few loaded seconds to answer. "It's in the chapel."

He picked up his cape, which had been folded neatly on the chest, then settled it over his shoulders and made for the graveyard.

I watched him leave before I clutched my head and considered bashing it into the wall.

Fool! Idiot! Stupidity incarnate! What were you thinking, Lena? I had to bite my tongue to keep from screaming.

Did I chase after him or did I wait until he disappeared? Instinct told me the moment of true danger had passed—*a slap on the wrist? Really?*—but he could just be drawing out the suspense. Would he turn around and sink his fangs into my neck when I least expected it?

I wrestled with myself, knowing there was really only one decision I could make.

"Wait!" I caught up at the base of the stairs. "Is that it, a slap on the wrist? I tried to kill you!"

He glanced down at me. "Would you prefer to be flogged until dead?"

"No, I just ..." It would make more sense. A little contrite, I said, "You don't even seem upset."

He hummed, noncommittal, and took the stairs two at a time.

"Don't you care?" I asked, trying to keep from tripping over my own feet at the pace.

"Life is too short to stress about such things, don't you think? Besides, now that you've got it out of your system, we can both move on."

We entered the chapel, and I lingered near the trapdoor, unsure of what to do with myself.

He straightened the Dawn Lord's broken statue, frowning as it shifted the altar's weight back and forth on uneven legs. He swatted the statue to the ground, where it cracked into even more pieces.

An inappropriate smile started to hitch the side of my mouth, but I instantly wrenched it down.

And I thought *I* was a heretic.

"There you are," he said as he spotted the basket I'd left on the pew. His face brightened, and he snapped fully awake.

I didn't want to stare, but I couldn't help it.

I hadn't realised how tired, how very gaunt he'd appeared at our first meeting. He looked impossibly healthier now, stronger and as enthralling as I'd expect a devil to be.

He uncorked one of the bottles, smelling the blood, and I didn't know what it was—whether it was that particular unhuman action or just a trick of the night—but it made me flinch. For a split second, it was like something slithered beneath his skin. Like something lay in wait beneath his outfit of flesh and bone.

"Are you feeling better for it?" he asked, and I had to mentally replay our conversation for the words to make sense.

"No, not really." In fact, it felt like I'd rubbed filth over a wound. If I left it there too long, it would begin to fester.

He took a swig of blood, and my stomach gurgled in protest. He was like the leeches we kept in a jar back at the clinic.

Forget about eternal youth. Vampires were disgusting.

He licked his lips and nodded, which I took to mean the blood was acceptable. A knot unravelled in my chest.

"What should I call you?" I asked, then instantly regretted the word choice. If he said something like 'My Lord', I would be liable to lose my sanity. He turned to me with a little flourish.

"Oh dear, I have been scattered. Little thief," he said, and I did not take kindly to the title, "you may call me Ansel."

"Ansel," I repeated. "My name isn't little thief."

"Are you sure?" He took another drink of blood before draping himself across the pew.

"Pretty sure. I'm Lena."

"Well, if you say so. What happened to your hand?"

My palm tingled in response, and I flexed my fingers. "An accident. I wasn't paying attention when I should have been."

Ansel twirled a piece of hair around his finger and asked, "Can I smell your blood?"

"What? No."

"Just a drop?"

"*No.*"

He raised his hands in surrender. "Fine, fine. But if you're so averse to the idea, perhaps you'll answer me this instead:

Was it you who woke me up?"

I scuffed the toe of my boot against the ground. "Not on purpose."

"No, I should think not. A belated thank you, anyway. I would have slept through the next millennium, otherwise."

I'd had my suspicions, but hearing him confirm it set my teeth on edge. I didn't want to be thanked for such a thing. "And how long were you ... sleeping?"

"Ninety-six years." He looked thoroughly put out.

"*Ninety-six?*"

"Oh, you know how many that is, do you? And here I presumed you wouldn't know how to count. What else can you do?" He sounded genuinely impressed, like I was a puppy that could roll over on command.

I tried to wrap my head around it. Ninety-six years, far longer than the average lifespan, unmoving in his sarcophagus. And then I came along and ruined everything.

I groaned into my hands.

I'd made a complete mess.

When I looked up again, Ansel was an arm's length away, bent at the waist to stare at me. I froze.

"Delicate girl, aren't you." He gestured to his neck, and I swallowed, tugging my collar up. The bruises he'd left would take days to fade, even with the creams I'd been applying.

"Maybe," I said, sudden fear teetering me between brave and stupid. "But I didn't get these bruises on my own."

A thoughtful expression passed over him, and he straightened to his full height—a foot taller than me, at least. “True,” he murmured and returned to his pew.

My knees wobbled with relief.

“My thanks for the blood, but three bottles will not last me long,” he said. “You’ll need to be back within the week. And now that we’ve both tried to kill each other, I do wonder, could we call a truce?”

My first instinct was to tell him to go take a walk in the sun. But then, a truce? I considered the idea, fidgeting with my bandage.

“What would this truce entail?” I couldn’t hide my scepticism.

“What any truce would entail, I’d expect. The ceasing of death threats, tentative peace between enemies.” He sounded amused as he said, “I do not care much for conflict.”

He wasn’t fooling me. His eyes were too innocent, smile too innocuous. But there was nothing I could do about that when my attempt to rid myself of him had failed, embarrassingly so.

“I won’t try anything if you don’t,” I said. It seemed too good to be true.

“Splendid!” He stood, clapping his hands together. “Well, I shall look forward to your next visit. Do be careful on your way back, for I hear there’s a vampire in the area.” He pushed the basket into my hand, scooping out the two remaining bottles and cradling them in the crook of his elbow.

I raised an unimpressed eyebrow. “Don’t say that too loudly. You might scare your blood source away.”

"Not to worry. There's a high supply of them if anything goes wrong."

I barked a single, morbid laugh. He had a point.

Ansel smiled. His fangs looked incredibly sharp. "My source seems a hardy girl, though. I do not think she will scare so easily."

I wondered, as he turned and made for some hidden destination, black cape flaring out behind him, whether that was a compliment or a promise of things to come.

CHAPTER SIX

A few mornings later, I padded downstairs and was greeted by the sight of Markus stuffing clothes into his travel sack. My hair fell out of its lacklustre knot, catching on the coarse wool of my nightgown as I idled in his doorway.

"Is it that time already?" I asked. I'd been so distracted lately that the day had crept up on me.

"'Fraid so." He picked up a loose piece of parchment from his desk, checking it over, then shoving it in his pocket. "Greenwood's got some new lads that need breakin' in. You lot will be fine here without me."

"But what about ..." I couldn't finish my sentence.

What about me?

Was it too much to expect him to stay an extra week, just until a little more time had passed? To wait until my hand was fully healed and my bruises had faded?

I looked down at the wooden floor. Of course it was. This wasn't about me. Markus had his responsibilities, not just in Myrtle Gully, but the bigger surrounding towns. And sickness waited for no one, something I knew better than most.

"I won't be gone as long as last year. Back before the close of autumn." He rubbed his back. "You get those supplies you were gonna?"

"What? What supplies?" Had I forgotten something else? But then I understood he was talking about my weekly trip to the inn. A trip I usually enjoyed but now found myself avoiding. I sighed and leaned heavily against the doorframe. It was time to face the music. "No, not yet. Do you want me to go?"

He grunted his assent, and I trudged back to my room to change. It took me longer than usual, my fingers fumbling over the buttons of my dress. I gave up on doing anything refined with my hair, simply leaving it down. Never mind if it made me look like an underfed milkmaid.

I hurried downstairs when I'd finished and called out a goodbye. Only Hugo deigned to answer, and I rolled my eyes to the ceiling in exasperation. I was going to pick up a cartload's worth of items for Markus—the man could at least pretend he was grateful.

I had to dodge a stampede of children as I shut the door behind me. They ran up and down the main street, squealing as they splashed each other with a bucket of dirty water. Old Man Kenny walked out from behind a house, two hares swinging from a cord around his shoulder.

The gravel crunched beneath my feet as two boys, Louis and Lucus—or was it Liam and Luka? I always got their names wrong—exited the butcher's shop, laughing. Their voices grew hushed as they spotted me, not at all subtle, and I tried not to let it bother me. It was a natural reaction. If I were them, I might gossip about me too.

They shot me dirty looks as I passed. I shot an even dirtier one back.

A rat snuffled at the door of the inn as I approached, and I shooed it away, cringing.

It was a quiet morning at the Gully Inn. Light shone through the windows and illuminated the wooden interior, the worn, empty tables, and the stag head resting as a trophy on the wall. Two men lounged at the furthermost table from the counter, their long, ashy hair pulled back in messy braids. Their beards were overgrown, their clothing dirt-splattered and worn. Travellers, I decided, who were passing through the village, making an insignificant, forgettable stop on the way to their true destination.

I nodded at them. They paid me no attention, too busy staring down their tankards.

At the counter, I called out, "Good morning, Marie."

A tall, middle-aged woman popped her head out from behind the stockroom door, and I gave her a little wave. She paused, then caught herself.

"Morning, Lena," Marie said, wiping her hands on a rag and throwing it on the bar. She put an arm beneath the bundle tied to her waist, hoisting it up before moving a flap of material out of the way. "Say good morning, Elain." Elain scrunched her face up at the light.

I leaned forward, resting my elbows on the counter. "Hey, Elain, didn't see you there. Looking cute, as usual." About four months ago, Hugo and I had delivered Marie's fourth daughter. Neither of us had delivered a baby without Markus before, but the man had insisted something along the lines of 'If you don't do it now, then you're never gonna.'

Marie said, "I was wondering when I'd see you next. You must have run out of half the pantry by now." There was a slight edge to her voice. She, at least, was trying to hide the disdain.

My chuckle was forced. "Mm. That, and Markus is leaving again."

"So soon?" Her gaze darted to my neck, and I touched my collar self-consciously. "I would have thought that ..." She trailed off, bouncing on the balls of her feet. Elain bobbed with the motion. "But duty calls, I suppose. What can I get for you?"

I gave her Markus's order, as well as a list of my own personal items, being generous with the quantities. Not only could Markus use the extra food on his trip away, but Marie could use the extra money. She took my basket, then disappeared into the back rooms. I sat at the bar, swinging my feet against the wood of the stool.

The two men muttered to each other, voices slurred, and I did my best to keep from eavesdropping.

I had a busy day ahead, made even busier by Markus's departure. I couldn't believe I had forgotten. The days were slipping by faster than I could keep up.

The carpenter was dropping by the clinic later to replace some shelves that were rotting, so I needed to make sure I was back in time to greet him. But then, little Agna Miller was vomiting, and I had promised Markus I'd deliver her some dried chamomile. Did I have time to do so now? Markus would want his supplies as soon as possible, so maybe waiting would be better?

A guttural voice interrupted my thoughts.

"Bar wench," called one of the men, the more thickset of the two. "Where's the woman gone?"

My top lip curled up. I glanced around the room. "Are you talking to *me*?"

The two men were so similar in appearance, they had to be brothers. They shared the same hooked nose, heavy brow —and the same atrocious manners, I discovered, as the second man, greasy-haired and wiry, whistled. "How much you cost, girlie?"

I blinked. He did not just say that.

"You look like the type to tell me how to do my job," I said rigidly. "So, unfortunately for you, there's not enough gold in the world to tempt me."

"Gold?" he muttered, rifling through his pockets. He almost fell off the chair at the shift in weight, and I clenched my teeth to keep from scoffing.

The thickset brother smacked the table. "The woman, bar wench, where did she go?"

"She's busy. Stop being so rude and just *wait*."

He stood, toppling his chair.

"What are you ..." My throat closed up as he started towards me, and I jumped off the stool. It occurred to me that I was a fool. I could have avoided this situation if I'd spoken with a soft tone and well-placed smile, but the stress had been building within me, constricting, until I couldn't help but snap at someone.

"Don't touch me," I said as he stomped close enough for me to smell his body odour. I reached over the bar, grabbing a tankard. It wouldn't do much damage, but it was better than nothing. "Marie," I yelled. The man caught me by the wrist. His brother moved out from behind the table and started towards us. "Marie!"

There was a pounding of footsteps, and Marie appeared from the back rooms.

"Lena, what's going on?" She looked from the bear of a man hunching over me to the tankard I held poised to strike. The man had halted at her entrance, his fingers tightening on my wrist until I couldn't feel my fingertips. "Sir," Marie said, cheeks flushing, "what are you doing?"

He stared at her, then me, his gaze assessing. Wordlessly, he dropped his hand and took a step back.

My heart was hammering, and I was cold with shock at the sudden danger, but also at the fact he'd actually backed down. I'd called Marie out of desperation, not because I thought it would do any good.

The man turned to stalk away, gripping his brother by the back of his neck as he passed. The door slammed shut behind them.

Elain let out a cry, breaking the silence.

Marie sighed. “They’ll be back, unfortunately. Been lodging upstairs for a few days now. Should have seen the gear they came in with—some kind of hunters, I’d say, though I don’t know why they’re looking for game around here. Maybe looking for the beast that ...” She cleared her throat and eased Elain upright.

I stared at the door, a tumult of emotions raging through me. Anger, fear, indignation. Pride in standing up for myself, stupid as it was.

But hunters? I wouldn’t have thought so.

“Lena?”

I sucked in a breath. “Pardon?”

Marie levelled me with a suspicious look. Elain had quieted, sucking on a tiny fist. “Lena, are you okay?”

“Yes,” I said too quickly. “Yes, I’m fine. Sorry. I didn’t mean to cause a scene.”

“It’s okay. But that’s not why I was asking.” Her gaze ran down my body, catching on my neck and waist. When she met my eyes again, it was like she’d never seen me before. “You look tired. And thin.”

This was why I had been avoiding leaving home.

“It’s just the stress,” I lied. “I’ll get over it soon.” I laughed at the end to soften my words, and she nodded, still concerned.

“I can send one of the girls over to help at the clinic if you need it. Angela would be happy to.”

Angela’s name sent a jolt through me. I hadn’t thought of her since we’d parted in the forest. How fortunate she hadn’t been with me when I ran into Ansel. Her presence would have made things infinitely more complicated. More dangerous.

"Thank you," I said and picked up my basket, now full of flour, cheese, milk, and other items. "I'll let you know."

I paid her the copper coins then left, checking over my shoulder once outside, almost expecting the two men to be waiting for me.

But no. Everything was tranquil, though the children still squealed from somewhere far away. The main street was as it always was.

I started for the clinic but stopped as I passed by a narrow lane. There, lazing in a shaft of sunlight beside a house, was the lizard I'd come across the night of the festival. He watched as I came closer.

"Hi, lizard." I pulled a berry from my basket, dropping it a few inches from him. "If you're hungry."

I was at the edge of the lane when his head shot down and he scurried forward, tongue shooting out. Satisfaction filled me as he swallowed. He was a pretty little thing, layers of brown and yellow running up his torso to line his black eyes.

It would be nice being a lizard, I decided. Lounging in the sun and watching the world go by. I sighed and stepped out of the lane, leaving him in peace. It was almost mid-morning. Markus would want to be off soon.

The clinic was in a flurry when I returned. Markus was yelling to Hugo from the surgical room about the trocar he'd misplaced, and Hugo yelled back from the kitchen that he'd thrown it in one of the medical bags. Hugo rolled his eyes as I began filling the pantry and mouthed a word to me that I couldn't make out.

I shrugged. Making myself heard would be too much effort.

Markus's shouts petered out as he entered the room and saw me. I held the basket out to him. He hesitated—strange for Markus—then covered my hand with his.

"I don't want to be seein' any more of this when I'm back next," he said, running a finger across his neck. "You be a smart girl, like I know you are."

It had only just set in that he was leaving again. Next to us, Hugo acted like he wasn't listening.

"And if you *are* bein' smart and somethin' still happens," Markus continued, "you send that heap of dung to the deepest pits of the afterlife." He slipped something cool and smooth into my hand.

The knife was small enough I could conceal it within my pockets—within my hand, even—but, with the proper force, long enough to penetrate a man's heart. Maybe I should have felt disturbed at such a gift. I didn't. All I felt was loved.

"Lena?" Markus prompted.

"I'll be smart." My voice broke. "You too, okay? Don't die of old age while you're gone."

Hugo smothered a laugh, and Markus glowered. That he didn't grumble anything back meant he was feeling particularly affectionate.

"You two look after each other," Markus said, then cleared his throat. He untangled our hands and pushed past me to the hallway. "Dawn Lord knows you're both disasters."

Hugo didn't hide his laughter this time, and neither did I.

Markus left without fanfare, giving me a rushed, one-arm hug before plodding out the door. He was heading west to Greenwood City, riding with a merchant acquaintance who stopped in at Myrtle Gully every few months. When summer turned to autumn, he would go north to the town of Haycock.

I watched as he rode on the back of the wagon, puffing away at his pipe. He was invaluable as a healer here; it was why the villagers put up with his moods, why people spoke fondly of him even when there was not much good to say. They would miss him for his expertise. I would miss him because I knew him.

Hugo and I were kept busy the following days without Markus, and though I felt guilty, I learned to enjoy my mentor's absence. It meant I didn't have to sneak nervous glances over my shoulder when collecting blood. Predictably, the people that came to be treated weren't as friendly as usual. I overheard a couple of them tell Hugo they were happy to wait as long as necessary if it meant he would be the one treating them. Until then, I hadn't been aware Hugo possessed such a colourful vocabulary.

I did not cross paths with the two men from the inn again, for which I was particularly glad.

I wasn't as nervous when the time came again to visit the castle. I reasoned that if I couldn't anger the vampire by trying to kill him, there would be very little I could do to receive his ire.

Not to mention we had a truce.

Hugo had gone to visit Trudi, so I estimated I had until midnight before my presence would be missed. I rugged up in a shawl and hooked my basket over my arm, bottles of blood clinking together.

I didn't announce my presence as I entered the castle but headed towards the library. It didn't seem too out there to presume Ansel had some supernatural sense that would let him know I had arrived. I was proven right when, minutes later, he swung the library door wide open and announced, "Thief, I have an errand for you."

I placed down the book I was flipping through and crossed my arms. What did he want me to say—yes, master?

Ansel balanced an ochre rug on his shoulder, and it teetered from side to side as he walked to me. "Now, I need you to fetch me some books, preferably historical in kind, though certain scriptural accounts may work just as well."

"You want books?" I cocked my head. "Do you even know which room you're in?"

"Books that are not entirely archaic." He unrolled the rug as he spoke, shaking it out, and a great plume of dust hit me in the face. He called out an apology, but it was made insincere by the fact I was sure he'd done it on purpose.

I coughed, pulling a vial of amber liquid from my pocket. I opened it, then paused.

"Will you hold this for me?" I asked, trying to swallow through the scratchiness of my throat.

Ansel didn't look at me as he smoothed down the edges of the rug, then held out his hand.

"Thank you," I said and gave it to him. Except I was clumsy, artfully so, and a trickle of liquid landed on his thumb.

He hissed and dropped the vial.

I recoiled at the sudden outburst. "What's wrong?"

Standing, Ansel crushed the vial beneath his boot. He covered his mouth as if sheepish. "Oh dear, I'm sorry about that. What a dreadful mistake. And this rug is ruined now, pretty as it is, for we shall never rid it of the smell." He wrinkled his nose. "Take it with you, yes? I do not want it clogging up my halls."

A muscle in my jaw twitched. "There's no smell."

He sucked in his cheeks and studied me, trying to ascertain if I was exceptionally dumb or exceptionally clever. "Do not take me for a fool, and please do not do that again. It was quite rude, considering our ceasing of threats."

I struggled against the warming of my cheeks, hating that he was so astute. I'd known exactly what I was doing when I placed an infusion ripe with garlic in his hands.

"Sorry," I muttered. "I was curious." I sat on the other side of the rug, feeling like a child that deserved to be chastised. This would be my time-out.

"Then might I suggest you ask next time?" He sighed. "A perfectly good rug, utterly ruined."

"Surely, it's not that bad." But then, it probably was that bad for him. That knowledge, at least, meant my little experiment hadn't been a complete failure. "There's a nice rug upstairs in one of the cabinets—blue and white with a pretty flower pattern."

"No, it won't suit the ambience." He sat on an embroidered footstool, twisting his ring around his forefinger. "Maybe ... No, that one won't work either."

"Sorry," I said again, taking the moral high ground. Slaughterer though he may be, I was better than petty payback. When I was caught in the act of it, anyway.

"What?" His attention snapped to me. "Oh. Yes, yes, that's fine. It didn't touch my heart, so all is forgotten."

I hesitated, wondering how he'd react to my next words. "You know, you're very forgiving for a spawn of evil."

"One of my many virtues."

I quirked an eyebrow. He copied the action.

"Don't look so sceptical," he said. "Even the very vilest of sinners has at least one."

I pulled out a loose thread from the edge of the rug. It really was a pretty piece—it would fetch five or six silver coins at the market. "And do you count yourself amongst their ranks?"

"Me, a vile sinner?" He tossed his head in a practised act of dismissal. "Not in the slightest. I've always been generous. I like the hope that flares in broken people's eyes."

My fingers paused on the thread. "The hope that flares before you break them again?"

He rolled his eyes and went to pull a piece of stray hair from his cheek but jerked his hand back and scowled. "That really is filthy," he said under his breath. Then louder, "You are wilfully misinterpreting me, and I dislike it. Stop."

I laughed, surprising us both.

Should I write a list for him, detailing the *generous* ways he'd broken the people of Myrtle Gully? Perhaps I could put it in song and dance to it over his grave one day. The villagers were at a loss without Father Snow, a flock of sheep wandering the wild without their shepherd. As kind as Father Pentaghast seemed to be, he didn't, and would probably never, inspire the same kind of love that his predecessor had.

"But in answer to the question you're really asking," Ansel continued, eyeing me like I was one tomb short of a graveyard, "contrary to popular belief, vampires are not inherently evil. And I am usually very kind to my food."

"Victims," I interjected. At his blank look, I said, "They're victims, not food."

"Oh?" His voice was wry. "And that's what you call the little lambs you butcher, is it? How self-aware of you."

I opened my mouth, but nothing came out. His expression turned smug, and I huffed.

"The point is, you can survive without killing anyone. You're doing it right now."

"Yes, well, not many vampires have the benefit of a blood delivery service. You should be grateful, thief. I've given you a business opportunity."

"I already have a job," I snapped and then felt stupid for saying it.

A closed-lip smile. "I know."

I looked to the ceiling before counting the book spines on the highest bookshelf. A ladder rung soon obscured my view, and I gave up.

"Are you all right?" Ansel asked, leaning forward on his elbows.

I took a deep breath. I wasn't usually like this—this volatile mess of a person, itching for a fight but too aggravated to see it through. I tried to release my pent-up feelings on my exhale.

"Yes," I said. In need of a good scream but all right, nonetheless. "I should go."

"Wait. Please." The words left his mouth so fast I wondered if he'd meant to say them at all. "Perhaps you might ... stay here a while longer? There's an ancient pot of tea leaves in the kitchen, should you be so inclined."

I didn't think I'd heard him correctly. Me, stay here longer?

With him?

"I don't know," I said slowly. "People might notice I'm missing. And that would be dangerous for both of us." The first part was a lie. No one would notice my absence for a little while yet. I didn't like how naturally deception was beginning to come to me. "Why?" I asked.

His brow furrowed as he considered his words. "I am a social creature and have been left on my own for far too long. I could do with a distraction."

"You're lonely?"

"No. Though it would be much easier were that the case."

I took stock of the situation. My body needed rest. I felt it in the rusty hinges of my limbs, the slight weight of my eyelids. But my mind, on the other hand—my conscience—

felt inclined to join him. Not for his sake, but for the sake of the villagers.

A happy vampire was a happy village, after all.

"All right," I said, then folded the edge of the rug to roll it.

"No, no, *no*, forget that silly thing. I was being dramatic." Ansel's voice came from right above me, and I stiffened.

"You want it still?" I asked.

"Oh, yes. The smell will come out after a good wash."

"Okay." I stood, keeping my gaze on the black jewel pinned at his throat. He was too close.

"Thief?"

I moved my gaze up to his mouth. "Mm?"

"You will stay?"

"Mmhmm. Not for long, though."

Finally, our eyes met. His irises were just as I remembered —the flat, solid slate of the ocean. The last colour a drowning woman would ever see. But I noticed more this time. He had the slightest of crow's feet and a single silver eyelash tucked in amongst the woodland of black ones.

These things made him appear more of a person and less of a monster. I didn't like these things.

I stepped around him, closer to the door. 'So," I asked, trying to hide my wariness, "what do you want to do?"

He thought about it, tapping his jaw with a finger. Suddenly, his expression lit up. "I have just the thing. Would you prefer honey, cinnamon, or lemon?"

I blinked. "Lemon?"

"Good choice."

Ansel guided me to the chapel, pointing out little upgrades and alterations he'd made along the way. The chapel itself remained unchanged, and I was grateful for that fact. The castle had been mine before he'd woken up. I wanted at least one part of it to remain familiar.

"I'll just be a moment," he called out behind him, disappearing down the trap door. I sat on a pew, glad the tension between us in the library had dissipated with the change in setting.

Ansel returned with an armful of items and, without thinking, I went to help him.

"Thank you," he said, handing me a bowl, a thin branch from a lemon tree, and a bag full of eggs. "On the altar, please."

When I turned back to him, he passed me a pot plant. I looked between him and it.

"You had pot plants on your window," he said, as if that were a feasible explanation. "I thought you would like them."

They were purple pansies, nearly at the end of their life. Still, they were pretty. "I do like them."

He nodded like he'd expected as much.

"Where did you get this?" I asked, watching as he unfolded a towel and examined a cluster of mould at its corner. He shrugged and laid it across his shoulders.

"Off the back of a trading wagon, somewhere between here and that city over there." He pointed in the vicinity of the door unhelpfully.

You stole it, I thought.

Ah, well. It was mine now.

"Now," he said, turning to face me, "usually we'd wash our hair first, but there's not enough water for the two of us. We shall just have to hope for the best. Would you like to go first, or shall I?"

"What are we doing?"

He gestured to the various items as though it were obvious. "Hair treatments. I don't stay this fine with vampirism alone."

I pulled a face before realising he was serious. "Oh," I said at his expectant look. "Okay."

I watched him mix the ingredients, wondering if the eggs were rotten and if this was payback for the garlic incident, but everything seemed normal. He spoke to me as he prepared, explaining that he'd love to add a bit of milk to thicken the consistency, but the farmers' cows would run whenever they sensed him coming, and he didn't want to cause any heart attacks by chasing them through their paddocks. I listened, torn between fascination at his likable manner and utter confusion as to how my life had taken this bizarre route.

He offered to let me go first again, and I quickly declined, not wanting his fingers near my neck. That meant, of course, my fingers would be near *his* neck. I was used to uncomfortably close proximities with people, but this was a completely different beast.

C'mon, Lena, I thought to myself, shifting into the clinical mindset I'd practised for years. Ansel leaned back on the pew, taking his earrings out and tossing his hair over his shoulders. *If you can treat Old Man Kenny's toenail fungus, you can treat a vampire's hair.*

I pushed my sleeves up, wetted my hands, and got to work.

Minutes later, I had decided it really was like treating a patient I wasn't fond of. If I pretended that I didn't mind, they would do the same. And Ansel didn't even have the need to pretend, for he spent almost the entire time recounting a story from before his slumber. Something about trying to evade a group of vampires, getting lost in a cornfield, and spending the daylight hours hiding beneath his cape and a very fat horse.

I didn't want to laugh at first—I wanted to stay cold and aloof—but I couldn't keep it up for long. His words were too engaging, and even if he *was* the current bane of my existence, I was terrible at holding a grudge. Besides, it felt good to laugh. Healthy, almost.

I had been gentle in my ministrations up until that point, but there were some wayward hairs refusing to meld beneath my hands. I tried not to pull too hard as I got them under control. Tugging at his hair would yield a similar consequence to tugging the tail of a sleeping wolf: it would get me eaten.

"I do hope you're being kind to my hair," he said as if he knew my mind.

"Your hair is fine." I added another glob of treatment to prove my point.

"'Tis better than fine, I'll thank you."

We were both quiet for a while, Ansel deep in thought, me intent on my task. I hummed one of the tunes the musicians had played on festival night. The song was a staple for every festival, its melody buoyant and suited for choreographed claps and spinning steps.

The liquid on my hands was chilly, as was the breeze sifting in through the open ceiling, and I cut the tune off, fighting a shiver.

"Are you cold?" Ansel whispered.

I shook my head, then remembered he couldn't see. "I'm okay." Finished with the mixture, I wiped my hands on the towel around his shoulders. "Why do you keep your hair so long, anyway? Did it used to be the fashion?"

He craned his neck to look at me. "I keep it long because it is the only outward sign that time has passed."

"What do you mean?"

A dark look passed through his eyes like gathering storm clouds. The look dispersed as fast as it came.

He explained, "A vampire never ages. A vampire never scars. Physically, a vampire can rarely progress. I wear my hair long to remember that time has passed and that time will continue to pass. To remember that I am not entirely set in stone, nor completely invulnerable, and that although time is constant in trying to leave me behind, it will never quite manage." He smoothed a clump of wet hair behind his ear. "Also, I think it's rather fetching."

I laughed beneath my breath. "Of course you do."

I hadn't thought what it would feel like for time itself to abandon me. To have the knowledge I would never grow a day older, never settle down one day.

Or perhaps I *was* familiar with that knowledge, only in a different context.

"It's ready to rinse," I said, picking up the basin of water. Ansel followed my movements, starting when he spotted the empty bowl of hair treatment.

"You used all of it." The words were accusatory.

"Yes."

"But what about your hair?"

I shook my head and placed the basin on the altar, water sloshing from side to side. "My hair is happy to sacrifice itself for yours."

His scoff was half laughter, half disbelief. "You've thwarted me."

"Have I? Turn back around, please, so I can wash it out."

He shot me a reluctant look but did as I asked. The water was freezing, relatively fresh from the river, and I took no small amount of pleasure pouring it down his scalp.

"How did I thwart you?" I asked, combing my fingers through his hair and wincing as beads of icy water ran down my forearms.

"Hm?" His eyes were shut.

I sighed. "Never mind."

His hair was soon rinsed and dripping onto the stone floor. I towelled off the ends, glancing up every now and again to see the moon rising.

"I really do have to go now," I said once I'd finished. I blew on my fingers, trying to turn them back to their normal colour.

Ansel stretched on the pew, rolling his head on his shoulders. He gathered his hair to the side, delighted. "You were so thorough."

I nodded, a smile playing about my lips. Seeing the dark, wet strands drip onto his shirt, glisten against his skin, felt oddly more intimate than having my hands on his scalp. Almost like I was catching him in a rare, vulnerable state.

Happy vampire, happy village, I thought, gathering my basket and placing the pot plant inside. *Job completed for the night.*

Yet I hesitated to leave.

I said, "I'm sorry again, about earlier with the garlic. I shouldn't have done that. Even if you *were* being dramatic about it."

He made a little sound in the back of his throat, one of amusement, and before I could control it, my smile grew. His gaze met mine, and I made my face go blank. If anything, it amused him more.

"I'll see what I can do about those books, but don't get your hopes up," I continued, ignoring the heat that rose to my cheeks. "Also, please don't eat anyone in the meantime."

He tilted his head to the side and looked at me through his eyelashes. An incomprehensible expression passed over him. It made me nervous.

He said, "Only if you hurry back."

CHAPTER SEVEN

I ransacked Markus's bookshelf with very little luck.

Only a handful of other people in the village knew their letters, and so I was forced to decide between spending a week's pay by taking the trip to Haycock or making a visit to the church.

I practised smiling in my hand mirror before leaving, unable to fool even myself. When I finally came to the conclusion that my efforts at sweet-talking would be futile, I reached beneath my bed to the linen sack hidden there, pulling out a silver coin.

Bribery wasn't really the action of a saint, but I wouldn't exactly call it a sin either. And besides, even the Dawn Lord would warm to me with this amount, let alone his priest.

The grey stone church was the centrepiece of Myrtle Gully, the head of the main square. Its spire was visible from the very outskirts of the village, like a constant sign to guide our way. Or, depending on the point of view, like a particularly persistent voyeur.

The arched door was open as it always was throughout the day. Open in invitation for prayer, for worship, for luncheons and knitting circles and arm-wrestling competitions. Father Snow had allowed anything, really. Said it helped create unity among us.

Personally, I think he just got bored.

The chapel was sparsely filled. A more conventional priest would frown on using the Dawn Lord's church as a place akin to the local tavern, so my guess was that this—this quiet, solemn place of worship—was how it would stay.

I waved at the little boy seated on the back pew, fiddling with the pages of a prayer book. He ducked his head. I tried not to be hurt, but instances like this were growing more common.

The door to Father Snow's office—no, it was Father Pentaghast's office now—was shut, muffled voices fluctuating behind it. I waited for a few minutes, taking a seat and twiddling my thumbs, but it soon became obvious this wasn't going to be a short visit. A woman's voice grew in volume, an angry edge to her words, and I decided it was time to step in if only to save the priest from the wrath of us small-time village folk.

I had already knocked when I finally figured out whose voice it was, and by then, it was too late. The door opened, and the stonemason's mother shoved past me to snatch the little boy's hand.

"Come, Paul," she barked.

No wonder the boy had averted his eyes. I recognised him now and felt for him. I wouldn't talk to me either if it meant dealing with the discipline of that woman.

A sigh came from beside me.

"Off trots the devil on her cloven hooves," Father Pentaghast drawled, then chuckled at my wide-eyed stare. "Or perhaps I'm being a little unfair? It has been a trying time for all." He motioned me inside. "There's no need to loiter in my doorway. Come in."

I had not been in this room for years, and yet it matched my memory almost exactly. A humble desk sat in the corner, and sparsely filled shelves lined the walls. A mosaic of the Dawn Lord hung on the mantelpiece, surrounded by incense sticks. Their floral blend was a little too strong for my liking.

Being here bothered me more than I thought it would. This was where Father Snow had spent most of his time before ... well, before Ansel got to him.

And here I was, in Father Snow's old office, running an errand for his murderer.

Father Pentaghast fetched a cup and water pitcher from one of the shelves. "I'm glad you're here. Please thank your friend Hugo for me."

"Hugo? Why?" I hadn't seen him this morning. He'd been out making a house call before I'd even left my bed.

"He did not tell you to come?"

"No."

We watched each other, waiting for the other person to speak. He was dressed in a black tunic, no sign of the Dawn

Lord's gold on him. I wouldn't have known him to be a priest or a religious man, even, but for the small effigy around his wrist.

As far as I knew, Father Snow had rarely spent a day out of his vestments. Father Pentaghast cleared his throat pointedly. "Well, you're here now." He passed me the cup.

"Thank you," I murmured as he poured the water. "You were looking for me?"

He nodded and sat on the desk, placing the pitcher to the side. "Yes, I had a question for you, but you were out when I stopped by. I ran into Hugo on the way back, and he assured me he'd pass on a message."

"This was last night?" My voice rose in pitch.

"That's right."

Last night when I'd been at Ansel's. We must have just missed each other. And now Hugo knew I hadn't been home, which wasn't a huge problem, but ... well, it wasn't ideal.

I racked my brain for an excuse. "I was treating someone. They thought it was an emergency, but everything's fine now." Lying in a church. What would be next, vandalising an effigy?

Oh wait, I'd already done that.

He waved a hand, dismissive. "You don't need to explain. You're all busy in this place. But if that's not why you came, then what are you doing here?"

I frowned, shocked by his bluntness.

He rolled his lips together like he was trying not to smile. "Please do not take offence, Miss Lena, but you do not come to weekly worship, and you do not seem like the kind of person interested in my help, offered or not." His accent turned my name from two simple syllables into the whisper of a song. He would be wonderful at sermon, if only for the fluency of his voice, the rolling of his vowels.

I shook my head slowly, indignance a fire in my chest.

I didn't like it when people presumed. Experience had taught me that most of them were too self-centred to see the truth. "I didn't realise I came across as such a martyr."

"No, I wasn't suggesting you do," he conceded. "Now, you have a bag in your hands, so I suppose that means I have something you'd like?"

I took a quick drink of water—to cool the fire—and pasted my smile back on. "Books, Father, history ones if you please. I know they're precious but"—I pulled the silver coin from my pocket and held it out; no point being subtle about it—"I do hope you'll accept this donation as a token of my sincerity."

Father Pentaghast's forehead crinkled as he plucked the coin from my fingers. I resisted the urge to snatch it back and hide it down my undershirt.

"So, the Dawn Lord and I are to steal your hard-earned money?" He sighed and stepped forward to slip the coin back into my pocket. "Keep it. I think you'll need it more than Him." He jerked his chin to the mosaic of the Dawn Lord.

Was this really the same man who so reverently committed Father Snow's soul into the Dawn Lord's hands?

To reject a donation, especially one so large, in a village as small as this ... I didn't know what to think.

"The books are through there," he said and walked me through the chapel, gesturing to a door opposite his office. "I haven't found the time to clean them up yet. Or the will, to be perfectly honest." His cheeks dimpled at my questioning glance. "I hope you're not averse to a bit of dust."

It wasn't as bad as his words had me envision. The castle had obviously scarred me with its wiggling piles of dust and cobwebs that bordered on sentient. The mere memory alone made my eyes burn and my nose itch.

Father Pentaghast leaned in the doorway as I pulled the grime-encrusted tomes from their shelves.

"About why I came to see you," he started, and I glanced over my shoulder to show I was listening. "Well, have you travelled to Haycock much?"

I blew the dust off a black, leather-bound title. "Quite a few times. With Markus, of course, and then with some friends." *Once with my family,* I almost said.

He didn't need to know that.

"And did you like it?"

Did I like it? It was small compared to the other big cities I had been to, and a little dirty, but that was to be expected. The people were nice enough. Trudi enjoyed the shopping there. I hadn't made the journey in a couple of years, but there was nothing really to dislike.

"I guess so. Do you?" He had been stationed there for a while, from what I could remember.

"No."

"Oh." I turned to look at him again, but his expression was mild. "Sorry to hear that." One book into the bag and then another. They were all thick. I wouldn't be able to fit many in.

He said, "But if you don't mind it—well. How would you feel about a short visit there from time to time?"

I almost laughed again. "No, I don't think so."

There was a beat of silence.

I had the sudden urge to hide within the towering shelves, burrow in between the books until I too had been there long enough to be covered with filth and become unrecognisable.

The feeling was gone as soon as it came.

I heard his teeth click together before he said, "I'd think it would be helpful to you."

"Really? Why's that?"

"Time away. Time when no one will look at you like you're a disease or wait for you to crumble from the load your brittle shoulders seem to carry. The clinic there could always use the help, and you could come back with Markus at the end of autumn."

I turned to him as he spoke, watching as the energy seemed to drain from him. Absently, he stroked the beads around his wrist.

It was rude of him to say, but I liked that he called things as they were.

I shoved the last book that would fit into my bag. "It's kind of you to think of me, but I can't. I couldn't leave Hugo to tend to everyone on his own."

"Oh, I don't know. I think he'd do all right."

I rolled my eyes at the books, then hitched the bag over my shoulder and closed the distance between us.

"Thank you for the books, Father Pentaghast." I tilted my chin to look him in the eyes. "And I'll think about Haycock"—no, I wouldn't—"but I just don't really think it would work."

"I understand," he said quietly and moved out of the doorway to let me past. I left with what I thought was a decent haul.

Ansel, when I next delivered blood, did not seem to echo the sentiment.

"Oh, they didn't," he moaned. "I hate this book." He was leaning back in the rocking chair, recently placed within the library, a book covering his face. His heel tapped an agitated rhythm against the footstool.

"Apparently they did." I continued skimming the pages of the tome. Nearly eighty years ago, a renowned priest had warned the people of a certain artisan city against loving their crafts more than they loved the Dawn Lord. The people chose to ignore the warning. Three months later, the city was overrun with plague.

"He did it on purpose." Ansel's mutter was visceral, and I wasn't sure I quite heard right.

"Pardon?"

He shook his head, plucking the book from over his eyes to drop it on the floor. "Just read, please."

I blew a raspberry. "The next section looks to be a compilation of sermons."

"Next."

"Divine healings of the sick."

"Just skip the goodwill babble and find something of interest."

I marked down the section for later, then shut my eyes and opened to a random page. "The Purging of Evils?"

"Hm. Perhaps. Anything grizzly in there?"

"Hang on." I followed the words with a finger. "A priest quashed some kind of religious rebellion, a priestess slew a wicked beast ... Oh, and some deacon supposedly managed to banish a horde of demons that were wreaking havoc within the towns. Deacon Zar—" I stopped, squinted. "Zardirovak? Is that how you say it?"

"*No.*" Ansel gasped. "Show me that."

I passed him the book. He read through it much faster than I had before laughing the most startled and elated of laughs. "That sly dog. He actually did it."

"You knew this man?"

"Knew him? I was the one that suggested the position to him. Do you have any idea how difficult it is for a vampire to receive any kind of priesthood? Near impossible, that's how difficult." He passed the book back to me as he spoke, and I almost lost my grip on it in shock.

"That deacon was a vampire?"

"And a very pious one at that." He shrugged. "Of course, the church wouldn't have known that. I imagine he feigned sickness or some weakness of the body you mortals seem to have. I once walked in on him reprimanding a room full of vampires after they'd celebrated the winter solstice by eating half the local county. He had them on their knees, begging for forgiveness by the end of the night. It was quite the spectacle." Ansel bit his lip, fangs pushing deep into the pink flesh. "I wonder if he'd be terribly upset with me for the death of your priest?"

The sounds, smells, and images of that night didn't assault me as they usually would when Father Snow was mentioned. I was far too disconcerted.

"So," I said, trying to make sense of the senseless, "banishing the horde of demons?"

"I imagine he politely asked the vampires residing in that specific area to leave. No doubt they found his plight amusing and agreed to cooperate. We can't stay in groups in one place for too long, you understand?"

I nodded blankly.

He kicked back again and said, "I always knew he could do it. What happened to him? Does it say?"

"Um." I glanced down. "He went missing a couple of years into his travels."

"Ah, an early retirement, then. A pity, but always the safest option. I shall have to meet with him again someday."

I shut the book gingerly and placed it on the ground. If it held any other startling revelations that skewed my perspective of the world, I didn't want to know. "That was over fifty years ago. You think he's still around?"

"Oh, yes. In fact, I think he probably moved somewhere near the sea—a coastal town, perhaps—and if he's no longer in the church's service, then he's opened a flower shop. He always did love growing things."

"Huh. Would you ever become a holy man?" I would think it impossible before, if not due to his vampirism, then due to his blatant irreverence, but he may have practised his own brand of piety. Who was I to judge?

He snorted. "Heavens, no; the pay is terrible."

I grinned, able to relate. The clothes I wore were testament: trousers with a hole in one knee and a white dress shirt that had both sleeves ripped off at the shoulders. A consequence of working in a clinic that needed a constant supply of rags.

Absently, Ansel gathered his hair together and began a loose plait. I watched, entranced by the fluidity of his fingers. He threaded the three pieces of hair in complete symmetry. What would it be like, I wondered, to be able to produce perfection? To be able to create, knowing the creation would be infallible?

I shook my head at myself. It was just a hairstyle.

Ansel tied off the end with a ribbon. "What's next?"

I sighed, plucking the next book from the pile. "The Legion Plague."

He groaned. "Anything but that."

"Why? It looks pretty grizzly. I thought that's what you wanted."

"Look at the date."

I looked. "Oh." He would have been awake for this particular calamity. "You were there?"

"That's one way of putting it," he said wryly. "Anything else, please. Go back to the healings or sermons if you must."

I shut the book with an audible thud. "No. I think I've had enough of this particular history lesson."

His gaze rested on me, calculating. The look told me we were only moving on because he was allowing us to do so. "How about recent history? What's the most outrageous thing that's happened in your lifespan?"

My answer was instant. "Meeting you."

"I said outrageous, darling, not outstanding. Try again."

I faltered at the term of endearment, then quickly recovered. "Why don't you leave this place and go find out? You'd learn more than you would sitting here, reading dusty books."

He tapped a finger against the rocking chair, nail clicking on wood. "I suppose." He was thoughtful before saying abruptly, "Well then, where shall we go?"

"No, not *we*. I'm not going anywhere." For now, at least.

"Why did you suggest it, then?"

I flopped my legs over the armrest, fanning myself with the book. It was too thick for any kind of airflow, and I quickly gave up. "I didn't suggest anything. I said *you* should go."

"And you're happy to just let me eat how I like, are you? If they're not from your dirty village, they don't matter?"

Horror dawned on me. I dropped the book, almost winding myself in the process.

"This isn't a lifetime deal I've made," I blurted. "I'm not going to follow you around, providing blood for you whenever you feel like it."

Ansel nodded soberly. "Nor would I want a little thing scampering around my boot heels."

"Then why would you ..." I shook my head. "Never mind. As long as we understand one another."

He spread his palms. "Naturally. Now, about where we're going. Do you have any aversion to fishing?"

"I just told you—"

"An aversion to stabbing a hook through all the poor, innocent fishes, perhaps?"

"No, but—"

"Excellent." He uncurled from his languid position and stood. "Put your shoes on, and I'll fetch you something warmer to wear. Will they like rabbit meat, do you think? I'm not convinced, so I'll only catch the one, but I can always find another if they seem to enjoy it. Also, do you know what we could sit on? No? Don't worry, I'll find something."

I scrambled to my feet. "I can't come."

"Why?" he asked before his brows rose in realisation. "Ah, I remember. You worry people may notice you are missing. Tell me, do you often entertain guests past midnight?"

That was beside the point, and he knew it. He must have seen the distinct 'no' on my face, because his tone turned soft and cajoling. "Come. I'll tell you stories. You enjoyed that last time."

He was right, I had enjoyed it. But that wasn't the issue.

"I don't want to be in the forest with you," I said plainly.

He cocked his head, frowning. "You think I would hurt you?"

I didn't answer.

Something darker than annoyance passed over his features, an echo of malevolence. Adrenaline shot through me, and I locked my knees to keep from rearing away.

I blinked, and he was back to normal.

"I won't hurt you," he said quietly. "We have a truce, remember? And so far, I am the one who has best kept it."

I cringed at the reminder, embarrassed, but still not quite at the point of regret. Discovering that garlic could hurt him was too valuable a prize.

I tried to think objectively. Apart from that first nightmare-inducing night, he had only ever been civil. I had tricked him, argued with him, tried to kill him, and there had been no real consequence. In our current situation, he had no reason to hurt me. It was only lingering fear that tried to convince me otherwise. He may have mocked my self-awareness, but I had enough of it to admit I found him charming. Intriguing, even.

It frustrated me. A demon should not have been so easy to like.

Ansel moved closer, stepping over the pile of books between us. "Would you rather sleep away the midnight hour than behold it for yourself? The stars really are very pretty this time of night."

His hand skirted over the back of the chair I'd been sitting in. I stared at his fingers, feeling the ghost of pressure around my neck. The bruises may have healed, but I wasn't sure how long it would take the trauma.

"Fine," I said, hoping that facing my fears would expel them. "Fine, we'll go. But I can't stay out too long. It's market day tomorrow, and I don't want to be falling asleep while I'm picking through skeins of yarn."

No one would miss me. Hugo was staying in tonight, and I'd told him I was going to bed early. No one would notice that I was gone. No one would even look.

Ansel unclasped his cape—this one was a rich, red velvet to match the blood he glutted himself on—and wrapped it around me. I stood still, breathing through my nose, so as not to undo the delicate balance between us.

"Tonight is unusually cold," Ansel said, smoothing his palms down my shoulders. "We don't want you shivering at the water's edge, teeth clacking. You'll scare off all the fish."

I turned away, trying not to trip over the excess of cape on the floor. "Hm. Thanks."

Ansel watched my unsubtle retreat with an intensity that made me uncomfortable. Awareness tingled up my spine.

A brilliant smile, wild and intoxicating, lit his face. "My pleasure, little thief."

CHAPTER EIGHT

The stars were indeed pretty that night, so it was a shame I barely noticed. I was too busy squinting at my feet through the dark, trying not to fall flat on my face.

Being out in the forest with Ansel for the first time since he'd nearly killed me was ... surprisingly okay. I noticed myself inching away every time he got too close. He'd noticed as well, if his bright-eyed joviality was any indication.

It also didn't help that he seemed to disappear every few seconds and then reappear as if he were a sheepdog rounding me up. The third time he did so, he returned holding a dead rabbit by the ears, manoeuvring it into the large bag of supplies we'd brought. I paused, balancing on a tree root, and asked whether it would have been better to just dig up some worms—to which he muttered something about only the truly evil using live bait. I'd sighed and looked to the sky for help.

No help. Only pretty stars.

We wandered up the river's edge for almost an hour until Ansel finally found a pocket of grass scattered with leaf litter and deemed it an acceptable spot. I was so tired I would have sat on a rose bush by that point.

The river here was wider than Myrtle Gully's snaking, narrow bed, and the water flowed sedately, sloshing against the rocks. Ansel stood at the edge, glaring at the running water, and it took all of my self-control to resist pushing him in.

It would be funny until it wasn't.

Ansel turned and landed his heavy gaze on me. "You forgot the fishing supplies, didn't you?"

"Vampire," I said, and his brows rose at the word. "I was with you when you packed the bag."

"What bag?"

"The one you've hidden away somewhere. The one with all the supplies. The one I saw you carry the whole way here and put your dead rabbit in."

"You could, at the very least, pretend to play along," he said but moved to get the bag from wherever he'd hidden it.

I sat on the grass, pulling Ansel's cape tight across my shoulders. The crisp, sweet scent of myrtle blossoms wove through my senses, a familiar companion. It calmed me. Beneath it was the smell of honeysuckle, rose oil, and ... a distinct layer of rot.

I inhaled deeply.

It was the cape. I pushed my nose into the lining, hissing as the cloying burn shot up my nostrils. The fragrance suited Ansel, I decided. Flagrant and corrosive. It was more pleasant than painful, even with the burn.

The bag landed beside me, and I yanked the cape down.

Ansel made himself comfortable on the grass, pulling out items. "A cushion for me to sit on—I hope you remembered to bring your own—a few books in case the fish don't deign to show themselves, some cord, my fishing hat and"—he plucked out a bottle of blood—"a midnight snack."

"We seem to be missing a few key things," I said, staring at the pile of books he'd brought.

He swept a stray lock of hair behind his ear. "Oh? But I thought I'd brought all the essential things. You must have too, seeing as you were with me when I packed."

I wrestled with annoyance and lost.

Pointing to the other side of the river, Ansel continued, "Look, is that hemp nettle over there? Pity, I could have spun us a bit of fishing line if I'd had the forethought." There was a raw gleam in his eyes. He was trying to rile me on purpose.

And he was enjoying himself *immensely*.

"Ansel." I sighed, any wariness I might have felt overpowered by irritation and the kind of tiredness that makes one impervious to caring. "Go find a stick or something we can use. I'll take care of the rabbit."

He thought on it for a moment, then acquiesced, throwing the rabbit at my feet and moseying off to I-didn't-care-where.

It was lucky I had my knife from Markus, because Ansel sure hadn't been thinking about the logistics of cutting up the bait. By the time he returned, I'd cut neat slices of meat from the rabbit's hind legs.

"Our rods," Ansel said, holding two slender tree branches to his chest, "and everything else we could possibly need." In his other hand were sharp splinters of wood—makeshift hooks—and a couple of small stones.

I nodded. They looked serviceable enough.

"As for the bait ..." He glanced between me and the rabbit. "You've butchered it."

"Yes."

"But you weren't supposed to."

I wiped the blade on the grass. "What did you think we'd do, throw it in whole?"

"Well, that's how it used to be done. How am I to know if fishing techniques have progressed? Are you wilfully forgetting I've been indisposed this past century?" He reached over to flick my nose, and I caught his hand with my own bloodied one. His skin was cool, yet I burned.

"Now you're making up nonsense," I said, pushing him away.

He shrugged like he knew it was true and it didn't bother him to admit it. His gaze, though, became stuck on the bloody marks I'd left on his skin. With a curious tilt to his features, he swiped his tongue up the back of his hand.

His face scrunched in disgust. "That's revolting."

My expression mirrored his. "Yes, it is."

Without another word, he dropped the cushion into my lap. Then, he plonked what looked to be a woman's straw hat on his head, tying the green bow beneath his chin. I shook my head at him, hugging the cushion to my chest.

Ansel said, “Let us hope the fish aren’t picky.”

We sat together—him on the grass, me on the cushion—at the edge of the river and dropped our lines into the water. It wasn’t long before Ansel breathed out a sigh next to me and wedged his makeshift rod into the ground. He tapped a finger against his crossed arms, muttering beneath his breath.

I would have thought an immortal would possess the patience to sit still for at least a minute, but alas, he’d surprised me yet again.

I passed him my rod. “Hang on.”

He watched as I rifled through the books he’d brought.

“Here, why don’t you read this?” I opened the weathered book and frowned. “What language is this?”

“No idea. I thought the pictures were lovely.”

I flipped to a detailed illustration of a girl riding a bull and whistled. “You like art?”

He made a noncommittal sound, returned my rod, and continued his finger tapping. Time passed without even the barest of tugs on my line, and I started to drift off. I imagined myself floating somewhere in the warmth of an ocean, sun dappling my face as the blue of the sky seared into my eyelids. The air carried the scent of brine. The gulls called to each other, just as they had when I was nine years old and visiting the southern coast with my family. But most wonderful of all was the strength of my body, the confidence I had in my muscles as I glided through that ocean.

The rod jerked in my hands, and I snapped to alertness.

"Ansel! Hey, I think I have something!" It was only when I started pulling the line that the silence hit me. Confused, I turned. "Ansel?"

He stood in the centre of the clearing, facing the endless gulf of forest. Mist undulated at his ankles, writhed like spirits upheaved from hell, and it occurred to me that this was the kind of moment bards plucked from reality to spin into song. A beautiful man gazing longingly into the darkness as though he had lost something.

As though he was about to find it again.

"Is something there?" I asked quietly.

His head angled towards me. The rod bounced in my hands again, and I finished pulling up the line. The fish gleamed bronze in the moonlight. I wrapped a hand around it, biting my lip at the slimy sensation.

"Oh, good catch," came Ansel's voice from beside me. He was squatting to my right, chin resting in his hands. "She's only a little thing, though. Best throw her back."

My skin prickled at how close he was. I leaned away. "Yeah," I agreed, throwing the fish back. It vanished into the murky chasm of water. "Anything interesting over there?"

"A snake is gorging itself on a mouse nearby. The rodent's squeaks were doing my head in."

I sniffed my hands, frowning at the fishy smell. "That's how it goes, I guess."

"Indeed." A pause. "But not always."

We stayed a little longer, until my shoulders were sore and my legs numb. Ansel made good on his promise of stories, telling me tales of the north. He let slip that he'd been born in a time of war and that his parents had moved around much before settling somewhere safer. I tried to piece together how old he was with the information but came up blank. He spoke of the world and society with the kind of authority that suggested he'd seen and done everything either had, and would ever have, to offer.

In the end, Ansel caught only two fish to my five, claiming I must have cast a spell on the river for it to favour me so. I said nothing to the contrary but chalked it up to the fact that I actually replaced my bait. For someone so enthusiastic about wanting to fish, he didn't seem very well-informed about it.

I was tired when we packed up and left, but I walked with a spring in my step. Three of the fish I'd caught were long and fat. They hung on the bag from a length of fishing cord, slapping against it with every step.

We were entering a denser part of the forest when a shout in the distance sliced through the quiet night. I frowned at Ansel, who shot me a long-suffering look.

"I have nothing to do with that particular sound of terror, I swear," he said.

But the sound didn't seem to be terror, I thought, as the echo of laughter settled over us.

I pointed to a game trail that cut through the trees. "We should go that way to avoid them."

"No, no—come now, quickly, or you'll be left behind." Ansel strode ahead, and unease sank like a stone in my stomach.

Smoke billowed up from a campfire as we drew closer. The smell of burnt meat permeated the air. Ansel moved like a spectre through the undergrowth, halting only paces away from the camp and the five boys.

"They're probably from Haycock," I whispered, noting their fine clothes and easy smiles. It wasn't unusual, girls and boys from privileged backgrounds making the trip up and into the forest as though wandering around lost for several days proved something to society. The people of Myrtle Gully were the ones who found them, fed them, and looked after them. It was how the inn got a small percentage of its business.

The five boys were all intoxicated, each one nursing a bottle of liquor. A blond boy, at the catcalls of the others, started pulling off his shirt.

I bit my lip to keep from laughing. Trudi would be sorry she'd missed such a sight.

"Let's go," I said. "That's one show I don't want to see."

Ansel didn't seem to hear me. He stared at the boy with preternatural focus, a wide smile slashing his mouth open.

I felt the blood drain from my face.

"Ansel?" The word was drowned out by the boys' laughter.

Ansel ran his tongue along his fangs, saliva dripping from their points.

"Ansel."

Reluctantly, he dragged his gaze away, and the glee faded from his countenance. Still, he chuckled softly. “Shall we give them a fright?”

“No.” I shook my head. “No, we should *not* give them a fright.”

“Ooh, now, just a small one. Where’s your sense of fun, Lena?”

That was the first time he’d called me by name. I knew it was meant to stump me, and for a moment it did. I wanted to scoff. As if he needed more of an advantage than he already had.

I took a damning step in front of him, arching my neck to get in his space. “My sense of fun? Silly me, I must have left it back at Father Snow’s corpse.”

He blinked slowly, his tongue prodding the corner of his mouth. “Is that why you’ve been such drab company, scurrying away at every opportunity?”

“Drab? Are you seriously—” My voice rose over the treetops. “*Drab*?”

“Shush, shush, shush.” He clapped a hand across my mouth and, faster than I could follow, whirled me around. The back of my head smacked against his shoulder as he leaned forward—over me—and gestured to the boys, still drinking and jibing and oblivious to our presence.

His jaw brushed over my hair as he whispered, “Careful. We don’t want them running off just yet.”

“You mean *you* don’t want them running off.” The squawk was muffled gibberish, stifled by his cold palm.

"You shouldn't talk with your mouth full, darling," he said as I tried to bite his fingers.

He held me gently, lips caressing the shell of my ear, and poured sweet little venomous nothings into me.

Something about it only being a fright.

Just a little fun.

And then praises for coming with him, for playing along. About the colour yellow and how he much preferred it to gold. The slick barrage of meaningless words scraped indents between my ears. I had to stop listening eventually, had to stop fighting.

It was on the tip of my tongue to say no.

I *should* have said no.

Instead, when he finally cut off mid-babble and freed me, I asked, gasping, "Is a fright all it's going to be?"

A soft hiss. "*Yes.*"

I scrubbed my hands down my face. If he was determined, there was no way I could possibly stop him. At least a fright was better than a funeral. "What did you have in mind?"

Ansel smoothed the hair back from my temple, placed his hat on my head. He took his cape back, setting it across his shoulders.

Then he smiled.

It was a lilting, haunting melody Ansel hummed as he approached the boys with steady footfalls. Even as inebriated as they were, it had taken only seconds for them to register his presence. At that moment, Ansel's unnatural visage seemed to fill every void and crevice of the forest.

The air was so thick with him I could barely breathe.

"Hello," he said. His smile was almost shy—at least, the closest approximation Ansel could get to shy—as he brought a hand up to his chest. "My, you startled me."

I shuddered, feeling as though I was watching a common tree snake shed its skin to reveal the viper underneath.

One by one, the liquor bottles dropped from the boys' hands. The last one shattered against the hard earth, and the frog-eyed boy who'd been holding it flinched. "Who are you?" he asked.

Ansel averted his gaze. "Nobody of consequence. Nothing compared to you boys, I'm sure."

I pulled a face. What was he trying to do, court them?

But his words seemed to have hit their mark, because the half-naked boy flushed, blood rushing to his chest and neck. He stared up at Ansel as though he was the most breathtaking sight he'd ever seen, and while the vampire may have been equal parts attractive and terrifying, the boy's expression was too vacant to be really in the moment.

Ansel stood a little straighter. "Well? Are you going to offer me a seat, or shall I stand here for the five of you to gawk at all night?"

The frog-eyed boy shucked his jacket and arranged it by the fire. "Here you go, sir. My Lord, sir."

I scoffed, and Ansel peered back at my hiding place, a wicked tilt to his mouth. He had kept his chin tucked until that point, hiding his teeth. That he now ran his tongue across them and lifted his head chased away any levity I may have felt.

"You know, this would have been fun, once," Ansel said, voice deepening with displeasure.

The air around me crackled with sheer power, an all-consuming pressure that pushed down on my back and demanded I drop to my knees. I gripped the tree trunk in front of me, determined to stay on my feet.

The shirtless boy wasn't so lucky. He dropped to the ground with a crunch. His friends didn't move to help.

"I would have smiled," Ansel continued, starting a slow circle around the camp. Each step was measured, purposeful. His boots scraped across the ground. The sound sent adrenaline rushing through me. "You would have preened. And then, as awareness came rushing back to you, I would strike. Not all of you, of course. One needs to be alive to tell the tale. But look at you all ... You're not even trying to resist." Ansel rapped his knuckles on the frog-eyed boy's head. "See? Utterly empty."

It *was* an unnerving sight. Five boys staring silently, bewitched, as though it was the Dawn Lord himself in their midst.

"Stop toying with them and leave," I whispered, managing to stop my legs from shaking. "You've scared us all enough."

I knew he heard me. His body angled towards me in a gesture that seemed unintentional. But he didn't leave.

The noise he made was ripe with frustration. "And delicious as you all are, I'm afraid my little thief wouldn't forgive me if I were so indulgent as to partake."

The boys' eyes turned glassy. They didn't understand.

"But, well ..." Ansel breathed through his nose, rolling his neck to the side. His bones cracked. "Maybe just a *taste*."

"No!" I shouted as Ansel stalked to the boy on the ground, the weakest, easiest prey.

I didn't think. Thinking would have made me hesitate as I rushed into the clearing, and thinking would have stopped me from crashing into Ansel, ripping the boy from his grip.

The boy staggered to his feet, took one terrified look at Ansel, and turned a sickly shade of grey.

I reached out to steady him, but Ansel's arms wound around my middle, cradling me. I felt a tremor run through him at the contact.

"Hush," he murmured in my ear, voice fluttering like wings as the shirtless boy fled. "Hush, hush."

I wasn't the one making the noise. It was the boys' screams that echoed throughout the trees and rattled my brain like a tooth in a jar. Birds took flight at the sound. The shirtless boy lost his footing and soiled himself.

I was familiar with the kind of terror that could set one running for dear life. It was of consolation that they wouldn't be chased, for Ansel was too busy laughing.

I untangled myself from him, moving to the fire to pick up a liquor bottle.

I took a swig, liquid scorching its way down my throat. "You're so scary, picking on children."

He shook his head, covering his mouth. "What pathetic specimens of humankind. I used to have to bite someone for them to scream like that."

Better a fright than a funeral? What was I thinking?

I snapped, "Do you realise how badly this could go for you? What are you going to do if they come back with a mob?"

"Why, I imagine I'd invite them all to dinner."

I glared at him.

Ansel set his hands on his hips. "Do not worry so, little thief. What will they say they saw, drunk in the middle of the night? Will they say they saw a vampire, only for them to flee back to their wet nurses, tails tucked between their legs? No, I do not think they will be a problem." He laughed again. "My dear, I have so missed that look of terror."

It wasn't what would happen to him that bothered me; it was what would happen to me. Those boys had seen me. Their minds, fogged with terror and Ansel's brand of mind poison as they had been, wouldn't have been so far gone as to dismiss me entirely. What person ran to a vampire instead of from him?

Me, apparently.

I corked the bottle, as well as the others that were strewn around, and did my best to wrestle them into the bag.

Ansel, acting downright jubilant, took them from me and hitched the bag back onto his shoulder. "After you," he said.

The flame of the campfire died down to coals as we started our walk back to the castle. I stayed several paces ahead of Ansel, the desire to pretend he didn't exist overwhelming the self-preservation that insisted I didn't want him at my back.

By the time we'd passed through the back gates and into the servants' quarters, the sky was beginning to lighten.

"Of course you had to wake me up in the middle of summer," Ansel said as he dropped our things on the kitchen table. "Long hours of sunshine with barely an overcast day."

I rubbed the tiredness from my eyes. "Don't worry, I regret it as well."

He shot me a look that was, dare I say, affectionate.

And it distracted me, but not enough that I didn't balk at the sight of him.

Powering ahead as I had been, I'd failed to notice the obscene number of friends he'd made along the way.

Bats. All over him, *bats*.

They nuzzled against his neck, hung from his collar, and snuggled into the opening of his waistcoat. What came out of my mouth wasn't quite a word, but Ansel seemed to grasp my meaning.

"They came to say hello." He petted one clutching his forearm.

I nodded, at a loss for words. "I've never seen one up close before." I went to move closer, but a bat on his shoulder spread its wings and hissed at me.

"Manners, Iris," Ansel chastised.

"Do you know they're carriers of disease?"

"Excuse you, they are not. Ignore her, girls; she doesn't know what she's saying." He scratched the hissing bat beneath the chin, and it squeaked at him. "Now off with you, quickly. Can't have you nesting in here, as lovely as you all are." The bats must have made some noise I couldn't hear, because Ansel shot back, "No, it's time to go. I'll walk you back to the forest, but then you're off, yes? There are only two of us here, and the castle is already overcrowded."

"Wait," I blurted. "Could I look a bit closer?"

Ansel pursed his lips. "Hasn't she changed her tune. What do you think, Iris? Are you willing to give the little mortal a chance?"

"Have you met them before, or are you making up these names on the spot?"

A flat look. "Iris says she's not interested." He petted the one on his forearm again, and it leaned into his palm. "Magnolia, however, might just oblige us."

I went to peer forwards, but Ansel shook his head. Gently, he placed her on my shoulder.

"She'll like smelling your hair," was his explanation to my panicked look.

Relaxing my posture, I peeked at the bat from the corner of my eye as she shuffled around and tried to find purchase on my dress. It was obviously too much effort for her—she promptly flew back to Ansel, nearly slapping me in the face with a wing.

Ansel welcomed her back, unrepentant. "They recognise the night creature within me."

"Well," I said, shaking myself out, "I have enough dead fish to console myself with, at least."

"Yes, do enjoy your spoils. Now, you'll have to excuse me, for I am to walk these ladies home."

"Be careful," I said, stretching my arms above my head in an attempt to soothe the pinch in my back. "Sun will be up soon." Although, maybe sunbathing would do him some good after his practical joke. Put life and death experiences in perspective.

There was a beat of silence. I could feel him looking at me, like nails raking down my front.

"What is it?" I asked.

"Nothing." He jerked his chin. "You are pale. Go. Rest. I will take care of things here."

I grunted but trudged up the stairs, planning to be halfway home before he made it back. The library was unchanged, and I knelt to straighten the pile of books we'd left in disarray.

I didn't mean to rest my shoulder against the armchair or loosen my grip on the books. The world spun, like girls capering around a maypole, and I curled in at the ugly truth of having overexerted myself.

Just ten seconds, I thought. *Just ten seconds of rest.*

My muscles relaxed.

Seven, six.

A piece of hair was tickling my neck, but I couldn't muster the energy to move it.

Five ... four.

Sleep was a siren's song. My eyes shut.

Three ... two ...

A long, languid scraping brought me to consciousness. I tried to fall back into that blissful state of nothingness, but a piece of hair—that same piece of hair—tickled my neck, and I remembered where I was and why I felt like a human pretzel.

I jolted upright so fast I nearly lost my balance.

Ansel was back from his sojourn in the wilderness and was sitting in the rocking chair, embroidering. I started to ask exactly what he was doing, but my voice came out scratchy, and I had to swallow.

"Just getting in a bit of needlepoint practise before bed. Look." He brandished the embroidery hoop. "Can you guess what it is?"

I ran a hand down my face, blinking away the remnants of sleep. He was two-thirds through what appeared to be an orange circle.

"Is it the sun?" I asked, grimacing at the cottony texture of my tongue.

"Drat. It was supposed to be a tangerine."

"A what?"

He waved a dismissive hand. "It's a fruit. Oh, and there's tea if you want it. Should still be hot."

It was then I realised how warm I was. I looked down.

Ansel's cape was draped over me.

Quickly, I pulled it off. "How long was I asleep?"

"Long enough to start drooling," he said before easing the teacup into my hands. His fingertips brushed the side of my palm—the cut was healing well, beginning to scar—and the touch woke me up properly.

I had lingered too long.

Swallowing the tea in three gulps—it was bitter, nasty stuff—I ran my hands through my hair. Ansel's gaze followed the movement, intent on my collarbone.

"If I find those boys stumbling through the forest, I'm sending them your way," I said, gathering my basket.

"You'd do that for me?"

My mouth curled up. "With a stake. I'm sending them your way with a stake. Also, go drink some blood."

He snapped his fangs playfully.

I stopped in the doorway, taking in the overcast light of the dawn, the way it turned Ansel's skin a milky blue.

"See you next time, Ansel," I said, waiting for the dread that normally accompanied the idea. It didn't come. Instead, there was hope. Optimism, even. He hadn't killed those boys when he had the opportunity. Maybe things would work out, somehow.

Ansel tapped the embroidery hoop against his chin. "Enjoy market day, Lena."

For the first time in weeks, my walk through the forest was almost pleasant.

CHAPTER NINE

The traders were setting up in the main square when I arrived. One of them tried to catch my eye, but I shook my head. Would Ansel really notice if I took a couple of things from the castle? I didn't know, but if he ever found out, he'd make me pay him back tenfold.

The lizard, who I had settled on naming Balthazar the Magnificent, sat in the shade of the post office. I cooed at his unimpressed face in greeting.

The bell chimed at my entrance, and Trudi peered up from the ledger she was poring over.

"Lena!" She threw her reading spectacles onto the counter and rushed to embrace me. "You're early. Are you that excited for market day?"

"No." I laughed, returning her hug and taking a seat. "I was up earlier than usual and thought I'd see if you were around."

"Up earlier than usual?" She sat on the stool next to mine.

I hummed, jerking my chin towards the book in her hands. “Your father ran off again?”

“Yeah,” she said and sighed. Trudi’s father was kind and charismatic and a complete deadbeat when it came to work. He preferred the company of his tankard over that of his daughter.

Myrtle Gully didn’t receive many letters, not when less than half the population could read, but it was how Trudi chose to occupy her time when she wasn’t coordinating the traders and figuring out the logistics of market day. Markus had been the one to teach her how to look after a business, I had been the one to teach her letters and numbers, and Hugo had been the one to kiss her and profess undying love, so in that way we were all one big family.

“This is for you,” I said, pulling the brown paper package from my basket. “Caught fresh this morning.”

Her face lit up. “You went fishing? With who?”

I shrugged. “You can’t smell it on me, can you?”

“No, but you’re looking ...”

I raised an eyebrow.

“Nice,” she finished lamely.

“Yeah, I’m feeling ‘nice’.” It wasn’t a complete lie. I felt buoyant, barely even sore anymore.

“It’s terrible what everyone’s been saying—but I know you don’t believe in that kind of thing. I didn’t think it would bother you that much.”

I blinked, trying to understand the non sequitur. “What?”

“You know. What they’ve been saying? About festival night.” She froze when I shook my head. “You haven’t heard?"

No, I had not heard.

She hesitated. "So, you know how the villagers like to gossip?"

"Yes."

"And how sometimes someone says something and so everyone else just repeats it until no one knows who said it in the first place and everyone thinks it's real even though it's not."

I scraped my tongue across my teeth. "Trudi, what have they been saying about me?"

"Well"—she shifted nervously—"it's not specifically about you."

"Then what's it about?"

"You remember how everyone thought some kind of animal attacked Father Snow?"

"Uh-huh." I didn't like where this was going. Trudi must have sensed as much because she finally got to the point.

"The thing is ... and don't laugh at this, because they're just scared and coping how they can, but they're saying it was a vampire, the one that used to terrorise the village. They're saying it came for Father Snow and it's going to come back for the rest of us."

Something inside me cracked. The fragment of hope shattered.

A noise wrenched out of me that Trudi must have mistaken for laughter.

A rueful smile touched her lips. "They don't mean any harm by it. Father Pentaghast has been trying to calm the gossip, so ..." Her eyes went wide. "Are you okay?"

I was extremely far from okay.

There was a rasp echoing throughout the room, and it took me a moment to realise, no, Trudi's drunken father wasn't hiding passed out behind the counter. It was me. My laboured breathing.

"Um," I started, and my voice broke on the syllable. "Not really."

Trudi grasped my hand. "You don't have to worry. I don't think anyone actually thinks it was a vampire; it's just a coincidence because of the night it happened. You know that the farmers start telling tales when they have nothing else to gossip about."

I nodded dully. I hadn't even considered the villagers' superstitions would get the better of them. It was obvious now that I thought about it.

The village priest goes to ward us all from evil, but the evil has other ideas.

Trudi was still talking. I barely heard a word until she said, "And besides, it didn't look like a vampire bite, did it? See? They're just making up stories."

"No. It didn't look like a vampire bite."

Trudi nodded as though she had been triumphant in expecting this answer.

I couldn't handle the secrecy. The stress of it would kill me before anything else would. The villagers were revelling in the thrill of a vampire, taking advantage of Father Snow's death to add excitement and meaning to their humdrum lives. To burden someone else with the knowledge of Ansel's existence was cruel, but I couldn't do it alone anymore.

I tightened my hand around hers. "Trudi, I have to tell you something. And it needs to stay a secret, because if anyone else finds out, we're all going to be in a lot of trouble."

The lines around Trudi's mouth grew deeper. "Are you okay? Is this about—I mean, is it getting worse?"

"No. Nothing to do with that." It would be simpler if that were the case.

She studied me, confusion and a touch of wariness in her eyes. "What are you talking about, then? What kind of trouble."

I shrugged and smiled wanly. "The fatal kind."

"What?" Trudi blanched. "But you just said it wasn't about ..."

"And it's not. Trudi, I need you to listen. And don't hate me. Please."

She exhaled through her nose. Her expression turned grim. "Tell me."

And I told her.

About the trapdoor I'd discovered, the giant crypt I'd stumbled across beneath the castle. I told her what really happened festival night—running into Ansel and finding Father Snow's body. The deal Ansel and I had made.

Her face was ashen by the time I finished talking, like my words had sucked the life from her. Doubt started to sprout in my mind, but I rooted that weed out. If I couldn't trust Trudi, then I couldn't trust anyone.

"Are you serious?" she said finally. "You are seriously telling me there's a vampire out there who killed Father Snow and is blackmailing you to get blood? Lena, are you *serious*?"

"Yes," I said fervently. "Yes. Trudi, I wouldn't make something like this up."

Trudi swallowed. Opened her mouth, then shut it again. She raised a hand. "Just one second." She scurried off the stool and ran into the mailroom. I rose to follow, but she smacked the door shut behind her, so I just stood there, staring blankly at the wooden panels of the wall.

There were no other exits in the room. It was just a tiny storeroom where they kept the mail and other miscellaneous items. She couldn't run off and tell someone. Even if she wanted to, I would try to dissuade her. I would make sure she understood the ramifications of people finding out, but it would be her choice to—

A muffled scream came from the other side of the door.

"Trudi?" I called, trying the door handle. "Are you okay?"

"Yes, I just need a moment." She started screaming again.

I bit the inside of my cheek to keep from smiling. Hadn't I thought the very same thing—that I was in need of a good scream—only nights ago? I should have joined in with the Haycock boys earlier when they'd had a go of it.

The door opened, and Trudi emerged, thoroughly shaken.

"Didn't see that coming, did you?" I said.

She looked past me, dazed. "Everyone always said that castle was evil."

"Yeah." My amusement died at the tremor in her voice. "I know."

"And now you're a vampire's familiar. Or, I don't know, his pet."

I ran a hand through my hair and sat back down at the counter. "No, I'm not his pet, I'm his ... caretaker makes it sound like he's an invalid."

"Lena, you're his pet. You do his bidding, you fetch him things, take him food." She blinked. "No, he's *your* pet."

I snorted. "He should be so lucky."

"So, let me just get this straight." She stumbled back to her seat. "He's a vampire ... but he hasn't killed us all yet?"

"That's one way to think of it. Should I applaud him for refraining from mass murder?"

"Oh, ha-ha. You know what I mean." She blew out a massive breath. "I just can't believe it."

Indeed, she looked like she needed to lie down.

"Give me a second," I said, jumping up to rummage through the cupboards. A weight had been taken from my shoulders. The fear that had gripped me in its chokehold had been banished by Trudi's listening ear. "If we're going to continue this conversation, you're going to need some food in you."

"An actual vampire."

"The real thing." I found some almonds and dried apples, handing them to her. Colour returned to her cheeks as she chewed.

"You sound like you—" She bit her lip.

"Like I what?"

"Like you don't mind him too much."

I thought about how I'd described him. Was that really what it sounded like? Even if it was the case, I was loath to admit it. "It was either bend or break," I said. "I've had to adapt."

Trudi watched me, wisdom in her gaze. She may have been two years younger than me, but beneath all her layers of idealism, she was an old soul.

I asked, "Why do you look so disappointed?"

"What? I don't."

"Trudi, this isn't going to end like one of those books you like."

"I know that."

"We're not going to run off into the sunset together. He would burn to a crisp—well, I presume he would—and I hate running."

"That's not what I was thinking," she mumbled and shoved a fistful of almonds into her mouth.

"Really?"

"Yes."

I picked up her quill, running my fingers down the goose feather. It was looking worn. Maybe I'd buy her a new one. "Then what were you thinking?"

It took her a moment to answer, her jaw still working on the almonds. Finally, she swallowed and said, "You should go, you know?"

She may as well have just poisoned my herb garden. "Go?"

"You should. It may be too late, soon."

Oh. *Oh*. She didn't mean leave her alone, she meant—

No. She couldn't be serious. Me, leave Myrtle Gully? Now? After everything I'd just told her, that was the very last thing she should think.

"Lena," she said, "think about it. If the legends are true, then this vampire won't grow old. Time is different for him, and that's time that you don't have. You need to tell Father Pentaghast. Or—or I could take him the blood. I could get Hugo to collect it for me and then—" She cut off abruptly at my expression.

"No one else can know," I said. "Not the priest and not Hugo. No one."

"But you'll ..."

"There's still time," I said. "I promise you. There's still time."

"Okay." She scratched at a bit of dirt on the counter. "Then you should take Father Pentaghast up on his offer."

I'd told her about Father Pentaghast's idea to have me stay at Haycock a few days ago in passing. We'd both agreed it was a strange proposal. That she brought it up now made me wonder if she'd been listening to any of our conversation.

"Trudi," I said and licked my lips. "I feel like we just went over the fact that me leaving isn't going to help anything."

She huffed. "I don't mean you should actually go to Haycock, but just tell people you are. And then spend a week in the village and a week in the castle, so you actually have a chance to rest." She clasped my hand. "Lena, you look exhausted."

"You think I should go? Even though you hate the castle?"

She looked straight at me. Her words, when she spoke, held weight. "I would rather you be well-rested there than suffering here."

I rolled the idea around in my mind.

Trudi was devout. Loved and worshipped the Dawn Lord not only like a god, but like he was the father she'd always wanted. When she talked about morals, about morality, I listened. As far as I was concerned, she'd just given me permission to lie as much as necessary. I hid my smile behind a mouthful of dried apples.

Trudi nodded to herself, coming to a decision. "I'll cover for you so no one will suspect. But in terms of the vampire, what can I do to help?"

Ah, Trudi, I thought, *the best friend a girl could ask for.*

I hugged her. Well, it was more of a tackle. And then I outlined exactly what I needed her to do.

CHAPTER TEN

"What is your name, little thief?" Ansel asked as he easily lifted a bookshelf that weighed at least two hundred pounds.

We were rearranging furniture in one of the cabinets. Adjacent to the library, it was one of the first rooms I'd tackled by myself, almost a year ago now, while Ansel was deep in his beauty sleep. I'd arranged the armchairs, settees, and desk in what I'd thought was a perfectly acceptable fashion, but Ansel had taken one look at the room, scoffed, and declared my taste in decorating to be non-existent.

It had been days since my conversation with Trudi and therefore days since I'd visited Father Pentaghast to take him up on his offer. Arrangements were made, letters were sent—all of which were intercepted by Trudi in the mailing room—and I left Myrtle Gully to take up temporary residence with a vampire.

Ansel hadn't seemed put out. In fact, he seemed delighted by the prospect of company. It wasn't until the day I'd arrived, travel bag in hand and a nervous ball twisting in my chest, that I'd figured out why. Turned out that my stay at the castle was conditional on how well I 'earned my keep'—his words, not mine.

Hence, the rearranging of the cabinet.

I threw down the rag I was using to dust and glanced at Ansel. His hair was pulled back in a bun, and the sleeves of his tunic were rolled to his elbows. I was candid enough to admit it was a good look on him. Then again, he'd probably look good tarred, feathered, and quacking like a duck, so it wasn't saying much.

"You know my name," I said through my kerchief. I may not have been coughing much lately, but the precaution was necessary.

He grunted, shoving the bookcase into place against the wall. "No, no, your last name."

"Montgomery."

"Montgomery?" He turned, swiping the rag up to wipe his hands before tucking it into his back pocket. His gaze lingered over my hair, down to my eyes. "You don't happen to mean Montgomery as in Mercantile and Co.?"

"No," I said, "because Montgomery Mercantile went bankrupt several years ago."

"Bankrupt? Oh, dear. You know, they sold me the very best potpourri packet I ever did buy. ''Tis a pity they're no longer around to sell me another."

I snorted. "My uncles and aunts would say the very same thing."

His eyebrows inched up. "So that's why you're so well educated."

I shrugged, untying the kerchief from my face. Growing up as a child of the continent's largest trading group certainly had its advantages—advantages I wish I'd taken more seriously before my extended family sought out a foolhardy venture that placed them in so much debt, not even the king's coffers in the Holy City could have pulled them back out.

"And you settled in your charming hovel, how?" Ansel asked.

I sighed and sat on one of the couches. Dredging up the past was never very pleasant.

"My parents preferred to travel rather than stay cooped up with the books. They took me with them."

"Dead, are they?"

My expression must have been severe, because he looked momentarily confused.

"Sorry," he said. "That was impolite."

"Yes, it was. Anyway, Mother has passed. Father lives near the Holy City."

He came to join me on the couch, eyes alight with curiosity. "So that's how it is."

"What do you mean, 'that's how it is'?"

"Father dearest leaving you here." A smile curved his lips. "Let me guess—his grief proved too strong, so he dumped you here like a bad smell and is now living in the lap of luxury with his new wife and annoyingly perfect twin daughters."

I wasn't even going to pretend like that didn't hurt. I clicked my jaw from side to side, fighting against a bone-deep ache spreading through my body. "That's an incredibly cruel thing to say."

"Only if it's true."

It was true. At least, true enough that I didn't bother to defend my father. He was by no means rich any longer and from what few letters he'd sent, his new wife and son, my half-brother, were both sincere, dignified people.

The opposite of my dead mother.

The opposite of me.

I wished them every happiness. But then, sometimes I also wished they'd all catch gout, get evicted from their thatched-roof cottage, and spend the rest of their lives hating each other. It depended on the kind of day I was having.

I said, "Think what you like. Father's better off wherever he is than if he were stuck here, threatened by the likes of you."

He nodded. "You're right."

A thoughtful silence descended then, interrupted only by the quiet growl of my stomach. I'd been hungrier recently, much to my pleasure.

I looked around at the unfinished room. There were books in need of dusting and candles in need of replacing. Ansel had wanted to get an early start on the day, so we'd pinned the drapes shut. Living for the night was a strange contrast. The village was silent by midnight, yet with Ansel, midnight was the middle of our day.

My stomach growled again.

"I'm hungry," I said.

"And I am parched." Ansel stood and gestured for me to follow. "To the kitchen, then."

The kitchen was balmy with evening warmth. Ansel opened the door wide, leaning a chair against it to keep it in place, so we could hear the crickets chirp and watch the progression of the moon across the sky.

A hefty wooden table took up much of the room, and as I shimmied around it to the sizable larder, I considered my meal options. I'd made sure to bring enough food with me to last the week—dried meats, potatoes, mutton pie—and was pulling out various bags full of nuts and seeds when my hand slipped. The sound of rice raining upon stone made me groan.

If I didn't know any better, I'd say the Dawn Lord had given up all pretence and decided to poke at my wounds. Rice wasn't cheap. Weeks ago, before Ansel and the increased need for austerity, I'd traded five copper coins for this measly bag.

"Do we have a broom down here?" I asked Ansel, already resigned to trekking back upstairs to find one. Feeling decidedly too lazy to do so, I knelt and scooped up a handful. Ansel dropped next to me. I was about to thank him for helping when I noticed the rigidness of his shoulders.

"Are you okay?" I asked.

Slowly, he reached out a trembling hand and plucked out one rice grain to sit in his palm.

Then he did it again. And again and again.

His mouth moved in time with his hand, words I couldn't hear. All the same, I knew what he was doing. He was counting the rice grains.

Hesitantly, I tapped him on the shoulder. "Hey. Ansel."

His voice grew louder, leaving his mouth in a caress of breath. I left him alone, and his words turned silent once more.

How interesting, I thought with no small amount of glee.

Scooting close enough for our knees to touch, I plucked one of the grains out of his open palm and dropped it on the floor, where it became lost in a sea of them. Ansel's hand twitched, as did a vein in his forehead, before he let the rest of the rice fall through his fingers.

He started again.

I almost applauded myself there and then. I'd found another weak link, a chink in his armour. Excitement swelled in my chest, made me cocky. I blurted, "You can't help it, can you?"

Ansel's head snapped to the side, his hand halting mid-air. His breath brushed my forehead when he whispered, dangerously low, "I can't *what*?"

A small plan of revenge had been forming in my head, one that entailed placing the rice grains in an unending spiral and watching as Ansel hoarded each one. He would be a dog led unwittingly to its kennel. Just a bit of fun, really.

But as his gaze met mine and I saw the black, burning shadow of malice there that he usually kept hidden—the *thing* residing beneath his skin I'd glimpsed once before—the blood drained from my face.

Maybe it wasn't the best idea I'd ever had.

Ansel, eyes still on me, got to his feet, pure control in the powerful lines of his body; he was a coiled spring, a bull about to charge. His steps were slow, painful in their preciseness. His hand jerked towards me—towards the rice—and he slammed it down on the table, a harsh crack ringing through the air.

I squeaked, watching as his mind and body warred with one another.

"Um," I started inanely. "I'll just clean this up, then?"

"*Please*." His voice sounded like it had been through a meat grinder.

I crawled around the rice pile to block Ansel's view, making my skirt into a makeshift bowl and scooping handfuls inside. By the time I had nearly finished, Ansel was looking slightly drunk and sounding even more so with his slurred, endless chain of, "Clean it up, clean it up, clean it up."

I poured the last handful into my kerchief and knotted it closed. Placing it on the shelf, I shut the larder door behind me.

I said, "So, the rice thing's true, huh?"

Look at me, hammering nails into my coffin.

The table groaned beneath his grip. "No, no. Throwing rice at weddings does not guarantee fertility. If couples truly want posterity, they should find a few babies to toss."

I wrinkled my nose.

Ansel sighed, curling his fingers through the hair at his temple.

"You were pretty scary there," I admitted.

"And you were very *cheeky*."

I presumed he used a far less polite word in his head. I sat at the table, resting my feet against the chair legs. "Why is this legend true when others aren't? I don't understand. It doesn't make sense."

Ansel looked to the ceiling, opened his mouth, and then shut it again. I'd seen Ansel be a lot of things, but I'd never seen him struggle for words.

It put me on edge.

He muttered, "I cannot believe I'm about to tell you this." And as irked as he appeared in that moment, when he glanced up and saw the anticipation in my eyes, his features softened. It occurred to me how wrong I was when I thought garlic and counting to be the only chinks in his armour.

It was an intimidating realisation.

"They're all true," he said eventually. "Well, most of them. I can't transform into a bat, but I can't say I've ever wanted to."

"All of them?" I asked. "But, no, they can't be. The Dawn Lord's cross did nothing to you." I thought back to our first conversation, the way he'd dismissed the symbols. "And I never invited you inside the clinic."

He tugged on an earring. "Yes, well, there are some misleading facts, I suppose. As for the invite, you must have given me some kind of welcome in the forest. Words can be slippery like that." He paused. "I'm a fool to admit all this. Pray tell what I get out of it."

"An eternity of my good graces."

He laughed. "Tempting, but not quite what I had in mind. Sate your curiosity in some other manner, will you? I'd rather not be the downfall of my entire species." He sat down, inspecting the crack he'd made in the table and clicking his tongue.

I asked the first question that came to mind. "Why were you stuck sleeping in a smelly old tomb for a hundred years?"

"Smelly." He huffed. "Leave me some dignity. I was meant to be awake and gone within a decade, but the man I hired to wake me died and left me in my slumber. I should never have hired the old, crotchety one."

"And you were slumbering because ... ?"

He made a noise, waved a hand in dismissal. "Next."

Hmm. So even that was a secret.

"I'm sick of asking questions," I said. "How about you save us the time and tell me something interesting instead."

"So, I am reduced to a mere amusement, am I? Very well, I imagine this will satisfy you. I once lived here. There. That village."

I tried not to show my surprise. "As a vampire or ... ?"

He shot me a wry look.

"A human," I finished.

I had wondered about Ansel as a human, of course I had, but there was something innately wrong with the idea.

Ansel could never be a creature limited to mortality. My gaze wandered over to the larder.

Though vampirism seems to have limits of its own.

I asked, "Were you very different when you were human?"

"I should hope so."

"Please. I really want to know."

He leaned back, crossing his legs. "I was different, I suppose. Though admittedly, I can't remember parts of that life too well." He flicked his gaze to me. "Ask me something specific and we'll see where it takes us."

That life, he'd said. As though he wasn't talking about himself.

I took a few seconds to think. "What did you do for work?"

"Many things. I built, I designed, I planted crops, I ... travelled." He cocked his head. "Or maybe the travelling came after. Who knows? It's been far too long to remember such miscellaneous things in real clarity."

"Then what do you remember?"

His eyes took on a faraway sheen. "I remember a hut that would lend no warmth in the winters. A limping dog that would eat straight from my hand. The smell of clean linen, forced to mix with stale alcohol and smoke. I remember nothing good."

The silence sat heavy on my ears. It would have grown painful if I hadn't broken it. "And you started terrorising the villagers after that, why?"

The Festival of Providence and the tales surrounding it had sprung from somewhere. If he really had done all those terrible things—stealing people from their beds, leaving their corpses in the forest—there would be a good reason.

At least, I hoped there would be.

His eyebrows rose. "Figured that out, did you?"

"There weren't many other vampires around to choose from."

"That you know of. For being such a good little helper, you do ask the difficult questions."

I waited.

Reluctantly, he said, "My family were refugees in a village that'd never heard another language, had never seen black hair or a woman wearing breeches. They were wary of us from the start. So, naturally, when they discovered that man for the evil he was, they wanted us gone." Ansel's fingers twitched like he wanted to crush something. "We were abnormal, they said. Bringers of bad omens. We were not worth the dirt on which we put our feet. And that was true for *him*, at least. He used to hit us, you see. Her and me, over and over again until we'd both bleed ..." He trailed off, staring at his hands. Staring through them.

"Was the woman your mother?"

"Which woman?" It was a whisper.

"You said 'her'. Was she your mother?"

He raised his head sharply to look at me. "What?" He grimaced, placed a hand on his temple. "I think I've had enough of this conversation for one night."

The disturbed twist of his mouth made me wonder if I'd opened a floodgate of memories that should not have been touched.

"Sorry," I said. Before I could talk myself out of it, I reached across the grimy table and laid my hand on his arm. The softness of his shirt made my skin tingle and itch.

Cautiously, as if not to scare me away, he laid his hand over mine.

Pressure built in my chest, and I marvelled at the strangeness of it all. The unnaturalness. Whatever camaraderie had developed between us, it was enough to assuage fear and dull self-preservation. If I were here with anyone else, them sitting in Ansel's spot, having just told me of their childhood, I would have called them a friend.

That's what this is, I realised. *Almost a friendship.*

Ansel's hand tightened on mine, and for one heart-stopping second, I thought I was about to say or do something really, really stupid.

Then something worse happened.

A tickle formed in my throat, both strange and familiar, but one I couldn't ignore. I coughed, once, twice, and then took a deep breath. The pressure didn't dissipate. Instead, I could feel it rising, convulsing my lungs and stomping its way up my windpipe. My gaze shot to the door.

I couldn't let Ansel hear this vulnerability of mine.

"I'm going upstairs," I wheezed, not letting myself breathe.

"Thief?" he asked as I turned, a curious note of hurt in his voice.

Covering my mouth with a hand, I escaped to the entrance hall, then up the stairs, gratitude flowing through me when Ansel didn't rise to follow. My heartbeat thudded in my temple, and by the time I reached the bedchamber I'd taken as my own, I was flushed and oxygen deprived, collapsing on my knees before the large bed.

I coughed and coughed, until I couldn't see through the tears running down my cheeks, and being able to breathe was not a right but a privilege. I scrambled to my basket and unstoppered one of the vials inside, gulping down the bitter contents.

There hadn't been such an abrupt attack in ... I couldn't remember.

I'd expected a relapse, for my appetite to wane and my body to grow tired, but something so extreme, coming from what was seemingly nothing...

But I knew better than that. There didn't need to be a reason.

Everything will be okay, I lied to myself.

I'd just overextended myself today, that was all. It could be a freak happening. It could be.

I barricaded my door, hid under the covers, and cried myself to sleep.

CHAPTER ELEVEN

I returned to Myrtle Gully the next morning, a full day earlier than I'd originally planned. Hugo winced when he saw me. I optimistically put it down to my sudden arrival rather than the unhealthy pallor of my skin or the bags beneath my eyes. I'd taken the coward's way out, simply leaving Ansel a note on the chapel altar telling him I had business back at the village that couldn't wait.

I had no desire to be questioned, nor did I need the reminders traipsing through a graveyard would bring. He had enough blood. He'd be fine without me.

I threw myself into work, barely coming up for air, so I wouldn't be reminded of the many things I was hiding from. I prescribed medicines, sewed cuts, pulled out teeth, rewrapped dressings of wounds, and shooed children from the front door in a poor imitation of Markus when they came to bother the peace. I threw myself into work so my bad mood couldn't dominate me. So I wouldn't despair. It even worked for a couple of days. But then reality—the hussy—blew her horn at me in a way I wasn't expecting but was no less unpleasant than anything else in my life.

I'd been back at the clinic for only three nights when I found the pig's head in my bedroom.

It had been an uneventful afternoon. Hugo was exhausted from a week of non-stop work, so he jumped at the opportunity to rest when I offered to take the shift alone. I found myself coughing only rarely and nothing so severe as at the castle. Barely a villager came and went, and I found myself knitting a pair of socks at the kitchen table, bored out of my mind until the sun finally decided to set.

I lit a candle and made my way upstairs, knocking on Hugo's door to rouse him. He groaned something unintelligible, and I smiled, knocking louder and harder until I heard the tell-tale sound of rustling sheets and the thud of feet hitting the ground. He had a date with Trudi, and I wouldn't be responsible if he looked like a mess.

Nothing had seemed out of place at first. My room had been warmed by the afternoon sun. The pansies I'd received from Ansel were still clinging to life from their spot on the windowsill. I decided I would change, then go downstairs and get some water for them.

Humming to myself, I opened my wardrobe.

Lifeless, beady eyes stared up at me. The pig's tongue was lank, its ears torn. Blood had soaked into the wood beneath and was that—was that a spine jutting from behind or—

I screamed.

Hugo ran into the room, banging the door against the wall in his haste. He grasped me by the shoulders, asking what was wrong, why was I screaming, if I was hurt.

I pointed a shaking finger to my cupboard, and he turned. He blanched, throat working.

Where did it come from? Who would have done this—*why* would they have done it? I scanned the room for anything else out of the ordinary. The hair on the back of my neck stood on end, and a shudder wracked my frame. My stomach churned.

Hugo leapt to shut the wardrobe door, and I covered my face, trying to clear my mind. It must have been one of the villagers. With the way some of them had been treating me, talking behind my back or even outright ignoring me, I wouldn't put it past some of them to take matters into their own hands and—

"*Lena*," Hugo said. It obviously wasn't the first time he'd called my name.

I licked my lips. "What?"

"What happened?"

I swallowed bile. What did he mean? "Someone put a pig's head in my cupboard."

"No, I know that." He smoothed a hand down his face. "I mean, are you okay?"

"Yes." No.

"Do you know who did it?"

I pulled a face.

"No. No, of course you don't, sorry," he muttered, walking towards me. I flinched, and he paused mid-step.

A voice from downstairs broke through the tension.

"Hugo?" Trudi called. I shut my eyes, cursing her timing.

"Go downstairs," Hugo said softly, and I opened my eyes. "Tell Trudi I'm not finished with work and that you'll go with her to dinner instead. I'll clean this up."

"But I don't want to go to dinner." There was no way I could eat, not after that.

"Please, Lena." Hugo took a step forward, caught my cold hand in his clammy one. "I'll fix this, I promise, but don't tell Trudi."

Trudi called for Hugo again, louder this time.

"Go," he said.

I grabbed my shawl from where it lay over the bedframe. "Fine. But I'm not coming back here tonight. I'll stay with Trudi and leave for Haycock in the morning."

"But—"

"I'm going," I said, voice hard. Then softer, "Thank you."

He nodded.

"Hugo?" Trudi came to a standstill in my open doorway.

I pasted a smile on. "Sorry, Trudi, but it looks like you'll be stuck with me tonight. Hugo has some work he has to finish. Those poultices don't make themselves."

"Oh." She looked between us. Her hair was curled, and she'd pinched colour into her cheeks. She was ready for a date, not a consolation dinner. "They can't wait?"

"No," Hugo said. "Sorry, love."

Trudi glanced at me, and I shook my head. I'd tell her later.

"Well, okay then," she said, pulling a brave face and clasping her hands in front of her. "I've been to dinner with worse-looking people."

I attempted a laugh. It didn't come out right.

Hugo tossed me a silver coin, and I clenched my scarred palm around it, ushering Trudi out.

As we descended the stairs, I murmured to her, "I don't think I can eat anything." I needed to, though, or at least drink some water. I hadn't eaten since lunch, and the single boiled egg had left much to be desired.

"Why not?" she whispered back.

"I just ..." I looked up at the ceiling, to where my bedroom was. "I'll tell you at the inn."

The Gully Inn was ripe with the sounds of merrymaking as Trudi and I took our table in the corner. It was a full crowd tonight, every seat filled, the servers being run off their feet. My body warmed as I melded into the hustle and bustle, the boisterous, chaotic strains of life. The smell of ale and roasting meat permeated the air. Rather than make my mouth water like it usually would, the smell landed like a dead weight inside my stomach.

I looked around the dimly lit room as though the perpetrator would be dragging the rest of the pig around on his belt. I'd have to do some digging later and see if anyone could account for the missing animal.

We gave our order to a serving boy before I whispered the events of the evening to Trudi.

"*What?*" she all but shouted, and I shushed her. "Don't shush me. What do you mean he said not to tell me?"

"Really?" I snapped. "That's the part you're stuck on? There was a pig's head in my wardrobe, Trudi, so get over it."

She flushed. "Right. Sorry."

I groaned. "No, I'm sorry, too. I didn't mean ..." Before I could finish, a dishevelled-looking Angela came with our food.

My eyebrows flew up. I hadn't seen her since the funeral and even then, we hadn't spoken. I hadn't been up to much talking that day.

Angela stumbled at the sight of us but recovered quickly. "Hi, Trudi," she said shyly. "Hi, Lena."

"Hello, Angela," Trudi said and averted her gaze. I'd hurt her feelings.

Trudi and I waited for Angela to drop off our food and continue on her busy way, but she just stood there looking for all the world like she was trying to gather her courage.

I asked, "Is that food for us or ... ?"

Angela looked down at the tray. "Oh! Yes, sorry." She put each dish on the table and smoothed a stray lock of hair behind her ear, then turned to me. "I'm sorry to interrupt, but can I talk to you for a second? Maybe outside or—or upstairs if that's better?"

"Right now?" I asked.

Angela laughed nervously. "That was stupid of me. Of course you want to eat first."

Trudi shrugged. "It's fine."

"Oh, um. Are you sure?"

"Mmhmm." She ripped off a chunk of bread roll with her teeth. I tried to bury my annoyance. This wasn't how either of us wanted to spend our evening.

"I can talk now," I said to Angela, pushing my chair from under me. The grating of it blended in with the villagers' laughter, the scraping of cutlery.

"No, that's okay, you don't have to," Angela protested, even as she moved to give me more room.

"It's fine." I turned to Trudi. "Be back soon."

She nodded and took another bite of bread.

Angela led me past the bar, up a narrow set of stairs, before stopping in front of a door at the end of the hallway. "My room," she said, wringing her hands like she thought I might turn my nose up at her. "Sorry, it's a little messy. The twins were in here earlier, and they're terrible at cleaning up after themselves."

"Don't worry about it." Mess didn't faze me, not after dealing with decades worth of filth at the castle.

A small bed was pushed against the left wall, its blankets tangled and discoloured. Wooden dolls were scattered across the floor, and a crude rocking horse stared out from beside a chest of drawers. The hubbub of the floor below muted as Angela shut the door behind me.

I gestured to the bed. "Do you mind if I sit?"

"No, of course not. Here, let me fix it. Sorry, you must think me such a slob." She smoothed the bed sheets down, then did the same with the blankets.

"I don't," I said. "What did you want to talk about?"

It was as though she'd been waiting for me to ask, because she blurted, "I'm so sorry. I should have stayed with you the whole time, that night in the forest, and then you wouldn't have been alone when—when you found him."

Surprise but also relief flowed through me, because I hadn't considered she'd feel that way. This would be a good distraction.

"There's no need to apologise. Anyone could have found him out there." As difficult as it was to come to terms with, I was glad to be the one who'd found Father Snow. If anyone else had made a deal with Ansel, the village might have been razed to the ground by now.

Or perhaps I was merely flattering myself. After all, Angela's discomfort in the forest that day hinted at a sensitivity to danger I didn't possess. Maybe, subconsciously, she had known Ansel was out there, whilst I, on the other hand, went blundering towards the threat at full speed.

Regardless, it was a blessing Angela hadn't been there.

Angela was speaking, apologising again. I rubbed the back of my neck, uncomfortable with the sincerity of her feelings. When she didn't show signs of stopping, I decided desperate measures needed to be taken.

I placed my hands on either side of her head and mussed her hair so thoroughly she squealed.

"Now, listen to me," I said, holding her cheeks. "Stop apologising. It's all in the past, all right? In fact, I've forgotten about it already. What were we talking about?"

Angela gulped. “Really?”

“Really.” My mouth hitched up. This was what I’d always imagined a younger sister would be like to talk to. Angela even looked like me. “But anyway,” I said, “it’s time for me to get back downstairs. Trudi may just leave if I’m any longer.”

“She did seem a little quieter than usual.”

“That’s being diplomatic,” I muttered and stood, only to grab onto the bed frame at the last second to keep from keeling over. The room spun, and I shut my eyes, waiting for it to pass.

“Lena?” Angela sounded distant. “Lena, are you okay? You look sick.”

I took a deep breath and opened my eyes, blinking until the floor stayed where it was supposed to. “I’m okay.”

“Are you sure? You can lie down if you need to.”

“No,” I said, sharper than I meant to. I heard Angela’s intake of breath and cursed myself. I should have been able to keep my temper under control, no matter how trying a night it had been. “Sorry."

She hesitated but nodded.

Trudi was still at our table when Angela led me downstairs. She had almost finished her meal, so it was easy to take two bites of my chicken and palm off the rest to her.

The coughing, dizziness, abrupt loss of appetite, then the pig. All these secrets I was keeping, all the pressure that was building—I didn’t have to be a gambler to know the odds of everything collapsing around me were high.

Trudi and I finished quickly and left. Although she didn't say anything once we were on the street, she did hold out her arm for me to take and started leading us back to her place. I was grateful for the warmth she provided.

It was chillier than it had been in months and, subsequently, there were few people out—which was why, when I spotted two familiar men trundling towards us, I wrestled Trudi in behind the closest building.

"What are you doing?" she managed to splutter before I smacked a hand across her mouth.

"*Shh.*" I peered around the wall.

The men were clad in more layers than the cooling weather permitted, their thick tunics and surcoats fastened together by a strange assortment of buckles. Their rucksacks were full, close to bulging, and hung off shoulders corded with the type of muscle gained by constant manual labour.

They were obviously drunk, loud and vulgar in their ramblings, and I knew they probably wouldn't recognise me, not with the weeks that had passed. But on the off chance they did and wanted to pick up where we last left off, I just couldn't be bothered.

Could. Not. Be. Bothered.

It took thirty seconds of apologetic eye contact with Trudi for them to stumble past our hiding spot and around a bend in the road, towards the church.

"I thought they would have left by now," I muttered.

Trudi smacked my hand away and whispered, "What's going on? Who were they? You're not in even more trouble, are you? I swear, if you tell me there are men trying to kidnap you now, I'll have to start screaming again."

"What? No. Where do you even come up with this stuff? I ran into them a few weeks ago, and we got into an argument."

"What did you do?"

My jaw dropped. "Why do you think it was my fault?"

She raised her eyebrows.

"It wasn't! They—you know what, don't worry about it. Who knows what they're getting up to this late at night."

"Like you can talk," Trudi said and promptly hopped out of smacking range.

We made it back to her place without further incident, though I paused when she opened the door for me to come in.

"I'm not actually staying," I said. I'd only come to ensure she got in safely.

Her face fell. "This isn't about earlier, is it? I'm sorry about what I said. It makes me so angry when Hugo treats me like a child, and the pig thing was awful, and I just—" She shrugged. "I'm sorry."

"That's okay. And I'm sorry, too. Give Hugo a good dressing down for me." I turned to leave, but she grabbed my arm.

"Do you really have to go?"

"Yes," I said, gently prying her off. "I'm unsettled, Trudi. Ansel may tease me, but at least I know I won't be waking up to any dead animals at the foot of my bed."

Trudi averted her eyes. "You don't need any blood, do you? He'll let you stay without it?" She tried to smile. "I've got some to spare if you need it."

My heart warmed, even as I clutched my shawl tighter. The breeze was starting to pick up, whipping my hair to the side. "I think he'll be fine. But if I do, you'll be the first person I ask."

Trudi nodded, leaning against the open door. She said, "I've done what you asked, by the way. I don't know if it'll help, but I'll keep trying."

"Thank you. And me neither, but it makes me feel better."

I hugged her then and bade her goodnight before meandering through a narrow alley and out to a forest trail. The nightly watches, a half-hearted effort at best, had been put on hold after a month with no incidents. I snorted as I stepped over a fallen branch. All it took was mere weeks of quiet living and the entire village let their guard down. No wonder Ansel saw us as such easy pickings.

It was dark in the forest, and the farther I walked, the deeper I went, the more unsettled I became. The crisp, sweet smell of myrtle blossoms overwhelmed me.

My gaze snagged on the base of a tree trunk.

I'd found Father Snow at the bottom of a myrtle tree. For a second, the shadows made it look like he was still there.

I steeled myself and kept moving. It was cruel, the way the mind could play tricks. The way it was selective with fears and ailments. Walking through this forest at night had been bearable for me a week ago.

Tonight was evidently a different story.

The dense canopies of leaves blocked the sky and suffocated me. Each branch that brushed against my shoulder was a clawing arm trying to reel me in, chain me up, keep me still.

The dirt slid under my feet as I stopped.

It wasn't real. Nothing my mind was conjuring was *real.* I knew better.

And yet, the fear didn't cease.

The shadows taunted me with malformed creatures, and I rubbed my eyes, trying to banish them. My back turned slick with cold sweat. The tips of my fingers were numb. And over the pounding of blood in my head, I swore I heard a sound. A stifled exhale on the cusp of laughter. My skin prickled with awareness. Someone was here, I was sure of it, observing, enjoying.

"Lena?"

I whirled, clutching my chest.

Ansel stood before me, wearing a white shirt open at the collar and work pants stuffed into boots. His torso was covered in dirt, as though he'd been shoulder-deep in gardening.

I'd never seen him so surprised, nor so dishevelled, and my emotions exploded in a rush as my knees hit the cold earth. A sound escaped me, somewhere between a laugh and a sob.

Ansel knelt on one knee, placed his hand on my cheek. Gently, he rubbed a tear away with his thumb. "What makes you cry so, little thief?"

I sniffed and gestured to the forest around me. "I think you can guess."

"So, it is my fault?"

"*All* of this is," I shouted. My face was hot and sticky beneath Ansel's touch, and I pushed him away.

Ansel didn't move. Just knelt there and watched.

"Sorry," I muttered, voice thick.

His lips quirked in a crooked smile I'd never seen before. "For what, darling? Speaking your mind?"

I shrugged and stood. The castle beckoned over the treetops. "What are you doing out here?"

"Early evening stroll."

I gave him the side-eye as he kept pace with me. "Then why are you covered in dirt?"

"What, this?" He took hold of his shirt. "I was rifling through the garden earlier. Have you ever walked through a twelve-foot bramble? I must say, I cannot recommend it."

I hummed, not quite believing him, but too worn to care. The fear from earlier had melted away, replaced with tiredness and, strangely enough, a modicum of peace. Having someone else with me turned the forest into what it once was: a place of beauty, a hideaway. Dangerous still to those unaware of its many paths, but a place in which I felt at home.

The fact that 'someone' was Ansel was a spiteful kind of irony, but I'd take it.

The hoot of an owl accompanied our arrival, and in the moment before we crossed the stone threshold, I could have sworn I heard Ansel whisper something into the night.

When I asked him to repeat himself, he just shook his head and smiled.

I followed him up the stairs without thinking, matching his steps as though he could lead me away from the dark churning of my thoughts.

"You're early," he said, wiping dirt off his wrist.

"Yes. I'll bring more blood next time. Sorry."

"I never said it was a bad thing."

We were outside the library—it seemed to be the room we both gravitated towards—and I moved past Ansel to collapse in the rocking chair, dangling my legs over the armrest.

"Wait there," Ansel called from the hallway. "I'll be back soon."

I nodded, rocking back and forth, the chair creaking beneath me.

If my health got worse, what would I do? Leaving the village was out of the question. Ansel wanted his blood, and what Ansel wanted, Ansel got. Maybe I could actually spend some time in Haycock, try and make it work. Not that it would change much. Markus was the most knowledgeable medical practitioner for miles. If he couldn't do anything, then no one in Haycock could.

I had to believe that my efforts until now hadn't been a complete waste of time. That the huge amount of money beneath my bed wasn't sitting there collecting dust for no reason. I had to keep hoping or the despair would crush me.

Be grateful, I told myself. *Be grateful for this time. For Trudi, Hugo, and that one crazy old trader who winks at you. For jam sandwiches and the colour green.*

Groaning, I leaned my temple against the chair's back.

"Here you are," Ansel said, and I looked at him over my shoulder.

Looped over one hand was a cloth bag. Balanced on the other was a tray with a chipped mug, white teacup, and miniature jug.

He handed me the mug.

"What is this?" I asked, sceptical. My taste buds had yet to recover from the last time he'd made tea.

"Just try it."

Hoping I wasn't about to die of food poisoning, I screwed my eyes shut and swallowed. Flavour, rich and smooth, exploded on my tongue.

It was hot cocoa.

It was *delicious* hot cocoa, the expensive kind I hadn't had since I was a child. The warmth flooded me, brought strength into my bones and sharpened my mind. I felt like I could breathe properly for the first time in days.

Opposite me, Ansel took a seat and chuckled. "One sip and you're already looking better. Splash of milk?" He held out the tiny jug.

The image of Ansel chasing the villagers' prize cow for a jug of milk popped into my head, and I laughed. "You ended up chasing them, then?" I asked, referring to when he had bemoaned a lack of milk for his hair treatment.

Ansel filled the rest of the mug with milk, little finger raised. "The cows and I came to an understanding."

I shook my head, amazed that he had managed to lift my spirits so quickly. "Where in the world did you get cocoa from?" There were very few places throughout the continent he could have found it, and I was fairly certain Myrtle Gully wasn't on the list.

"I'd tell you, but I fear you would not approve."

"You stole it, didn't you? Don't tell me from where. I won't be able to enjoy it if you do."

Ansel watched me from over the rim of his teacup, a mischievous glint in his eyes. "Yes," he said, "I'm sure that new priest is missing it greatly."

I nearly choked on my mouthful. "You stole this from Father Pentaghast?"

"Oh dear, did I say that? What terribly loose lips I have."

"*Ansel.*"

"Yes, Lena?" His voice was low, gravelly.

Damn. I couldn't think of anything clever to say when he said my name like that. He seemed to know it too, because a smug kind of satisfaction settled over him.

"How old are you, Lena?" I gripped my mug harder. There seemed no harm in telling him, yet the answer made me self-conscious. "Twenty."

"Positively middle-aged. And yet you do not fashion yourself in love with a village boy? There is no beau you pine over at night?"

My face contorted. "What?"

"You are very pretty, aren't you? You must have a following of youths, each trying to earn your favour. And a mind such as yours must prove irresistible."

"Are you mocking me?"

He neither confirmed nor denied. Only sipped his blood.

"No," I said at last.

"No?"

"Yeah. No village boys." Of the few boys my age, one was my foster brother, another liked men, and the rest would see me stagnate as a village wife. The boys who had grand plans of leaving the village were already long gone.

Ansel raised his eyebrows as though I'd piqued his interest, but I didn't explain. He could read into it however he wanted.

I said, "And how about—"

"Quite unattached."

The interruption exasperated me. "What is?"

"Me."

My train of thought tripped over itself. I was going to ask him how old he was, not his relationship availability.

Ansel tapped his fingernails against the teacup, each *clink, clink, clink* ratcheting my nerves. What was going on right now? I thought I knew, but I also couldn't quite believe it. I sat up straighter, touched my feet to the floor and faced him.

"What's in the bag?" I asked, trying to diffuse the layer of *knowing* in the air. It worked. Ansel perked up, bending at the waist to rummage around.

"Here, I brought you this." He held out a pair of grey socks I'd been knitting, then passed me my needles. "I do hope you've got a pair in the works for me. Any colour but white, if you please. Anything too pale washes me out."

"Thank you," I said, thoughtful. "Why are you being so nice to me?"

Not that he'd been actively mean since our first meeting. I was starting to suspect his callousness that night was due to the headache he'd claimed.

It wouldn't have been because he was hungry, I thought dryly, disgusted but not surprised at the fact I could now be flippant about such a thing.

Like I said to Trudi, I'd had to adapt.

Ansel replied, "You seemed troubled. Not yourself. If death has taught me anything, it is that good company mixed with something delicious will cure most wounds. Or, at the very least, distract from them for a time."

Heat rose in my cheeks, and I tried to tamp it down. "Thanks."

I considered telling him what had happened. Explaining the details of the night, that someone had played a cruel joke on me, that I was scared and hurt and ashamed of myself for running away to the castle when I should have faced the situation head-on. But when I looked at him, all I noticed was the way his eyes were drooping as if content, and how his fingers curled lazily over the arm of the chair.

It was so rare for him to be still like this. I didn't want to ruin it, not after the kind gesture he'd made.

He cocked his head and blinked slowly. "What are you doing?"

"What do you mean?" I cleared my throat. "I'm not doing anything."

"You're turning red. Are you very warm?"

I frowned at him. "I'm blushing."

"Oh? Why?"

"I'm not doing it on purpose."

"Oh," he said again. He felt his cheek with the back of his fingers. "Blushing. Yes, I'd forgotten. Tell me, what does it feel like?"

I took another sip of hot cocoa, stalling. "Uncomfortable, now that you've drawn attention to it."

He pressed his lips together, gaze fond. He crossed his legs, trousers pulling tight across his thigh.

Eyes on his face, Lena.

Suddenly, he said, "I have to say, I like it. It makes you smell even better than usual. You've stopped taking that garlic monstrosity, haven't you?"

I nearly threw my hot cocoa onto him—that kind of comment deserved it—but managed to refrain. His eyes shone in the candlelight, blue and bright and for the very first time, warm. He looked happy.

I placed my mug down. "That's why I stick around—to combat the musty smell you're so good at cultivating."

The flash of his fangs as he smiled wasn't unsettling. It just was.

We sat together for a long, long while, him drinking blood while I sipped on my cocoa. He told me more of his life, about how he'd written poetry for a prince, designed gardens for a queen, and built a castle for himself when it all grew too tiring.

As I sat there laughing with him, feeling as if I were being healed from the events of the day, I wondered at whatever this was, this enmity turned teasing. It might have been strange and tentative and akin to prodding a bee's nest in the hope the honey was worth it, but it was even more than that. It was cosy and comfortably uncomfortable, thrilling and idiotic. It was both longing and contentment.

And if things weren't the way they were, it might have been a little bit more.

CHAPTER TWELVE

We fell into an easy rhythm as the weeks went by.

Ansel was a lover of spontaneity and so barely a night would pass where he wouldn't drag me out to keep him company on his little trips into the forest—midnight picnics, early-morning birdwatching, the occasional game of I Spy that would inevitably end in my defeat. If I was an outsider looking in, our level of domesticity would have been disturbing. The tension never disappeared, always lingering in the blood he drank and the way he spoke of a century ago as if it were yesterday. The tension was there, yes, but it was no longer as vitriolic.

Village life remained monotonous. Trudi, Hugo, and I all looked into the pig incident but found no evidence that could point us to the culprit. Trudi suspected the stonemason's mother—"The insult 'swine' can't be a coincidence," she argued—but Hugo had asked around, and the family hadn't owned a pig in years. That, and they couldn't afford to waste a perfectly good pig's head when they had a dozen bellies to fill.

I was wary in the clinic to the point of being unable to sleep, but the nights passed without incident, and my anxiety eased enough that I could almost pretend it had never happened in the first place.

My health didn't flare up again. On the contrary, I felt better than I had in a long time. I knew that wasn't necessarily a positive sign, but denial and I had become good friends, and I didn't want to rain on her parade.

All I knew was that one way or another and sooner rather than later, I would have to leave. The falling leaves were already ushering in autumn. I couldn't afford to wait for winter.

I was brooding on this late one night as I lounged atop my bed covers at the castle, playing with an old necklace of my mother's. I weaved the leather cord between my fingers, fiddled with the wooden cross. The bare walls of my bedchamber had become my canvas to which I'd slowly added colours. A trinket here, a woven ornament there. Ansel's tangerine embroidery was displayed proudly above my bed.

I shifted on the blankets, bringing one up to cover my bare thighs and tucking it around the black shirt of Ansel's I wore. I had pinched it from the drying rack in the courtyard, and it was proving to be one of the nicest things I'd worn for years. Perhaps I should have taken the ease with which I wore it as a warning sign, but all I felt was a thrumming sense of disassociation.

I still had nightmares, but I was starting to understand Ansel and his flippancy towards mortality. If I were to live forever, there would be a part of me that would throw away emotions like guilt or regret. To exist any other way for an eternity would be torture.

I heaved myself off the bed and lit a candle on the nightstand, opening an empty drawer to drop the necklace inside.

Ansel breezed through the open doorway, running a comb through his hair. He was dressed in shades of mourning, death, and hell, yet I'd wager there was no one who could possibly look half as celestial.

It was so unfair that he was prettier than me.

"Darling," he said, "have you seen my—" His mouth snapped shut.

His gaze roamed from the top of my blonde head to the tips of my toes. I looked down at myself.

Ah, yes. Wearing his shirt and showing an indecent amount of thigh.

Ansel took a slow step inside, the movement sinuous and charged. His pupils dilated, blue swallowed by black. "Is that my shirt?"

A sound left me, kind of like 'um'. The sound one makes when they know they're in trouble and are trying to think how to get out of it.

"Nooo," I tried. Technically, it wasn't. I had claimed it, so it was mine.

Lena, dictator of shirts. Hide your precious knits before she steals them off your backs.

Obviously, I was slaphappy.

Ansel paused at the foot of the bed, gaze moving reluctantly from me to the nightstand. He did a double take, and I craned my head around to look.

Abruptly, he asked, "Have you seen my red cape?"

"Your cape?" Was this his attempt at diversion? Were we really going to pretend he hadn't just been salivating over me? I wondered if I wanted it any other way, and panic overtook me.

Pretending it is.

"No," I said. "Did you leave it on the battlements?" We'd gone up to stargaze the previous night.

"I must have," he said stiffly. Once again, his attention warred between me and the nightstand.

"What are you looking at?"

"Nothing. Here, have this. I think you need it more than I." He tossed the comb onto the bed.

"A mirror would help," I said, "except one of us is sore about not having a reflection."

Ansel tapped his finger against his leg. He'd finally filed his nails so they no longer looked like talons. "On second thought, don't use it. Your hair is lovely as is."

I quirked a brow. "Okay. Thanks. Do you have ants in your pants or something?"

He was fidgeting like a schoolboy with a crush.

Ansel muttered something to himself, and I scowled. He knew I hated it when he avoided the question.

"I'm going to go ... drink something," he said. "Are you thirsty?"

I shook my head.

As his gaze raked over me once more, catching on the hem of his shirt, his mouth curled up. "I am glad to see you looking healthier." His exit was normal, lackadaisical almost.

Trying too hard.

I walked to the door and stood where he had.

How very curious.

I lazed the night away, a productive type of laze in which I finished knitting a pair of mittens for Trudi and mended a tear in my dress. Eventually, I ventured downstairs to find Ansel in the entrance hall, hanging a painting. A decrepit ladder creaked beneath his weight.

I had to hand it to him, he understood interior design like he'd given birth to the concept. The entrance hall had become the castle's crowning glory with its expensive furniture and freshly gilded sconces. In my absence one week, he had carpeted the stairs, and the maroon fibres reflected in the crystal chandelier he'd taken pains to repair.

There was no evidence on the outside, but the last two months had seen the castle begin to reclaim its former glory.

I marvelled at such a feat, trying not to gawk at the way Ansel's shirt clung to his biceps as he angled the frame or how the muscles in his back tensed as he balanced his forearm against the wall.

Attraction, I was discovering, was an all-consuming corruption.

He was finishing up when I cleared my throat and pulled the loose hair from my neck, holding it back.

It's a warm night is all, just a warm night, nothing to do with Ansel.

He glanced over his shoulder at the sound, an attentive expression passing over him as if he'd been waiting for me to announce myself. He was stepping down the ladder, was going to come over and say something witty or charming, when—

The bottom rung of the ladder broke beneath him, and he hissed as his foot slammed into the ground.

Well, there went that daydream.

He lifted his leg to reveal a thick, rusty nail penetrating his boot.

"Sit," I called, rushing to him. "Sit, sit—no, not on the ladder, on the ground." I knelt, propping his foot on my knee. "Okay, this is going to"—I pulled the nail out—"sting." I pried his shoe and sock off, exhaling through my teeth at the sight of the puncture. The nail hadn't penetrated the top of his foot, but it *had* been covered in rust. "We're going to have to wash this," I said. "Do we have any water left, or do I need to go for a run to the river?"

Ansel's forehead wrinkled as he studied me. He opened his mouth, about to say something, but the breath caught in his throat. He bit down on his bottom lip.

"Ansel?" I prompted.

"No need to wash it." The words were reluctant.

I held up the nail, head orange with rust, point red with blood. "See this rust here? You don't want this in your bloodstream. I know you're immortal, but people die from less."

"I understand that."

"Then what is it?"

He slid his foot out of my grip and leaned forward to take my hands. The nail clattered to the ground. "It won't matter. But thank you for trying." He ran his fingers down mine, spreading his blood across my hands.

It felt like he was painting himself on me.

His thumb swiped over my scarred palm, staining it red, and the touch sent sparks shooting up my arm. "That's a pretty colour on you," he said.

I grimaced, but even as I did so, I was internalising that I liked the way his hands could swallow mine whole. Liked the way they clasped me as if I were something precious.

I internalised, and then I repressed.

"Are you trying to tell me vampires don't get infections?" I asked, swiping a rag from his shirt pocket to wipe my hands.

"To be promised eternity, only to die by infection. You have to admit, it's not very romantic."

I rolled my eyes, mainly at myself. Of course, he would be fine. Instinct had taken over when instinct wasn't needed, and I'd gone and embarrassed myself.

"Here you go." I handed the rag back. "If it doesn't matter, just use this to clean the blood."

He was quiet for a moment. "Would you do it?"

I didn't answer.

"It's not quite healed yet," he explained, quickly, "and you know how brutish my touch can be. Best have you do it, so I don't make it worse."

"You're not going to kick me in the face, are you?" Because he was tricky like that, which I found entertaining, but not when it was aimed towards me.

He sighed.

"All right," I grumbled for the sake of grumbling, then placed his foot back in my lap. The wound had already closed, pink skin stretching taut across the bottom of his foot. "It's healed," I said, amazed. I had never seen him heal up close before. It was miraculous.

"Is it? But no, no, it still hurts. I need you to rub some ointment on it."

"Ointment?"

"Is that wrong? A poultice, then, or some happy healing herbs."

"Happy what?"

He wiggled his toes. "Darling, it *hurts*."

"Yes, okay, sorry." I wrapped the filthy rag around his foot to humour him. He could be up and walking now if he wanted.

"Thank you," he said once I'd sat back on my heels. He didn't need to say anything further, not with the way he was looking at me. I didn't have a name for the expression.

It was so very unlike the Ansel I knew that all I could manage in reply was, "Mmhmm."

"And I am sorry, you know. About your priest and that first night. About everything."

I blinked.

"I said it before, but I don't think you believed me." He shrugged. "With good reason, too. I was only being polite."

"You're sorry?" I echoed.

"Yes."

"About that night?"

His cheek twitched. "Very much so."

My eyelashes fluttered like dust was caught in them. Maybe there was. Maybe that was why my eyes were threatening to water.

"About Father Snow, too?"

Ansel hesitated, and pain lanced through me. He couldn't change. He was immortal and unfeeling, and he'd never be capable of change.

"Yes," Ansel said slowly, surprising me. "But please try and understand, I barely remember it. The smell of fresh blood was enough to wake me, but I wasn't ... all there. I had enough self-preservation to stay inside until it became dark, but that's all it was—base instinct. I would have killed my own brother in that state, not knowing who he was until I drained him." He shrugged again, shoulders tense. His expression was hope, I realised. Guarded and twisted beneath layers of defence, but hope, nonetheless.

"Okay," I said. "I believe you." It was lame as far as forgiveness went, but I didn't know what else to say.

The simple words were a balm for him. He relaxed, head tilting back and hair spilling down his side like pitch.

It hit me suddenly that I knew nothing about him. I had spent so long clinging to my own view of him, of how a vampire should be, should act, that my opinion of him was unreliable. Looking at him now, his foot wrapped in a filthy rag and an endearingly self-satisfied expression on his face,

I couldn't help but wonder at everything about him I'd missed.

Who *was* this vampire?

I blurted, "Do you actually have a brother or was that purely hypothetical? How do you sleep for a hundred years? Can all vampires do that, because it sounds amazing. Do you think if I studied you, I could cure sleep deprivation?"

Ansel removed the rag from his foot as I spoke, folding it away and replacing his boot. He took me by the elbow and gently tugged me to my feet.

"Well?" I prompted when he didn't answer. "Do you think so?"

He chuckled. "I think that it is getting early, and so we should go upstairs, where you're welcome to study me all you like."

"Oh, hilarious," I said under my breath as he pulled me up the stairs.

Ansel led me to my bedchamber—presumptuous of him—and set up a game of chess between us on the bed. I offered to get him some blood, but he went instead, returning with tea and a slice of buttered bread.

He was thoughtful, abounding in little acts of kindness. I could see that now.

I was pleasantly surprised he was not an adept chess player. He picked up the gist of it quickly, even though I took unashamed advantage of his beginner status, claiming a swift win on the first and second game.

By the third game, we could hear birdsong through the window, heralding the dawn.

I sighed, resting my chin in my palm. "It's been over a minute. Make your move."

Ansel shushed me, intent on the chessboard. A piece of his hair had caught beneath his collar, and he untangled it absently, revealing a black smudge beneath his jaw. I looked closely, noticing another on his temple.

"Have you been playing in the fireplace?" I asked, though we'd long ago agreed not to light any fires. Nothing screamed *'I'm here, come get me!'* like smoke from a chimney.

He rubbed his chin. "Nothing quite so risky. Just some sketches."

"Ooo, of what? Yourself?"

He laughed.

I sipped my tea, hiding a smile. Ansel finally decided which chess piece to move, and my smile widened into a grin.

"Again? Are you cheating?" he asked when I swiped another pawn from the board.

"No, but I'm fairly certain you are."

He averted his eyes. "I would never." He moved his rook this time, the crude rendering of a tower looking like it was about to disintegrate beneath his fingers.

"You're leaving your queen open," I muttered, placing my bishop in front of my king. "Why are you leaving your queen open?"

"She's a good distraction." He then took *my* queen with a knight he'd lost several turns ago.

My jaw dropped, and I fisted the blankets beneath me. "You *are* cheating."

"Take it as a compliment."

"Fine." I flicked his king over with a pawn that'd been halfway across the board. "Look, I win."

"I'm not sure cheating counts if it's so obvious."

I rolled the pawn between my palms. "Take it as a compliment."

Ansel nodded good-naturedly, and I set to packing the chessboard away. I paused at his hand on my arm.

He whispered, "The night suits you."

The world stood still. I didn't think either of us was breathing.

I stayed very still, telling myself it was pure fondness that spurred his words. Like I was his younger sister or a stray cat he'd taken in.

"That's because you haven't seen me in the sun," I replied, trying for levity.

"No, I don't think so." He smoothed the back of his fingers down my cheek, and I tried not to rear back. "Look at you. So lovely. So hungry. I could sate that hunger if you'd let me."

That's not how you speak to your sister, I thought.

I knew what this was. Ansel was growing tired of solitude, however much he may have denied being lonely, and I was the naïve distraction that kept him company. He was self-aware, but still male, which meant that after sleeping for a century and waking to a less than inspiring existence, it was no longer his brain he was thinking with.

It was only weeks ago that I'd admitted to friendship with him. There were too many variables, too many possible betrayals that made anything more than a fleeting attraction possible.

Anticipation glinted in his eyes. An invitation. He was asking me seriously, so I would answer in kind.

"How could you, though," I said softly, "when you're not what I hunger for?"

He looked like I'd slapped him.

"Ansel," I started, but aside from his name, no other words came to mind.

He shook his head and leaned back to run his hands through his hair. "I've been too flippant with you, haven't I. You don't believe a word I say."

"No, I do—" I cut off as his eyebrows lifted, derisiveness I hadn't seen since that first night at the village flashing across his face. It made my hackles rise. "You can't blame me for a little self-preservation."

"Call it what you will. I think we both know what it is."

I caught my breath, placing the chessboard on the floor for an excuse to look away. Too late, I realised what I'd done. There was no barrier between us now but for the blankets. "And what is it?" I asked.

He looked down his nose at me, and I was glad to find an absence where my fear used to be. Whatever opinion he held of the villagers, I knew now that I, at least, was safe from him.

"I'll tell you when you're ready to believe me," he said.

I didn't want to fight, so I stopped myself from scoffing. Instead, I took a pillow from behind me and hugged it to my chest. Restructured the barrier.

I swallowed. “Isn’t it past your bedtime, old man?”

“Not yet, though it is past yours, little girl.”

He wasn’t wrong. It was past my bedtime eight hours ago.

Ansel didn’t leave. Just spread out on the foot of the bed and said conversationally, “At least you don’t have to trudge downstairs each morning. I have weak ankles, did I ever tell you, and the endless stairs are doing them no good.”

The words, frivolous, normal for him, were an olive branch. Instantly, I reached out to take it.

“You could just stay up here,” I said, meaning aboveground. “I’m not going to open the drapes on you.”

A beat of stunned silence. “I beg your pardon?”

I shrugged. “I’d be sick of sleeping in that place too. Who’s buried down there, anyway? They’re not all your vampire brides, are they?” I wasn’t entirely joking.

He laughed again, but the sound was strained. “Heavens, no. They were acquaintances, I suppose, and it is more symbolic than anything, but you ... You are serious?”

“Yes?” We were in a castle. There were plenty of rooms to go around.

A feral smile stretched his mouth, and my heart plummeted into my stomach.

Death take me, I was dense sometimes. The other bedchambers weren’t yet made up—why would they be?—and he wouldn’t fit on any of the couches, not lying down.

Anyone would have taken that as an invitation, let alone Ansel, who was so obviously looking for one.

"No, I didn't mean it, that's not what I meant," I spluttered as he toed off his boots. "Ansel, wait."

I faltered at the look he gave me. It was a challenge.

"Problem, darling?"

Glaring, I hugged the pillow tighter. "This is my bed. Go back to your tomb."

"This is my castle." He started unbuttoning his shirt. "Go back to your village."

"I'll make a trail of rice as I go so you can come with me. During the dawn."

His fingers stopped. "Darling girl, I would catch you before you reached the door. But please, do still try."

He wouldn't budge? Neither would I.

I blew out the candle with more force than necessary and got into bed fully clothed. There was the rustling of fabric before the mattress dipped behind me. Ansel spread out, making himself comfortable.

I kicked behind me, aim hitting true when my heel connected with what felt like his shin. "This is my side. Move over."

He caught my foot between his knees. Trailed fingers up my leg. "Quiet now, I'm trying to sleep."

"You'd fall asleep faster if you kept your hands to yourself." Deep down, though, I enjoyed the feel of him discovering me. Craved more of it.

His voice turned soft. "Does my touch repulse you? Because I would be close to you now if you'd let me."

I shut my eyes and bit hard into my bottom lip. I didn't want to encourage him. I didn't know what I wanted.

Don't shatter his hope, some part of me demanded.

Mustering my courage, I took his hand from my leg and rolled over to face him. His breath hitched. Full of confidence one moment, vulnerable the next.

"Ansel?" I whispered into the darkness. Always, always the darkness.

"Yes?" He was frozen, as if any movement from his end would ruin the peace.

I hesitated. "Do you miss your old life? From a century ago?"

Minutes passed, and I accepted that he wouldn't answer. But when I was drifting off to sleep, fingers slackening around his, I could have sworn I heard him murmur, "Not anymore."

I was not at all surprised when I awoke to a body wrapped around mine.

Ansel's face was buried in the back of my neck, his front pressing me into the mattress. I yawned, blinking sleep from my eyes.

"Ansel." It was muffled against the pillow. "Ansel, I can't breathe." There was a fine layer of sweat down my back, on the inside of my legs. I should have bothered to change. "Wake up," I said when he didn't stir and kicked out with the leg he wasn't crushing.

A low groan came from behind me.

Success!

There was a pause in which I imagined him opening his eyes, registering the way his body sunk into mine. I heard him sigh. If anything, his arms became even tighter.

"Lena," he said, voice thick with sleep.

"Yes, it's Lena. And I have things to do, places to be, so ..." Truthfully, I was laying it on a bit thick. I would have been content to stay there if not for the consequences.

Ansel nuzzled deeper into my neck. I hunched as goosebumps needled down my spine. Softly, wetly, his lips caressed the spot between my neck and shoulder.

An alarmed squeak escaped me. I flailed, pushing at his arms and rolling over.

"Hello, darling," he breathed. His lips were slightly swollen, his eyelids heavy.

"Let go."

His grip loosened before he seemed to change his mind. "Why?"

"Because I'd like to get up now." I was acutely aware of his legs between mine, his chest—naked, due to his unbuttoned shirt—against my own.

Ansel smiled, and my face warmed at the thought of his mouth on me. Not even the sight of his fangs could dampen the heat.

"And what will you do to get me off you?"

Arrogant, I thought. He presumed he had me cornered.

He presumed wrong.

The nightstand was within arm's reach, and I grasped the only object within its drawer before Ansel, in his lethargic state, could comprehend my intentions. I shoved my mother's necklace between us, and Ansel hurled himself off the bed, landing on the stone floor with a *thud*.

As glorious as his reaction was, I instantly missed the weight of him. Annoyance stabbed through me at the feeling—*you know better than that, Lena*—and I shook the emotions off, chuffed that my suspicions had been correct.

Holding the necklace high, I crowed, "I knew it!"

"*Cover it up*," Ansel snarled.

"Oh—sorry." I tucked it into my pocket.

Ansel slammed a trembling hand on the bed. He rose to his feet, blanket sliding off his shoulders, the tattered remains of his shirt going with it. A sizzling sound emanated from him. It wasn't until he was standing at full height that I spotted the skin on his chest and face knitting back together.

"I'm so sorry," I said, covering my mouth, horrified at myself. "I didn't think it would be that effective." And why had I thought that? It was stupid of me. I had no idea what an item, once soaked in priest's blood and blessed, would do to a vampire.

He dismissed the apology, stretching to ease the new skin. "No, that was marvellous."

"It was?" There was a pink strip healing on his abdomen that I couldn't seem to avert my eyes from. He looked so alive, and it fascinated the healer within me. Blue veins beneath the skin, a freckle on his shoulder, and taut abdominal muscles. He was undead, but from the outside, he appeared incredibly healthy.

"Of course," Ansel said. "I do love someone who can keep me on my toes. It must have been an extraordinarily pious priest who blessed that little trinket."

The necklace had been my father's wedding pledge to my mother. My mother loved it, wore it everywhere she went. I didn't know who had blessed it, only that the blessing had once taken place and was done to bring the wearer good luck.

I supposed safety from vampires was the Dawn Lord's special brand of luck.

Ansel said, "I'm so glad to see you're enjoying the view, darling."

I started, shifting my gaze away from the skin of his abdomen, up to his face. Ansel tipped his chin up, and I scrambled for something clever to say.

I wasn't sure I succeeded when I blurted, "I see naked bodies every other day at work. Nothing you've got will surprise me."

"Oh-*ho*." A cat's smile curved his lips. "She says as much, but is that a blush I see tinting those cheeks?"

I slid from the bed, staring at the door and wondering if I could feasibly make a run for it. "No."

"She denies it, but her body cannot lie."

"Don't speak about me as if I'm not here."

Ansel inhaled theatrically. "And her voice. Is that a rasp I hear?"

"If you don't stop talking soon, I will knit you a muzzle."

He swiped his tongue across his teeth, looking like he didn't mind the idea at all.

Where had this blatant flirtation come from? I was treading on thin ice, I could feel it, and once that ice cracked, I was going to have to try my best not to sink.

I cleared my throat. "So, the necklace is a holy symbol, is it? A blessing makes it different than a normal effigy?"

"Perhaps. This changes the dynamic between us considerably, doesn't it?" He was thrilled.

"I guess." Not that I was about to start threatening him with it. One smell of his burning flesh was enough to last me a lifetime.

I threw Ansel out after that, threatening to spike his blood with garlic if he so much as stepped a toe inside while I was changing. We both knew it was an empty threat, but he played nice and left with only a put-upon sigh.

The hours that followed were ... unnerving. Likely because I enjoyed them so much, perversely so.

Ansel brought me breakfast in the cabinet as I sat hunched over the desk, poring over some notes of Trudi's. The Harvest Festival was only days away, and she had been inundated with stall proposals and offers from new traders. That Ansel brought me food was not strange in and of itself, but a month and a half ago he could barely sizzle a sausage. The display of honey-drizzled porridge he stuck under my nose meant he'd been practising.

When we went to sweep the colourful leaves piled up at the servants' entrance, he hurried into the forest, returning with a baby bat clasped in his hands. He held it out to me, as though presenting a child to the Dawn Lord for a blessing. I cooed over it but didn't miss Ansel's disappointment when I told him to take the poor thing back to its roost before its mother sought revenge.

And although he was subtle about it, Ansel miraculously found things to do in every room I was in. He shut a window the moment before I was about to stand and do so, like he had a preternatural sense of when I was cold. He covered me with his red cape, even though it was his favourite. Most surprising was that he considered my decorating advice.

His eyes were a little too eager, a little too excited every time I called his name. It had only been a short while ago that I'd admitted to friendship with him. If this was fast for me, it would be less than a fleeting fancy for him.

So, I kept my walls up.

When he laughed, I only smiled. When he teased, I only shrugged.

The final straw came just before dawn. I was sitting on the library floor, surrounded by books and braiding my hair. Ansel was drawing something on the couch behind me, the soft scrape of charcoal breaking the tentative silence between us.

I must have missed a strand, or maybe he pulled it out on purpose, but next thing I knew, Ansel's fingers threaded through my hair, caressing my scalp with each weave of the braid.

"You missed some," he said quietly, indulgently, as if my carelessness was the most enchanting thing he'd ever witnessed. I sat still, unable to move even if I'd wanted to.

All day I had tried to act unaffected, like his kindness meant nothing and I didn't care for the renewed life in his eyes.

My hard shell was cracking.

"You don't need to fuss over it," I said, relieved when my voice came out steady.

"But I like fussing over you." He said it with such openness, such casualness, as though *of course* he liked fussing over me, for what better thing was there to do?

The moment finished, and I made some excuse and fled from the room. The confused whisper of my name on his tongue followed me through the door and up the stairs, up and up, until I made it to the battlements. A gust of fresh air hit me like a physical blow. I knelt under the multihued sky, gripping my head and pulling at the hair Ansel had so carefully tied.

"An hour," I said aloud, voice cracking. "That's it, Lena, and then you'll go back to the village. Keep it in check." An image flashed, unbidden, of Ansel that morning, lounging in my bed, shirt open to reveal the indent of his hips. "Argh! No! Stop it, Lena, stop."

But I couldn't stop. Ansel was temptation personified, and the idea of having to go back down there and face him was torture.

I like him, I like him, I like him.

Therein lay the problem. Because I was mortal and in possession of a conscience, and what if he ran off at the first whiff of a lady vampire—*oh, and technically, he's still blackmailing me.*

I stayed there on the battlements, arguing with myself until the sun broke through the clouds and the temperature started to rise. Until I knew Ansel would have gone to sleep.

Then I hightailed it out of there.

CHAPTER THIRTEEN

The anticipation of the Harvest Festival breathed new life into Myrtle Gully.

The promise of food, music and dancing permeated the air, lightening it until everyone was practically bouncing in their boots. Traders were already arriving, early in the week as it was, selling masks decorated with antlers and horns and butterfly wings. This festival was the last thing Myrtle Gully had to look forward to in the coming months; the celebration that softened the inevitable blow of winter.

The villagers were happy and therefore nicer, actually greeting me instead of acting like I carried the plague. Even little Paul didn't avert his eyes when he came to collect an infusion for his father. I should have been excited. The Harvest Festival was my favourite celebration of the year.

But I wasn't excited.

I was on the Dawn damned warpath.

Ripping and tearing and splitting—I was going to annihilate the weeds that had the gall to take up residence in my herb garden.

"Stupid weeds," I said, hurling another plant carcass into the bucket. Next to it, Balthazar watched me, unbothered. "I will crush you and your stupid children and your stupid grandchildren, just like I did your stupid parents."

Evidently, I was working through some issues.

Issues like Ansel.

It had been three days since I'd scurried away from the castle like a sad, earthbound crow trying to protect its hoarded treasures—treasures that were in this case my last vestiges of pride.

I tore a weed to pieces. The feel of it shredding beneath my hands made everything marginally better.

There I was, trying to maintain the status quo and keep chaos from raining down upon us, but what did he go and do? Ruined the peace, that was what. Ruined the peace and made things awkward for me, because I cringed in pure, self-esteem crushing *awkwardness* whenever I thought of it. Thought of him. Thought of everything.

"*The night suits you*," I mimicked under my breath. "*Oh, and is that a blush I see?*" I snorted. "As if." I ripped another weed out of the ground, groaning when I accidentally uprooted the struggling mint plant wedged to its side.

Yet another thing to be annoyed at Ansel for, I thought, though somewhere deep, deep down, I knew I was being petty.

The mint plant was wilting. *All* the herbs, particularly the ones usually cared for by Markus, were dying, missing their real carer as much as I was. I could use a good inspirational smack up the head right about now.

The day was growing late. A bell chimed from the front of the building and brought with it the sound of Hugo farewelling the last patient of the day.

I breathed in the scent of earth and sweat, the fragrance of mint. The soil was hard and dry from neglect. I hadn't given it a proper watering in days, and knowing Hugo, he'd forgotten watering plants was a necessary component in gardening, opposite of a green thumb that he was.

Sighing, I got to my feet before pulling my gloves off and throwing them to the ground. "Back soon, Balthy."

Goosebumps broke out along my arms as I poked my head inside the back door of the clinic to let Hugo know I would be back soon—I needn't have bothered, for he was leaving to meet with Trudi—and I shook the unpleasant sensation off. I fetched a water pail from the stack and made my way to the outskirts of the village.

The moss-grown well sat like a lonesome soldier, a stalwart presence guarding the village from the forest's tree line. It was the farthest well out of Myrtle Gully, and its water was more likely to come out smelling sour than sweet, so it was largely neglected.

The pulley was stiff and took a few hits to dislodge, groaning as the pail descended into the black depths.

I wondered absently if Trudi had bothered to come to this well. We'd talked about her going to the other two, but I hadn't thought to specify. I considered checking with her but decided it wasn't worth it. No one drank from this well. It wouldn't matter.

I hoisted the pail into my arms. The water was as brown as predicted.

"Excuse me, miss?"

I flinched in surprise, and water sloshed over my chest, making me drop the pail.

Dawn Lord's flaming knickers, this stuff was *freezing*.

From behind came a timid, "Are you all right?"

I turned to find a lithe, straw-haired young man standing at my back. He had the gangly frame of adolescence, contrasted against the soft lips and large eyes that so often accompanied it.

It occurred to me that the last few times I'd met strangers in Myrtle Gully, it didn't exactly go well. Seeing as there was a festival on the horizon, added to the fact he was skinny enough for me to snap in two, I decided not to hold it against him.

"Fine," I said, peeling the wet fabric from my skin. "But that certainly woke me up."

"Me too," he said. His shoes and socks were soaked from when I'd dropped the bucket.

"Yeah, sorry about that." I picked up the water pail to send it back down the well. "But I guess that's what happens when you sneak up on a girl."

"I promise, miss, I wasn't trying to scare you."

"I know." I glanced back at him. "I'm just teasing. What can I help you with?"

He scratched the back of his neck. "I was trying to find someone who could help me. My brother and I broke a wheel on our cart on the way here, and we need it fixed before the festival."

I looked around at the trees, the obvious lack of civilisation. "Well, you're not going to find anyone out here."

"I know," he said, smiling. A shiver wracked my frame. I needed to change clothes. "But this is such a pretty place," he continued, "and I lost myself in thoughts as I wandered."

"Ah, I see. A daydreamer, are we?" I pulled up the pail and frowned. I had no desire for a repeat. "I'll tell you what," I said, tipping some of the water back into the well. "You come with me back to the clinic so I can change clothes, and then I'll point you in the direction you need to go." I paused. "Actually, maybe that's not such a good idea."

I wouldn't put it past certain people to ignore his stall on festival night if they'd seen him with me. He would be hated by association. "Okay, how about this—trail a little bit behind me as we walk to the clinic, then find someone to help, okay?"

He bit his lip—he had very nice teeth, blunt and white—and asked, "Do you not want to be seen with me?"

"No, it's just that village folk are good at holding grudges, and you really don't want to get in the middle of them."

He grimaced. "Sounds terrifying."

I probably would have thought so once, but that was before I woke up the resident evil.

As we walked side by side, the young man introduced himself as René and laughed when I explained again that he should really pretend he didn't know me. He countered that as we were both wet and I was the one holding the pail of water, we couldn't feign ignorance of each other.

We arrived at the clinic with a minimal amount of gawking from the villagers, and I invited him in to dry off and have a cup of tea. It was there at the kitchen table, as I listened to him talk about the journey here with his older brother, that I got my first good look at him.

The clean, plain clothes he wore, perfectly acceptable for a middle-class merchant, seemed underwhelming on this boy. Like a blooming lily shrouded in weary, shrivelled leaves. My gaze followed the gentle slope of his neck and shoulders, down his arm, to his hand; the tips of his fingers were smooth, unblemished. They were the fingers of a noble.

I brought my teacup to my mouth, and he gasped at the sight of my palm.

"That's a nasty scar."

"It sure is," I said.

The scar was purple, raised. Occasionally, it would pull at my skin, but it was no longer a hindrance. I almost liked it now. It was a reminder.

"You must have been worried," he said. "Blood loss and all that."

I tried not to chuckle, unsure if his sweetness came from his ignorance or vice versa. "Blood loss wasn't an issue. I was more worried about infection."

"Oh, of course. So, did it, then? Get infected?"

We spent the next hour talking about infections, blood poisoning and, strangely enough, Markus—both his expertise as a healer and his terrible bedside manner—until the boy ran out of questions and said he needed to leave before his brother gathered a search party.

I didn't have the heart to tell him those two words were bad news in this village.

He pushed his chair in politely and looked at me.

"You don't want to stay for dinner?" I asked. He was skin and bones.

"No, thank you. I'm running late as it is."

"Well, here." I moved to the bench, halving the loaf of bread I'd baked that morning, then pulling a small jar of relish from the pantry. "It's not much, but it'll get you through. Oh, and careful out there. Night-time around here can be kind of"—I tried to think of an appropriate word—"hazardous."

He nodded, smiling shyly, and accepted the food with a polite murmur.

He left, and I set about cleaning the table, washing the cups and placing them away. A headache thrummed behind my eyes, and I planned to lie down for a while in an attempt to quell it. Naturally, that's when Trudi came barrelling through the kitchen.

"Lena! Lena, I have the most wonderful news. You'll never believe it, but hang on, just, uh, let me catch my breath." She gripped the back of a chair, panting. She pointed at the bench. "Where's the rest of the bread? Did you eat all that by yourself? I brought stew for dinner. Hugo has it, he's catching up, and—" She took another deep breath.

I stared at her, trying to make sense of the bizarre verbal onslaught. "I gave it away."

Trudi was shaking her head, a giant smile lighting her face. She was practically blinding.

"Why are you smiling?" I asked, trying not to laugh. Even with my headache, her joy was infectious.

She squeezed my hand. "Because Hugo and I have something to tell you."

"About the bread?"

"What? No, forget about the bread." She turned and shouted, "Hugo, hurry!"

Hugo appeared at the door, bright-eyed and flushed, his smile the twin to Trudi's. Trudi held her hand up. Woven around her finger was a lock of auburn hair. Hugo's hair.

Oh. *Oh.*

My heart simultaneously soared and sank. I chose to focus on the former.

"You're engaged?" I shouted and nearly fell over as Trudi threw herself on me, squealing.

I asked all the right questions—*Hugo, how long have you been planning this? Will it be a winter wedding?*—and gave all the right answers—*Of course I'll be your flower maiden and, yes, I'll do the final stitches on your wedding dress for luck*—but selfish as it was, my heart wasn't in it.

Please don't leave me alone, I thought all the while. *Please don't get lost in your happiness and forget about me.*

"We didn't come to celebrate empty-handed," Trudi said, brandishing a pot Hugo had carried in. "Rabbit stew. I know it's your favourite."

It really wasn't, and I didn't know why she thought so, but it hardly mattered. The three of us hadn't done anything like this in a long time.

We lit candles and sat around the table. I smiled and laughed with the two of them, contributing to the conversation when it was appropriate but otherwise keeping my tangled thoughts to myself as I pushed globs of meat and gravy across my bowl. My stomach felt hollow yet uncomfortably full, and I'd only taken a couple of bites. I was craving something lighter, more invigorating.

Hugo was a seasoned gossiper, so I managed to glean that any rumours regarding Father Snow's death had been overtaken by the elopement of the cobbler's—of Ernst's—son and the butcher's daughter. That, and there was a garlic thief at large.

Good old Myrtle Gully. Always focussing on the important things.

But it was a relief, and I started to relax, my headache fading to a dull thud in my temple.

Hugo was saying something about needing a new pair of shoes when I took the last bite of stew I could stomach. The bowl was still half full, but I would make an excuse to save feelings.

I wish I could have said it was a rabbit bone that got stuck in my throat or a piece of gristle, but no. The twinge in my lungs, the unrelenting pressure in my chest, all came from me. Hugo was cut off mid-sentence as I pushed my chair out from the table, covered my mouth with a handkerchief, and coughed.

It was a wet, awful sound. If I heard it in a patient, I would be concerned.

I breathed in as deeply as possible, pulling the handkerchief from my mouth. I was trying to think of something witty to say, something that would make them forget what just happened, when I stilled. The noise around me grew muffled. My body exploded in a cold sweat. It felt like I'd been pushed down to the blackest, most barren part of the ocean.

There was blood on the handkerchief.

I was coughing up blood.

My chest tightened, and I moaned, crumpling the handkerchief before Hugo could see it. I was vaguely aware of him saying my name, pushing something at me. I blinked, finding a glass of water in my hand.

When did that get there?

I managed a single swallow before the water caught in my throat and I was coughing it back out. I dropped the cup, my hands slippery with spittle. I couldn't breathe, couldn't think past the hope of taking another breath. Everything hurt.

I couldn't remember when I slid to the floor, but I think it was before the tears started tracking down my face and sometime after I coughed more blood, bitter and salty, into my hands. I thought I might actually be dying there and then on the kitchen floor.

Finally, though, it came to a stop.

Slowly, I became conscious of someone running a hand down my back.

"Lena?" It was Hugo. "Lena, can you hear me?"

I groaned and cracked an eye open.

Hugo rubbed his face, moving to stop me when I tried to kneel. "No, lie down for a bit," he said.

Trudi was standing a few feet away, shoulders hunched. She was clutching the cup.

"Is that more water?" I asked, though it came out slurred.

Trudi looked at me, then at her hands. "Here," she whispered, setting it next to me on the ground. "I'll go get a blanket."

Hugo glared at me—I bet he didn't look at other sick people like that—and said, "I thought it wasn't serious."

"It wasn't. It's not. I'm fine."

"Lena, I just watched you nearly suffocate on your own blood. You are not fine."

I blinked sluggishly. "You saw that, did you?"

A pause. "Look at your hands."

It took me a while to drudge up the energy, but I eventually slipped my arms out from beneath me. Blood, bright and red as holly berries, was spattered across my fingers, thicker in the creases of my palms. It wasn't quite dry.

"Oh," I said, then swallowed. "Ew."

"Lena," Hugo began.

"What? What do you want me to say, that I didn't mean to?"

"You know that's not what I—"

"Stop, just—please, stop." I got to my knees, Hugo hoisting me upright when I teetered. He passed me the water, and I gulped it down, tasting metal. My stomach roiled. "I feel nauseous."

Hugo, much to his credit, had quick reflexes, which meant I spent the next few minutes vomiting into a bowl of half-eaten rabbit stew rather than the kitchen floor.

Small mercies.

Once my stomach was thoroughly emptied, I slid the foul-smelling bowl to Hugo and lay back down. Dust from the floorboards stuck to the sweat-soaked skin of my forehead.

"This is, uh, not so good," I said, more to myself than anyone else. A blanket fell on me—*oh good, Trudi's back*—warm but itchy. I considered asking Trudi why she chose this blanket when we had so many blankets that were both warm and *not* itchy, but then Hugo left the room and all I could think was, *maybe he's going to get me a different blanket.*

I yawned and scrunched my eyes shut, curling into a ball.

"Sorry about your stew," I mumbled. "But don't worry, it tasted just as good coming up as it did going down." When no reply was forthcoming, I croaked, "Trudi?"

A keening whine was the only warning I received before Trudi burst into tears.

"I'm sorry," she cried, falling to her knees beside me. "I'm sorry, I'm so sorry."

My breathing was laboured. She must have heard it because her sobs grew louder, coalescing into a mantra of *I'm sorry I'm sorry I'm sorry.*

"Don't cry," I said, moving to rest my head in her lap. "I'm okay, see? I'm so fine. In fact, I'm so, so happy, because my best friends are getting married and are going to be the happiest people in the world."

She shook her head violently.

I raised a hand that weighed twice as much as usual and tugged at her elbow. "Stop that. Hey, want some blanket? It's itchy but warm." I tucked the blanket around her knees, so my head was partially covered. My toes stuck out the other end. I wiggled them.

Trudi garbled something. I made sure I was comfortable before asking, "What was that?"

"*Your lips were blue,*" she screamed, and I winced, tilting my head up to meet her gaze. Her skin had turned a splotchy red, and wisps of hair were sticking to her tear-stained cheeks.

I bit down on my lip, intellectually knowing she was upset but unable to feel much after the shock of seeing blood. Or perhaps it would be more accurate to say I wasn't letting myself feel much. To let myself acknowledge even a pinprick of fear would be like unleashing a dam. I wasn't ready to start drowning again just yet.

Although, one emotion did manage to break through the numbness.

Irritation.

Couldn't she do this later?

I understood she was upset, but she didn't have to start sobbing at me like I was already dead. Her being so upset *now* would make it impossible for me to pretend I was fine *later*. I had managed to figure that out when I was eleven, watching my mother cough up blood. Trudi should have been able to figure it out too.

I squinted at her as she rubbed her face on her sleeve. Why was she still crying? Shouldn't she be the one comforting me? And it wasn't that I *wanted* to be comforted, I just wanted her to ... be quiet. Stop wailing.

My head was sore, and I wanted her quiet.

"What kind of flowers will you wear in your hair?" I asked. The words grated against my ears.

She sniffed. "What?"

"Flowers. What kind will you wear for the wedding? Can I have pansies?" I closed my eyes and snuggled into her skirts. "Do you like pansies? I won't wear them if you don't like them."

"You want pansies?" she whispered. The painful knot in my head loosened.

"Yeah," I said on a sigh. "Lots of pansies."

She sniffed again. "I guess I'd say dahlias, but they won't be in season. Primroses, maybe?"

I hummed, only half listening. Trudi would look beautiful if she turned up with potatoes in her hair.

Talking seemed to calm her. She murmured to me the dresses we would wear, the paints she would adorn me with, the way she would fashion my hair and cry with me as we entered the church.

Hang on, I thought. *Am I the one getting married?*

I dozed for what felt like an hour but must have only been minutes. Hugo returned and sat with us, a steaming mug in his hand.

"Drink this," he said, and I thought he was talking to Trudi until they both started manoeuvring me upright.

"Do I have to?"

"Yes," came the short reply.

The porcelain was deliciously warm against my mouth, and I took a sip. Promptly, I spat it back out. "Ginger?"

"And lemon. Just drink it."

"Liquorice would have been better," I said mutinously but drank it all the same. "Thank you." I went to lie down again.

"No, don't do that." Hugo slid an arm around my back, then one under my legs. "Trudi's going to give you a bath, and then you're going to bed."

"So bossy," I said. I could hear Trudi following behind us, up the stairs.

"Doctor's orders," he muttered.

Hugo filled the bath with tepid water. Trudi scrubbed my hands before undressing me and helping me into the tub. I caught her frowning down at my body through red-rimmed eyes. I followed her gaze.

I'd lost weight. Now that I looked properly, I didn't know how I'd missed it. The Dawn Lord may as well have thrown some bones in a bag and called it a person.

The idea that I was getting better had well and truly been crushed.

It was only once I was thoroughly towelled off, dressed in a clean nightgown, then deposited in bed that I was left alone. I thought I'd fall asleep the second my head hit the pillow, but my thoughts were relentless.

Do I really want to wear pansies to the wedding? Good thing I wasn't at Ansel's when this happened. I wonder how Hugo proposed? Propose, propose—any proposal would be better than the one Ansel gave me. No, I don't want to bring you blood, kind sir, good day. Is this it? Is this going to get worse? Of course it is; it's been happening for years. You're going to die. Get over it. But how do I get over it? Can I get over it by not dying? Because I choose that option.

My loudest thought as I fell asleep, the one I couldn't entirely ignore, was that Lena really was a very good name, and maybe my friends would name a daughter after me when I was gone.

I avoided looking at Father Snow's gravestone as I made my way through the cemetery. The grass beneath my feet was damp from the night shower, and my shoes sunk into the earth as though the soil was eager to pull me under and lay me with the other corpses. An early morning mist had settled over the village, so thick I could barely make out the bordering forest thirty feet away. I pulled my shawl a little tighter.

It was early enough that I was the only one in the churchyard. When I'd awoken hours before I usually would, I knew it was the only chance I'd have to escape Hugo that whole day. I was feeling marginally better after rest and had no desire to discuss the previous night's disaster.

There was a single grave in the corner of the yard, a weathered wooden cross that was surrounded by weeds and animal droppings. I meandered to its base, then sighed at the sight. I'd been a terribly negligent daughter.

"Hi, Mama," I said, finding a relatively clean patch of wet grass and making myself comfortable. Months had passed since my last visit. "It's been a while, so I'll need to get you up to date." I looked around, making sure I was alone. "Father Snow is dead, but if the afterlife really exists, you already know that. I found his mutilated body in the forest on festival night—that was rough—and am now good, uh, friends with his murderer, the jolly vampire, Ansel." I paused, making sure I hadn't missed anything crucial. "Oh, and I think I'm dying."

I let that sentence sink in. I'd never said it aloud before.

It felt ... like a bad joke.

"I'm dying. I'm going to die."

More than anything, I would have liked to pass the words off as dramatic, but I was fully aware of the reality. The symptoms I was displaying, had been displaying for a while now, were the same as Mother's before she passed away. Chest pain, loss of appetite, fatigue. Most recently, the expelling of blood.

"I guess that means I'll be joining you sooner than either of us thought. I almost had enough money to make it to the Holy City, but like I said—vampire. Frankly, I don't even know if I'd make the boat trip there. Certainly not in winter. Not with ..." I trailed off as it dawned on me properly.

I was going to die.

It wouldn't be the sudden, blinding terror I'd felt with Ansel that first time in the forest but would instead be a drawn-out, agonising process.

Even if I could afford a ticket to the Holy City, I still didn't have the funds to receive the necessary standard of healing. Ansel might have agreed to come, would have the money to pay, but a route without sunlight—being unable to travel throughout the day—would take twice as long and be twice as difficult to navigate. It wouldn't work. I wasn't going to make it.

I felt like throwing up again.

"Hey, Mama," I said and licked my lips. I clenched my fists, then unclenched them. Clench, unclench. "Mama, not to sound presumptuous, but I think Ansel considers himself in love with me." And while I liked him too in a guilty, thrill-seeking kind of way, that wasn't the point.

A vampire. A *vampire*.

"Do you think if I asked him ..." I couldn't even say the words. "That would be wrong, wouldn't it?" I shook my head, unsurprised that I'd managed to skip anger and go straight from denial to bargaining. Getting to my feet, I wiped my damp skirts. "I need to go, Mama. I'll come and see you again, sooner next time, I promise. It's just ..." I stared at the grave.

I wasn't talking to Mother. She wasn't there.

I was talking to a piece of wood. A piece of wood didn't care whether I was alive, dead, or any state in between.

"Miss Lena?"

I looked up to the sky. I wasn't happy with the Dawn Lord at present. Would it make me a terrible person if I were to take it out on his priest?

"Miss Lena," Father Pentaghast called again, closer this time.

Sighing, I turned to face him. "Good morning, Father," I said as he came to a stop in front of me. "Out for a morning stroll?"

He wore a billowing shirt and dark trousers, looking more like a pirate than a priest. His cheek dimpled. "Yes, nothing rejuvenates me more than a walk through the cemetery. Is that what you're doing here? Walking?"

I was tempted to leave, rude as it was. "Not quite," I said. "Father Pentaghast, meet my mother." I gestured to the grave. Father Pentaghast's expression fell, and I tried not to look vindicated.

"I apologise," he said, running a hand down his face, seeming to realise that, no, I did not traipse through a graveyard at obscenely early hours for fun. "I did not mean to intrude."

I crossed my arms and shrugged.

"I did wonder who Mathilda was," he murmured, gaze lingering over her name scratched in the wood.

I tensed. Nobody had said her name in a very long time.

"To be banished to her own little corner, you mean?" There was venom in my voice, and I enjoyed the way it felt on my tongue.

His gaze met mine. "Among other reasons, yes."

I looked back at the overgrown plot. When I was younger, I hadn't comprehended the insult insinuated by burying her so far from the other graves. My parents and I had been in the village for mere weeks before she died, a necessary stop taken for her health, and then her very last stop. We'd lodged at the inn until Mother's health grew so bad that Markus let us stay at the clinic.

No one mourned with us when she died, though the villagers knew of her by then. There was no ceremony or burial fast. Father didn't let me come when they lowered her into the ground. I didn't know why until Markus told me, years later, that there'd been no coffin to bury her in and no others to shovel the dirt on her cold, willowy body.

Father Pentaghast stepped back. "I'll leave you both, then."

"Wait."

He stopped.

I looked to the sky again, at the imminent sunrise. The crisp air nipped at my skin. "Do you think the Dawn Lord's really there? Or that he even cares?" Posing such questions to a priest was asking for a sermon, but I liked Father Pentaghast. He'd been honest with me before. I trusted him to be honest again.

"Oh, I know he does," he said, but it didn't sound like a compliment. "A little too much, sometimes."

I quirked a brow in question.

"Which would you find worse," he asked, "an absent father or one who smothers you to the point of desperation? If it were for your own good, which would you choose?"

"Neither."

"Yes, me as well. But what I'm trying to say is—" Father Pentaghast stiffened abruptly, teeth clicking shut. Frustration flashed across his face. "What I'm trying to say is if there's anything that brings you joy in this life, I suggest you take it."

It took me a while to answer. "But what if it's wrong?"

He smiled a small, secret smile. "Forgive me for presuming, but I don't take you for a great sinner, Miss Lena."

The words reminded me of the conversation I'd had with Ansel, about vile sinners and their virtues. That conversation felt like years ago.

I asked, "Is that because we're all just regular sinners?"

He chuckled. "Go and find yourself a little bit of happiness. You've been looking awfully tired of late. You deserve some peace."

"Tell that to your boss."

"Oh, he knows. It's why he sends souls like me to do the dirty work." There was a subtle sort of detachment in his eyes that seemed at odds with his kind demeanour. I found it disconcerting.

"Are you sure you're a priest?" I asked. "You lack a certain reverence."

"I'm sure," was all he said.

The seconds passed, and it was made obvious we were finished. I began to leave but turned on my heel as I reached the edge of the graveyard.

"Do you know anything about ..." *Vampires.* My throat closed up. I probably should have come to him at the very beginning, should have told him about Ansel, but I'd been foolish and proud and so very, very scared. Now, though, there was a completely different fear to consider, one that tugged at my heart and made evident why I had been so annoyed with Ansel.

"About?" Father Pentaghast prompted.

I smiled wanly and shook my head.

It was too late.

CHAPTER FOURTEEN

I threw all caution to the wind and returned to the castle that evening.

Leaving was irresponsible of me, and Hugo would be livid when he saw I wasn't in bed, but I couldn't lie there any longer, miserable, practically waiting to die. Facing Ansel, even with my embarrassment, was preferable.

The drapes were drawn in the cabinet, and I pulled a candle from a sconce in the hallway, looking for something mind-numbing to pass the time. I settled on writing a letter to Markus, one that would be full of half-baked truths about daily life. One that he'd probably fall asleep halfway through.

I was rifling through the desk, trying to find some ink, when I came across the sketches.

Gentle, smoky lines, the contrast of charcoal on parchment. Some areas were smudged, the dark particles rippled from being shoved into the drawer. It was because of this smudging I didn't immediately recognise the subject matter.

They were sketches of me.

I laughed in one, cried in another. Smiling, sleeping, eating. Every action was fluid, nuanced, and I could almost believe it possible that each girl was about to jump from the page and take on a life of her own. The wave of my hair, the curved cut of my fingernails—the details were so exact I could have been staring into a mirror.

I wasn't sure what alerted me to his presence. Perhaps the rustle of clothing or the awareness that prickled whenever he was near. Maybe my desire to not get caught had summoned him. All I knew was that when I glanced over my shoulder, he was there, leaning against the doorframe.

"Well, well," he said. "What have we here?" He wore a neutral mask, painted with shallow amusement.

I straightened my back, wishing away the sudden heat that eclipsed me. "I was looking for some paper."

"And find some you did. This *is* embarrassing."

"Yes," I said slowly, painfully aware of the divide between us now. I shouldn't have run away as I did. "You ... These drawings—"

"Not the drawings. They're genius. Best I've ever done. No, I mean how embarrassing for you."

I hesitated, grip tightening on the parchment. "Me?"

"You." He clicked his tongue. "I mean, to be caught snooping in someone else's things, how shameful. Really, I am so uncomfortable."

I almost scoffed but thought better of it.

Ansel sauntered into the room. “Spare us both the feelings of discomfort and, ah—” He waved a hand towards the door. *Leave.*

I wasn’t sure if I was more shocked or hurt. It wasn’t that I thought he would be happy to see me, but ... Well, I had thought that. With the way he’d been acting recently, I’d presumed my appearance would be met with delight.

He’d never treated me with this aloofness, not even at the beginning.

“Right,” I said, feeling oddly desolate.

I was almost out of the room when he asked abruptly, “Do you like them?”

I got the impression he wasn’t so much asking if I liked the drawings, but rather if I liked him drawing *me*.

He was asking for permission.

Was I willing to give it to him? It would be more than forgiving a few unsolicited portraits; it would be encouraging him in everything.

The villagers popped into my mind, and I banished them. This wasn’t about them, not anymore. This was about me.

What did I want?

Truthfully, I already knew the answer. It was why I’d returned here, even when I could have avoided Hugo easily enough elsewhere.

If I was going to die regardless, then I was going to live first. I was going to enjoy myself.

“They’re impressive, I suppose,” I said, bunching up my inhibitions and throwing them away, “but show me when you've done the rest of me. Then we'll talk."

Ansel's eyes widened, a surprised little "*oh*" escaping him. Then he laughed, a dangerous smile curving his mouth. He closed the distance between us, saying, "I know how much you'd love to hear me say I need to do a thorough examination of you to do such a work justice."

I didn't let on at the sudden anticipation pounding through me. I didn't let him know something between us had changed. "Would I?"

"Oh, yes." He twisted a piece of my hair around his fingers. The yellow was a burst of colour against his nails. "But—and you know I hate to do this—I'm going to have to disappoint."

I tipped my chin up, curious. "What do you mean?"

Amusement pulled at his mouth as he bent and whispered, "Full body portraits are in the bottom drawer."

"*What*?" My composure shattered, and I pushed past him to dig through the desk, pulling out sheet after sheet of blank parchment. At the bottom of the pile, tucked into the very back, was the drawing.

I gaped.

It was from the night I'd fallen asleep in the library after fishing and Ansel had draped his cape over me. The figure on the page was unmistakably mine, but I barely recognised this girl, peaceful as she was.

A shadow lurked in the background, where Ansel had sat, waiting for me to wake. I wondered if that was really how he viewed himself. Something that swallowed the light.

Ansel approached the desk, and a sense of awkwardness swelled within my chest, strong enough that it could only come from a place of romantic origin.

Say something. Don't let him see you flustered.

I blurted out the first thing that came to mind. "I guess creativity is another one on the list." It was something I'd already written off as false; the embroidery had told me as much. But maybe if I distracted him enough, he'd forget about the piece of parchment in my hand.

He looked at me quizzically. "What list?"

"The rumours list. Because creativity. No soul." I mimed drawing a picture. "No soul, bad creativity, so rumours."

He seemed to understand my gibberish, because he groaned. "Slander. The vampire who said that was a vicious hag who was terrible at the arts and wished for the rest of us to be, too."

"Oh." I took a deep breath, then went and put the parchment back in the drawer. The others were still scattered on the desk, and I couldn't help but look over them again. I steeled my nerves and asked, "What do you want from me, Ansel?"

I needed to be sure, because I refused to be only a footnote in the annals of his long life.

I would be everything to him or I would be nothing.

My words hung in the air. Ansel was watching, waiting, as he always was.

"Why are you here?" I continued when he said nothing. "Are you plotting something? Waiting for someone? Why are you still *here*?" I slammed my hands onto the desk, and the girl on those pages, the one who was meant to be me, slid loose and floated to the floor.

His answer was blunt. "Because you are here."

More, I thought. I needed to know more.

"Why?"

He knelt to collect the sketches, smoothing his fingers across my likeness.

Softly, he said, "I was to be gone within a month of waking. Enough time to recuperate and grant me a little fun with the villagers. Except it was the middle of summer, and the sun rose too early and slept too late for me to be truly safe when travelling. So, I decided to wait. Imagine my surprise, then, when summer turned to autumn and the darkening skies bid me leave, yet I was still here. With you.

"And the rest is history. There are no ill intentions lurking beneath the surface, nor terrible schemes I've been trying to oversee. There is no further reason I stayed other than I found you a fun plaything to while away a blink of eternity with. But I was foolish and fell too deep into a trap of my own making. And so now I am here. And whether you meant to or not, you have drawn me into your web."

Still not enough.

"I didn't mean for any of this to happen," I said.

His mouth twisted, something between a scowl and a smirk. "Didn't you? Because you play your role so well."

"We are not characters in a play," I snapped. "Don't belittle me by treating me as the witless heroine."

"Then how do you explain it?" He threw the parchment atop the desk. "You are a young woman from an insignificant village filled with insignificant people. Forgive me, but there must be some kind of black magic in you to be able to grasp even my attention."

Almost there.

"You are not a god, Ansel," I said. "You're not above anyone, no matter how highly you may think of yourself."

He drew himself up, rising to the challenge of my words. The air seemed to shimmer, trembling in his wake. Whatever the primal urge, he leashed it before it could escape. "And you?" he said. "Unless I've mixed up the nights, you're here early."

He counted the nights I was away. It bolstered my resolve.

"I needed to see you."

"You did? I wouldn't have thought so by the way you *ran away from me*."

That. *That* was what I'd been waiting for.

It wasn't only his pride I'd hurt, but his feelings. I'd pulled them from him unknowingly, cracked them open, butchered them and shoved them back inside for him to deal with however he knew how. My rejection had gutted him in ways I didn't think were possible.

Perhaps I'd started as a distraction, but I wasn't one anymore. I had power over this man. I was the one in charge. That, more than anything, made up my mind.

"I'm sorry," I said, but it felt inadequate. "I brought you something. More blood and ..." I searched my pockets, then held out the gift.

Ansel took it stiffly and sat on the rocking chair, which squeaked at his unusual lack of grace. He unwrapped it, careful not to tear the paper, before holding it up for inspection. "It's a candle."

"The villagers are burning them tomorrow at midnight." Praying for a good harvest at the festival. "I don't know how long it's been since you've celebrated something, but I thought that with this you could join in." Which, in hindsight, was ridiculous. What use did he have for a good harvest?

My embarrassment diminished as Ansel's expression caved in. He placed the small candle back in its wrapping and stood. Offered his hand. It no longer reminded me of the marks around my neck. I could no longer feel them.

"Come with me. Please." The words were ragged.

"Where?" I asked.

"*Anywhere.*"

I took his hand.

Ansel led me through the castle like a man possessed, an untamed energy pouring off him in waves. He abandoned me momentarily in the kitchen to retrieve his cape. I would have rolled my eyes at him for taking the time, but he wrapped it around me at his return, breathing me in.

We had only just entered the forest path when he grasped my shoulders, locking me in place against a tree.

It didn't escape me that the last time we were in this position he was trying to kill me.

"Ansel?" I said, and his breath hitched.

Slowly, he lifted his fingers from my shoulders to circle them around my waist. The pressure burnt through my shirt until the skin was sensitive and itchy. Ansel only made it worse by looming over me, my sky his silhouette, my horizon the width of his shoulders.

"What are you doing?" I asked.

His pupils were dilated, his lips parted. "Have I ever told you how exquisite you are?"

I shook my head. "You could start now."

He laughed, but it sounded pained. "Did you know you hum when you work? Or that you make faces when deep in thought? And sometimes when you think I can't see, you stare at me as though you understand. Like you want to tear my head free from my neck and discover how the blood drips before you sew it back on. You are agonising and pulsing and *iridescent*."

He said it with the kind of fervour I associated with religious zealots. And though none of his words sounded like a compliment to me, I had to blink a couple of times to clear the haze from my mind.

He panted. "Will you do something for me?"

"What?"

"Will you run?"

I frowned, a hundred questions on the tip of my tongue.

"Run," he said, fangs glinting in the moonlight, "so that I can catch you."

I pressed myself harder against the trunk. "No."

"Please," he said. "Please, please, please."

"I—okay." I drew the last syllable out, wondering what in the world I was agreeing to. "This isn't some ritualistic hunt where you're going to try and eat me, is it?"

"No," he said, sounding wholly insincere.

I squinted at him.

"Only if you want me to," he amended, which wasn't much better.

I mulled it over. "I'll do it. But you go that way"—I pointed towards the river—"and give me a head start."

His enthusiasm visibly ratcheted at my willingness to play along. "Fine, yes, good."

I knew this wasn't smart. There was danger in allowing Ansel free rein over me in the forest.

But that was what sickness was doing to me. Stifling me, strangling me, pushing me down deeper and deeper into suppression that the times it let go of its hold, even just marginally, I couldn't help but want to rise up and lash out. Be stupid. Have fun. Be free.

Live.

And so, it wasn't fear I felt when Ansel looked at me like he wanted to give in to those vampiric impulses he couldn't always control. No, what coursed through me was excitement, because regardless of whatever happened tonight, it was sure to make me feel alive.

Ansel sucked in a breath, boyish joy clashing with the feral glint in his eye. He reached out as if to touch my face.

I shut my eyes.

"Run," he whispered.

The wind tore through the trees, and before my eyelids fluttered open, I knew he would be gone.

Not quite daring enough to tempt fate by running, I enjoyed a leisurely stroll through the forest path, heading towards the castle gates where I stopped to survey my options.

I could just wait.

It would be easy and uninspiring but safe. Well, as safe as it could get at night with a vampire in pursuit. Quickly deciding against that, I refastened my hair tie, purposely throwing a couple of strands over the iron bars.

The moaning of the trees urged me to quicken my escape. My head start wouldn't last long, and I had no desire to deliver myself to Ansel on a silver platter.

I picked the tree that looked easiest to climb with its low-set, sprawling branches, and started the trek upwards. My arms burned, and I loved it. My body was fading, failing prematurely, but I could still do this: move and run and play and exist. It was a testament to how weak I was growing that by the time I was settled twenty feet in the air, hugging the tree trunk and feet dangling off the side, I was well and truly spent.

I straddled the branch, pulling Ansel's cape higher up my shoulders and diving into my pocket for the knotted kerchief within.

I *knew* it would come in handy eventually.

I leaned back against the tree trunk and admired how the moonlight lit the castle, casting away the perpetual gloom. It looked like a place of folklore and magic. No wonder Ansel wanted to clean it up. It would have been magnificent in its day.

Have I ever told you how exquisite you are? Now that I was alone, I didn't even try to hide my grin. He was a sweet talker.

I had just opened the kerchief, letting its contents spill out onto the wood, when boots crunched on the forest floor beneath me. I stiffened.

Ansel made that noise on purpose, the tease.

"I know you're here," he said. "The question is *where*?"

I was breathing too loudly. Blinking too loudly. Any minuscule action was too much.

"Quite cute, your little diversion tactic," he said, and a laugh followed. "But I know you don't really think I'd ever be so gullible."

I couldn't see him beneath me. The shadows were too dark, and he was dressed in a way to match. Sparks of anticipation jolted through my limbs and set my nerves alight.

"But, no, I know you wouldn't do that, now would you, Lena?" He hummed an unfamiliar tune. "*Lena*?"

I covered my mouth and counted to ten in my head. I made it to eight before his footsteps stopped.

The trees ceased their moaning.

The moon hid herself.

And then—

"There you are."

The tree undulated at the sudden shift in weight as Ansel appeared opposite me, at the tapering edge of the branch.

I swore, scrabbling back against the trunk.

Ansel's gaze scoured me, predatory and heated, before landing at my feet. His eyes widened, the whites of them bright.

"Good job," I said, doing my best to keep the words steady. "Better luck next time, though."

He glared at the pile of rice—the same rice I'd balled up in my kerchief weeks ago and stashed in the servants' quarters. I had made sure to nab it while Ansel went for his cape.

I stepped off the branch, onto the one below. Ansel's gaze darted between the rice and me, over and over again.

"You little she-devil," he rasped, and I blew him a kiss.

"The sooner you give in, the sooner you'll catch me."

He snarled, dropped to his knees, and began to count.

I climbed down, scraping my palms against the wood, and broke into the fastest jog I could manage as soon as I hit the ground.

In reality, it was too fast. Too foolish. My body started to ache, and my breathing turned wet, but I ran faster still, wanting to scream at the injustice of it all. More than that, I wanted to prove I could still do it.

It didn't matter that there'd be consequences later. Not in that moment.

When Ansel came, he came from nowhere. I didn't even know he'd caught up until I was flying through the air, fall cushioned by his body.

"Caught you," he purred once we'd rolled to a stop.

I was gasping, slightly wary, yet ready for whatever he'd say or do next. He lifted himself on his elbows to stare down at me. His fangs had grown long enough that he wouldn't be able to shut his mouth without penetrating his gums.

I stared back at him in sick fascination, because for the most perverse of moments, I had the urge to bring those fangs to my neck.

He slid down my body, left hand trailing over my waist and stomach until it reached just below my belly button. Heat pooled directly beneath his touch.

Seated between my legs, Ansel watched me with hooded eyes. "I do love it when you look at me this way." His fingers tapped against my belly impatiently. His tongue darted across his lips. He wanted to finish his hunt.

I went to ask exactly how I looked at him, but he took hold of my ankle, bringing it to his mouth and grazing the inside with his teeth.

I choked on the words.

"I have missed you," Ansel whispered against my skin. He pushed the hem of my breeches to my knee. "Do not go away like that again, will you?"

I dug my fingers into the soil at my back, trying to breathe evenly. I was about to disappoint him—I would come and go as I pleased—when he sunk his teeth into the back of my leg.

I couldn't stop the sound that escaped me.

"If you do, I might go mad," he continued. My blood pooled in his mouth, staining his smile crimson. I felt it trickle down my leg as I gaped, speechless.

I'd just been bitten by a vampire. By Ansel.

It hadn't even hurt. A brief piercing sensation and then nothing. How was that possible? Was there a natural numbing agent in his saliva, a kind of pain relief? It was possible, I supposed, but then—

I gasped as Ansel sunk his teeth down, harder this time, and higher up my leg.

He glared at me as he pulled his teeth out, drawing his tongue over the puncture. "Lena," he sang, "what lengths must I go to in order to keep your attention?"

"Sorry," I said automatically. My voice was husky. "You said you'd only eat me if I wanted you to."

He ran a finger from the bottom of my calf to the back of my knee. It set goosebumps crawling along my body. "You haven't seemed to be objecting."

"You haven't exactly asked." I tugged my foot half-heartedly, but he refused to let go.

"I wasn't entirely sure I needed to. I can tell when you're enjoying yourself."

My gaze caught on his lips, and a surge of possessiveness rose from somewhere I didn't know existed.

That's my blood on his lips. He'll never lose the taste of me.

I shrugged, and the forest floor dug into my back. It was a pleasant sensation. "And I can tell when you're grasping at straws. But I like it. Desperation suits you."

His hand scraped higher up my skin until it rested, splayed out, on the middle of my thigh. "There is no need to pretend with me, Lena. Do not think I haven't seen it."

"Seen what?"

Ansel lowered his eyelashes before freeing my ankle and crawling back up my body, legs tangling with mine. A dull ache had set into the places he'd bitten. I curled my toes, trying to lessen it.

He snaked his hand up my stomach, over my breasts, to fiddle with the button at my collar. "Your very nature is a lie, Lena Montgomery. All pouting and pure and doe-eyed." He unclasped the button with a snap. "But I know what lurks beneath this pretty mask you've made for yourself." *Snap.* "I saw it the first night we met." *Snap.* "I saw it the night you tried to kill me." *Snap.* "And I see it right now."

I caught his hand on the last button. "And what is it you think I'm hiding?"

He tapped my sternum with a finger to punctuate his words. "Utter. Ruthless. Desperation."

I held his hand at my chest, not letting it wander any further. "Maybe. Or maybe that's just what you want see."

"Why would I want to see that?"

"Because then we'd be the same. Kindred spirits. You've been watching me for days. You're so desperate, it's almost embarrassing."

A pause. "You see too much, and I dislike it."

I laughed. "I think that makes us equal."

He tapped me on the nose. "Every word of yours cuts me to the bone, and yet I am a dog begging for scraps. Any sign of affection, of approval, of desire, I would lose my soul all over again for them. So, no. I would not call any piece of this relationship equal." The way he said it was indulgent, but also like he was exasperated with himself. I knew they weren't empty words.

Ridiculous, dramatic, endearing man. He made me want to dive into this—whatever this was—headfirst, with a weight around my neck. Made me want to sink so deep no one would ever be able to fish me out.

This was it, then. This was the deciding point.

There was no returning after this, no going back. I would make my bed and lie in it, whatever the outcome. I wasn't sure what showed on my face, but Ansel, as if sensing my thoughts, wrapped my arm in his firm grip. And I realised I was wrong.

The moment had already passed.

He wouldn't let me go, not now. He would hunt me down as he had tonight, find me wherever I tried to hide.

It didn't scare me like it should have. In the end, he wouldn't be able to follow to where I would go. And perhaps that was the saddest thing of all. Everything was doomed from the start, whether I was healthy, whether he was a decent person or not.

"Lena?" he asked, a hint of darkness bleeding through. "It is time to return home now, I think."

He's not quite his usual self, I thought as his lips curled up cruelly.

"Lena, my lovely, why do you look so confused?"

"I look confused?"

He chuckled. "Oh, yes. You're like a cornered rabbit. It makes me want to dig my teeth in even deeper."

He had no idea, did he? I wasn't about to run off in fright, and his words couldn't scare me at this point. I had too little left to lose.

I couldn't imagine many people earning his devotion. I wanted to reward him for giving it to me so freely. Trailing my fingertips down the soft skin of his throat, I mused, "You always act like I'm the one being hunted."

Before he could form a reply, I kissed him. Plunged my hands wrist-deep into his hair and wrapped my legs around his waist. He made a noise of surprise, a soft whimper in the back of his throat that I echoed as I tasted my own blood on his tongue, salty and copper-like. Then he was everywhere, pushing me into the ground with the length of his body and forcing my lips open with his like he wanted to gorge himself on me.

I could taste him beneath the blood, saccharine to the point of decay, and I searched for the disgust but couldn't find it within me. It was him as I'd always known him to be, and I wouldn't want it any other way.

He shuddered when I raked my nails down his neck and gathered me in his arms. I tried to break away for air, but his mouth followed mine, even as he started walking us towards the castle.

Ansel wasn't the first man I'd ever kissed, but I knew he'd be the last.

CHAPTER FIFTEEN

The pre-dawn light filtered into the bedchamber, turning the stone walls a muted grey. I could hear Ansel, awake next to me, flipping through the pages of a book. I wanted to see him, desperately so, to make sure I was still sane and he was real, but a sudden pain in my limbs thwarted any attempt at rolling over.

I groaned into the pillow. "I'm an idiot."

Ansel had carried me to the castle, through the corridors, and up the stairs to my bed. I hadn't been ready to go any further with him physically, and he'd accepted that. Lying beside me, running his fingers through my hair as I drifted to sleep, seemed to content him just fine.

"You can pretend we did nothing but stargaze if you like," Ansel said. "But you'll have to face it eventually because I've never been very good at pretending."

"Like hell you aren't," I muttered, squeezing my eyes shut. "And I wasn't talking about your ill-advised hunt. I shouldn't have climbed that tree. I'm dying."

Literally and figuratively. Ha.

"I've heard vampirism is a good cure for that. Indeed, for any ailment."

I turned and cracked an eye open. "Except sun allergies."

He was shirtless, his dark hair spilling over the pillow. His skin was smooth. Pretty and flawless. The type of skin certain women in the village would have paid a fortune for in ointments and lotions. I laid my hand on his chest, right over his heart. His heartbeat stuttered beneath my fingers then calmed to its normal pace.

I frowned. Its normal pace was a lot slower than mine.

I met the abyss of his gaze and blurted, "If I cut you open, would your insides look the same as mine?"

"It's that look again," Ansel murmured. "I don't know why I find those words so provocative, but I do. I'm pathetic, and it doesn't even faze me." He placed the book down, took my hand, and rubbed his thumb across my scar. "But to answer your question, we would look the same. The consistency of our blood may be a little different, but the heart, lungs, and other internal organs are all in order."

And right on time, here came the guilt.

I needed to tell him. It was unfair of me to keep putting it off.

Ansel, our organs wouldn't look the same because mine are rapidly deteriorating.

No. That would be a terrible way to say it.

Ansel reached to the nightstand, giving me a moment of respite from his attention. I scrubbed at my eyes, pulled my undershirt's straps higher up my shoulders.

"I added some sugar this time," he said, passing me a teacup. "Careful, it's still hot."

Warmth welled up within me. More tea? That coupled with the sweet smiles ... Had I managed to domesticate a vampire? I should write a manual. It could simultaneously expand the marriage market and prolong the lives of mortals everywhere.

"What do you fancy doing today?" Ansel asked. "Another trip to the river when it grows dark? We could take the paints I recently acquired, and you could laugh at my dreadful rendition of a landscape."

"Only for you to hide the bag again, and we end up painting with mud? I don't think so."

He smiled crookedly, making a hand gesture as if to say *fair enough.*

I placed the teacup on the bedframe and winced, knowing he wouldn't like what I had to say next. "Actually, I have to go."

He turned rigid. "You do?"

"Tonight's the Harvest Festival. Trudi and Hugo—my friends—will be suspicious if I don't go. I'm sorry." It occurred to me that I was lying in bed with the man, yet this was the first time I'd mentioned my friends to him. For good reason, if his expression was anything to go by. I rolled my eyes. "I'm not running away. The Harvest Festival is my favourite, so it's just bad timing."

"Yes," he muttered. "I understand."

I pressed my lips together to keep from smiling.

He saw and heaved a sigh, the belligerent set of his shoulders slackening. "Yes, yes." He picked at a loose thread on the bed sheet. "I trust you. Go and have a merry little time."

"I will, thank you." I leaned over to kiss his cheek. "And I trust you, too. Kind of."

A furrow appeared between his eyebrows. He went to speak, hesitating at the last second.

"What is it?" I asked

"Nothing," he said finally. "Nothing at all. Here." He pushed the teacup back into my hands. "Drink your tea. We have the afternoon, at least."

I bit my lip.

His eyes went wide. "Not even that?"

"Sorry," I whispered, sipping my drink to avoid the accusatory look he was throwing my way. I sputtered at the bitterness. "Are you sure you added sugar? What tea leaves were they?" The tea he'd made had never been fantastic, but it'd never tasted quite this bad.

He eyed the drink like it had betrayed him. "I may have been a tad too enthusiastic."

I appreciated the gesture, so I finished it before throwing the blankets off and going to stand.

Ansel did not approve. He tugged me back by my undershirt until I was splayed out on the bed, knees bent and toes scraping against the stone floor. The hand that pulled me came to fiddle with my earlobe.

"Not quite so fast, my dear. Tell me, have you ever considered wearing earrings?"

I craned my neck back, wincing as an ache spread through my body and travelled down my legs. The punctures from where he'd bitten me had scabbed over, but I had yet to wash off the dried blood.

"No," I said, curling my fingers around his forearm.

"Rings?"

"They get in the way too much."

Ansel pushed my hair back from my forehead, chuckling when his own took its place as he leaned closer. I blew it out of my eyes.

He said, "Then I shall have to improvise. Your pretty holy symbol—'tis a necklace, yes? Would you be averse to adding a little something on there for me?"

I smiled. "You're giving me a gift?"

"Or trying to desecrate something holy," he said coyly, and I snorted.

"I don't think it'd be that easy."

"I'm not too sure. After all, you have a stain on your soul now." His lips replaced his fingers, caressed the shell of my ear. "And it brings me such joy to know it is in my image."

I stared at the ceiling, considering. I didn't like it, but he wasn't wrong.

"Okay," I said.

His teeth skimmed down my neck. "I'll find you the perfect bauble for it," he whispered into my skin.

I wanted to stay.

I wanted to spend the day with him, reading books or asking him questions or doing nothing at all, until tonight when we could go to the river. Even if it was with mud, I wanted to paint with him. Wanted to be with him.

But if I did what I wanted, this illusion of a life together would turn to dust.

"I have to go, Ansel," I whispered back. "But I wish I could stay."

"So, stay."

I caught the hair at his nape and drew his forehead down to meet mine. "But then the village savages would come at you with their ineffectual pitchforks. And I don't want to clean bloodstains out of the drapes in the vestibule."

"What?" Ansel pulled back, searching my face. Understanding lit his features. "Are those my words?"

"You don't remember?"

"I say many things, but I do not always hear myself when I speak."

I could have told him that.

Ansel planted a hand on my shoulder when I went to sit up. "One last thing." He paused, tongue prodding the corner of his mouth. "We should get married."

I covered my face, torn between laughter and tears. What a stalling tactic. "You do realize the whole point of marriage is holy matrimony, and you're basically devil's spawn?"

"Silly girl. I am not, as you like to call it, 'devil's spawn'. I made a deal with Death, who I must say, is rather personable once you get past his terrible impulse control."

I balked. He'd done what?

"You've met Death? As in, 'rings his bell, reaps your soul, and takes you to the afterlife' Death?"

"Hm?" He raised his eyebrows. "Have I not told you that story? It's a long one, I'm afraid, and its telling will take at least an hour. Maybe more, if you can bear to stay."

"Ansel."

"Yes, Lena?"

I shook my head in disbelief. "What do you mean you made a deal with him? Is that all you do in life, go along making advantageous deals with people?"

"Well, I had to die to become undead, didn't I?"

I pursed my lips. "I don't know, did you?" He had been painfully sparse with the details about vampirism. For all I knew, he'd done a kooky dance around a campfire and bam —vampire.

Ansel turned pensive, like I'd thrown a bucket of water on the flame of his mirth. "Yes. Yes, you have to die." His hand came to rest against my pulse. "Don't worry, though," he said. "That's not the part that hurts."

Later that day at the village, as I dressed for the festival in bright, hard colours and took a silver coin from my stagnant savings, I would think back to our time together. And I would realize that out of all the confessions he'd ever made, all the secrets he'd ever spoken, it was that last one I'd never forget.

CHAPTER SIXTEEN

"And so *I* said that if he wanted to walk me down the aisle, he'd have to give up drinking, to which *he* then said I'd be lucky to have my father present even if he turned up drunk, to which *I* then replied there was no way he was stepping foot in the Dawn Lord's church in that state, and that's when he—Lena, are you listening? What are you looking at?"

I snapped my attention back to Trudi, meeting her gaze through the white feathered mask she was wearing. "Sorry," I said. "I'm listening, I promise."

Trudi snorted, placing her plate of food on the table we were sitting at. "Barely. You're obviously feeling better since you're able to ignore me so well."

"Sorry," I said again. "What do you think that line is for?" I pointed to the crowd—young women mostly, though a few men were scattered throughout as well—loitering by a stall in the market strip. Their costumes bled together, mixing one animal mask with another, feathers to fur to scales. Candles hung from each stall frame and bathed the mass in a dim gold. Morphed the usual village rabble into a grotesque parade of limbs.

A quartet of parrots played a jig in the main square, and the table over from us entertained two jackals drinking ale and laughing loudly at nothing. The Harvest Festival was always the most fun, if only because you could pretend to be something you weren't.

"I can't remember—there are too many new stalls this year." Trudi took another bite of apple pie. "Dresses, maybe? Dyes?"

"No, look. Angela just left with ... is she holding a pastry? Really, that's what they're crowding around for?"

"Hang on, the line's starting to thin. Think the owner ran out already?"

I frowned, watching as two more girls walked away, arms laden with cakes and tarts. They looked behind them every few steps, giggling. I craned my neck, wondering what was worthy of such attention.

I froze at the sight of the man behind the stall.

"I have to go," I choked out.

"What? Why?"

It was difficult to pinpoint exactly what I felt at that moment. Alarm, for certain. Flustered, most definitely.

And yet, not even a little surprised.

"See that man over there?" I asked.

Her gaze followed my finger. She gasped. "Who is *he*?"

"He, at this moment, is many different things, most of all dead." Or he would be when I was done with him.

Trudi, managing to rip her glassy eyes away, turned to me. "Huh?"

"He's the vampire, Trudi."

The words didn't seem to register as she stared at me in that guileless way of hers, but then she blanched. I reached to steady her as she swayed.

"Oh," she said quietly. "Did you invite him?"

"No."

She swallowed. "So, he's here to enjoy the festival?"

"That better be why he's here," I muttered. "Tell Hugo I went to dance or something. And maybe don't walk this way."

"Wait!" She grabbed my arm. "You're not going to confront him, are you?"

"It'll be fine. I think." I hadn't told Trudi about the development in my and Ansel's relationship. Lover of romance though she was, I didn't think she'd approve.

Her disappointment would be one thing I couldn't come back from.

"Be careful," she said, letting me go. I nodded, pulled up my sleeves, and made my way over.

Unlike the rest of us, Ansel's face was bare, though no one would ever suspect his fangs to be real. He wore a tunic I'd never seen before, black with silver trimming—silver to match the circlet sitting on his brow, contrasting against the midnight of his hair. His half cape was made from textured silk. Most of the villagers would never have seen its equal in fabrics.

Ansel was shooing onlookers away from the stall as I approached.

I slammed my hands down in front of him. "What are you doing here?"

"*Me*? Darling, I'm breadwinning." He gestured between us at the honey-glazed pastries and jam-filled tarts.

"Where's the stall owner? What did you do with them?"

"I'm doing him a favour." He clicked his tongue. "Really, Lena, how do you expect an unconscious man to tend his own stall? Now, come sit with me. You're blocking all my potential customers."

"You knocked him out?"

Ansel nodded. "And threw him in the river. Right where we went fishing, actually."

"*What*?"

"And, dear, you wouldn't believe how heavy he was. Taste tested his wares a few too many times." He leaned back on his bench and beamed at me.

I dug my fingernails into the table, not letting myself appreciate the sharp line of his collarbone or the way his bottom lip curled as he tried not to laugh. He bit down on it, fangs digging into the pink flesh.

No doubt he thought dressing as a more obscene version of himself was hilarious.

I was about to let out a few choice curses when one of the musicians stepped in line behind me. I threw her an insincere smile, pointed to the first pastry I recognised and said loudly, "A blackberry tart."

"What's the magic word?"

"Just give me the tart," I whisper-hissed.

The musician shuffled on her feet.

"Are you sure that's all you'd like? I have a special deal, exclusive to my favourite customers."

I laughed. "What a flirt you are. Is this how you've been treating all the young ladies?"

"Darling, no need to be jealous."

"I'm not—" I spluttered as Ansel leaned to the side to address the musician behind me.

"Isn't my beloved adorable?" he exclaimed, which made several heads turn.

I covered my face, wishing the ground would swallow him whole.

"She'd be a lot more so if she hurried up," the musician said under her breath, which I was willing to let slide in the hope she would forget this encounter entirely. Ansel, though, could never be so generous.

"Did you say something?" he asked too politely.

She paled when she saw him. She had obviously come for the fine food, not the fine view.

"No? Nothing?" Ansel tutted. "I thought so. You should run along now. The last person who insulted this girl nearly got a stake through their heart."

A muscle pulsed in her jaw. "I don't understand."

Ansel smiled sweetly. "I don't want your filthy money. Go use it to buy a better costume, for you look like a colourful pile of dog sick in that."

The musician flushed, any indignation she may have possessed squashed beneath Ansel's stare. She stomped away in a huff, and I turned back to my vampire, past the point of exasperation.

"Did you have to?" I asked.

An upturned nose was my answer.

I heaved a sigh. "Back to what I was saying. What did you *really* do with the owner?"

"Should we try and find him? I hear there's nothing as romantic as moonlit trysts on festival nights."

"Just tell me he's safe."

"Perfectly so." He tapped the empty spot next to him. "Now come, sit."

And thus, my night was reduced to babysitting.

"I can't believe this," I muttered, shimmying my way between the stalls. He caught me by the waist and pulled me to him, depositing me between his legs. His hands settled on my stomach.

"Ansel, stop, what are you—the *villagers* are here."

Ansel tightened his grip at my squirming. "We'll tell them we met in Haycock if they ask," he murmured. "Here, eat." He plucked a blackberry tart from the table, bringing it to my mouth.

I hesitated but took a bite, making a mental note to pay the real stall keeper later. The tartness of the blackberries fizzled on my tongue, combatting the sweetness of the pastry.

"Oh my," I said after swallowing. "This is good."

Ansel smiled at me, unusually warm and so purely happy that I had to swallow again.

"It seems to be the favourite of the night."

"Yes, about that ..." I looked at the crowd. We were getting more than a few stares, one of which was Angela's, I noticed with no small amount of chagrin. She blushed when I caught her, ducking away. I asked, "You're not hungry, are you? And you're not going to play any pranks like last time? And have you actually been serving people baked goods?"

"No, to the first and second questions. As for the third ..." He lifted the tart back to my mouth, and I took another bite. "As for the third, yes. Look at all this money I've made us." To his side on the table was a small box. He opened it, taking a copper coin from the impressive mound within.

"Really? That's amazing." I tilted my head back to look at him. "The festival has barely started!"

He shrugged. "I just bat my eyes these days and they buy anything. It seems you've made me soft."

I leaned into him, resting my head on his chest and pushing away any mortification. Distantly, I knew my actions were reprehensible. The villagers had been speculating about who or what Ansel was for months, and here he was in full view while they were all none the wiser. Intellectually, I knew sitting here with him, giving in so quickly, was wrong. Emotionally, it was liberating.

Ansel said, "So, a fox."

I pushed the mask higher up my nose at the reminder. It was an elegant thing, bronze in colour, etched with whorls and sunbursts to honour the Dawn Lord. Trudi had bought it for Hugo at the last Harvest Festival—to match his hair, she'd said—and seeing as it wasn't a cheap purchase, I presumed he would wear it for many years to come.

As it turned out, Trudi and Hugo decided to go as a pair of swans this year, taking the whole 'mate for life' idea literally.

I said, "Well, it's no vampire, but I thought it fit in with the current circumstances."

"Your current circumstances require cunning? Charm? Screaming out in the night during mating season?"

"Ah, no," I said, laughing, and curled my fingers into his shirtsleeves. "I was thinking more in terms of outwitting predators."

I felt him nod. "Very wise of you."

"But really, what are you doing here?" It wasn't a complaint. The shock of him being here had left me buzzing and bright-eyed.

Ansel fiddled with the coin, rolling it over his fingers. "You gave me a candle, saying you wanted me to be able to join in with the festival. Did I take the invitation too liberally?"

Oh, he knew he did.

His smile grew as I told him as much, and I would have continued to needle him had I thought he was only here to give me a shock. On the contrary, he'd once called himself a social being, and out here amongst all these people, it was impossible to deny.

If a vampire could glow, he was currently doing so. It was a stark difference to the last time I'd witnessed him around anyone. Those boys in the forest wouldn't have recognised him.

Ernst moseyed over to us, and I went still, remembering where I was and the risk involved. Ansel squeezed my waist and, after a quick kiss to my temple, moved me next to him.

Ernst placed one hand on his hip and held a cup of water close to his chest with the other, giving the stall a once-over. The assertiveness he was trying for fell flat, dressed as some kind of fowl as he was. A rooster, if the red flap of material hanging from his beard was anything to go by.

"Where did Jan run off to, then?" Ernst said.

Ansel cocked his head. "Who?"

"Jan," he repeated, doing a double take when he noticed me. A scowl flattened his mouth. "The owner of this stall."

"Hmm." Ansel made a show of peering down at the various baked goods, the box of coins, the ribbon he wore that clearly identified him as a stall owner. "Are you sure that Jan"—he glanced at me, checking he'd got the name right, then nodded once—"yes, *Jan*, is the owner of this here pie stall?"

"Pastry stall," I whispered.

"Pie stall," Ansel said again.

"Well ..." Ernst tugged on his beard, jostling his makeshift wattle. "That is his apple fritter recipe."

Ansel turned to me, face twisted in a clear question of, *what is he still doing here?*

"Cut him some slack," I murmured. "His son just eloped with the butcher's daughter." To Ernst, I said, "Jan's a loud guy, right? Slender and a bit taller than you?"

I'd never bought much from him, but Marie at the inn swore by his plum streusel cake.

"Yes," he drew out, as though I'd asked if the sky was blue or cows went moo. He brought his cup to his mouth, took a swig, then muttered, "Dawn Lord's blessed behind, this water is foul."

I clapped my hands together. "Jan's gone to bet on the chicken racing. Apparently, there's a red hen in the mix with a whole lotta cluck."

Ansel laid a hand over his eyes. Ernst's forehead crumpled.

"Cluck instead of pluck," I explained, "because she's feisty, and she—forget it. He's over there." I pointed to the side vaguely.

"All right." Ernst jerked his chin at Ansel. "Nice teeth," he said before skulking away.

Ansel's attention slid to me, and I sighed. "What? It's not like you were coming up with any ideas."

He hummed. "And what pretty lines will you feed him when he doesn't find *Jan* cheering for his ..." He waved a hand in the air, trying to pick the words. "Clucky lady?"

"If he's that determined—which he won't be, by the way—I'll tell him to go try the inn. It's where most people will end up at least once during the night."

"Oh, good, because that's where I left him." His look turned innocent at my groan. "There were already two drunkards passed out. I didn't think they'd mind the extra company."

I bet I know exactly who you're talking about, I thought as we watched Ernst get swallowed by the crowd towards the main square.

Ansel said abruptly, "Why did he look at you like that?"

"Like what?"

"Like you're anathema."

I crossed my arms. "Oh, *that.* I'm not the most popular person around here, and some of them like to let me know it. Just when I thought they were moving on."

A power, ancient and ravenous, took hold of his features, and I nearly cried out at the bolt of dread that slammed through my body. His eyes were frigid. Like a veil had been torn away, I could see the monster lying beneath his pretty skin. The monster I had always known was there. The monster I had lulled myself into forgetting.

Ansel must have seen the unease streak across my face, because in the next moment, he was his normal self. If I weren't trembling, I would have thought I'd imagined the sudden transformation.

He rolled the coin across his knuckles again, back and forth, faster than my eyes could track. "So sorry to hear that, darling. Something the matter?"

I unclenched my hands, tried to relax. "No."

"Really? I'm not too sure about that. I think we've been noticed."

I followed Ansel's gaze in time to see Father Pentaghast, dressed in his full priest regalia, face painted with gold markings, spill his mead on a young woman. He was staring at us, bewildered.

I sank deeper into my seat. "There's no way he could know what you are from here, is there?"

"Some priestly sense, you mean?" The words were limned with sparks of fury.

"Mmhmm."

"No such thing. But, Lena?" The coin bent like butter between his fingers. "I think it's time for us to go."

It wasn't a suggestion.

We left the stall unattended and escaped to the forest, a stiffness that I wasn't used to bracketing Ansel's frame. His fingers dug into my arm occasionally, not painfully, but enough that he could feel my skin start to imprint beneath his nails. I wondered if he realised he was doing it.

We walked for so long, the silence thick between us, that I lost track of where we were in favour of watching the leaves crunch beneath my feet in a rainbow of hues.

As the forest grew denser and the night colder, Ansel slowed to a stop. We had wandered to the place where we first met. The exact elm Ansel had stood beneath fanned out above our heads, hiding the moon's soft glow.

A twig snapped far off, and I flinched out of Ansel's hold.

"Hey," I began, and he peered down at me. "Did we really have to stop here?"

There was a dead mouse nestled by a root of the elm. A stream of bulbous ants picked it clean. "You and me," I prompted at Ansel's blank look. "Last festival night."

"Last festival night," he repeated before massaging his temple. "Of course. I'm sorry, darling, I was led by habit."

"You've come here again?"

"Occasionally." He gestured to the elm, spoke as if he were commenting on the weather. "They hanged my mother here years ago. Left her corpse for the ravens to pick at."

I blinked. It took my brain a moment to recalibrate.

"Who did?" I asked, and he nodded towards the village.

"Them. Or their ancestors, I suppose, but there's no real difference. They have the same blood coursing through their veins, the same small-minded, ignorant need for validation."

A couple of flies had joined the ants, gorging themselves on the mouse's innards.

I swallowed through a dry mouth. "Why didn't you tell me?"

"It didn't seem relevant to anything." His actions betrayed him, the way he plucked the circlet from his head and ran a hand through his hair—pent-up energy needing an outlet. He said, "The village was little more than a block of mud huts back then. Primitive, compared to the northern cities my parents fled from, war-torn as they were."

I moved as he spoke, placing my hand on the sturdy trunk, feeling the dusty grooves of the bark. "Why did they hang her?"

"They did not need a reason." He chuckled. "But she gave them a good one in killing my father. One good knock to the head and he was gone. I would have been, oh, ten or so? That's very young, isn't it?"

I nodded, and he narrowed his eyes.

"Don't look at me like that, darling. Four centuries have done much to heal the sorrows of a little boy."

I only believed him because I knew that little boy was dead. Only a remnant existed in Ansel. Memories from someone else's life.

I ached for him, but he did not need my pity.

I swiped the circlet from his limp grip and crowned myself, saying, "So that's how old you are. Four centuries isn't as bad as I imagined. The Holy City has stood for longer than that."

"I am glad an age gap does not daunt you." He was amused. "But I did not bring you out here to regale you with tragedies of the past. There's something I must tell you, and I suspect you will not much like hearing it."

"That's never stopped you before."

"This is different." Gently, Ansel undid the ties of my mask. His thumb followed the curve of the circlet, ghosted a path across my skin. "How are you? You are looking well, but are you feeling it?"

I frowned. "Why wouldn't I be?"

"And you have had more strength recently. You have been happier."

If I hadn't coughed blood two nights ago, I could have agreed with him. As it was, I had no answer he'd want to hear. I stayed quiet.

He grimaced. "Darling, I've been feeding you my blood."

At first, I didn't understand the words. I went to contradict him because it was such a bizarre thing for him to state, and I couldn't remember ever asking or accepting blood from him.

Then I realised what he meant.

"You what?" I said, suddenly winded.

"I've been feeding you my blood. In the food I made you, the tea. As often as I could justify it, and I know you find it unpleasant, but there are no ill effects. Vampire blood strengthens, it heals."

"It heals?" I repeated blankly.

"Yes," he breathed. He took my face between his hands. "Yes, it *heals*. You have a weak constitution. You looked so tired all the time, and I knew that you would never agree, not back then, and so I did what I thought was best. To help, you understand."

Ansel was anxious. Ansel didn't get anxious.

He continued to speak, his words sweet as sugar to hide the rot underneath, but I heard none of them. I was spiralling, falling down a cliff that had no bottom.

"How often?" I asked, pulling away.

"It varied. Once or twice a week at the start. Now, at least once a day."

I was *falling*.

"It's your fault," I said. The last few weeks started to make sense. "This sickness, it's your fault."

"Sickness? No, it's not an illness, only—your body has been weak since I've known you. I can smell it on you; you're drenched in it."

I laughed. "It's not an illness? And so, what, you thought you'd try and fix it? Just like that?"

He looked so utterly confused it hurt. "Yes."

He had no idea what he'd done.

I understood now why I was terribly sick one day and perfectly fine the next, on and on. Why I'd coughed blood two days ago yet was able to run through the forest like a tree sprite the next night.

Fear had kept me from delving too deeply into these contrasting states.

My own fear had damned me.

And you call yourself a healer, a rusty, cobwebbed voice—Markus's—chided me.

To be fair, I never considered myself to be very good at it. The calling had been thrust upon me by happenstance. But even I, looking back, could see the pattern for what it was.

In a very short time, my body had grown dependent on Ansel's blood. Ansel, whether he meant to or not, had made me completely dependent on *him*.

"Here." He pulled what looked like a small vial from his pocket, the lid decorated with silver filigree. Inside was a liquid so red it was almost black. "The gift I spoke of earlier to add to your necklace. It holds my blood within, in case you ever grow unwell when I am not there to help."

I took a step back, behind the elm. He stepped forward, mirroring me. Exactly—*exactly*—like that first night.

"I don't want it," I said.

Ansel's voice was too calm. Placating. "It's just in case, darling, in case you start feeling tired or—"

"*I don't want it.*"

The wind in his hair, the scrape of my skirts, the ants feasting on the mouse's corpse; they pushed down on my shoulders until I thought my heels would crack. Crawled through my ears to nibble at my brain.

I wanted silence. I *needed* silence.

Before I could think, I lifted my leg and crushed the mouse beneath my foot. Its bones crunched, and the ants that still could, ran away. The flies stopped buzzing. All was blissfully quiet.

Ansel tucked the pendant away like its disappearance would bridge the sudden chasm between us. And it did help, a little. His eyes narrowed again, tracking my every movement.

This wasn't like the previous night, where his chasing me had been for fun. This was no game.

His blood could have changed me in ways I didn't want to consider. Was I entirely human still? Even if I did make it to the Holy City and receive healing, would I still be able to survive without his blood?

Did he care at all that I'd never given him permission?

"I'm going home." I didn't know if I meant Myrtle Gully or the castle. My feet made the decision for me, and I started towards the village.

"I don't understand," he said from behind me, quietly, imploringly, and I believed him. It was obvious. My heart felt like it might shrivel, because he couldn't be this cruel, not anymore.

Not to me.

He followed me as I stumbled back through the forest, watched as I fell on my knees at the outskirts of the village and swept the tears from my cheeks. I felt his confusion morph to frustration when the villagers burnt their candles and cheered for the promise of a better harvest. He didn't do anything as I returned to the clinic, didn't spirit me away or demand answers.

Didn't plunge his fangs into my throat or ply me with his blood.

He didn't do anything.

But I knew he was considering it.

CHAPTER SEVENTEEN

I woke up the next morning, tired and cranky, to find a letter slipped halfway under the door.

Scooting out of bed and pulling the tangled hair out of my face, I inspected the wax seal, failed to recognise it, and ripped the envelope open.

I skimmed the single, lightweight page before scrunching it into a ball and hurling it across the room where it landed with a damning crunch. Dawn Lord knew I loved the man, but Markus held the prize for the worst timing of the century.

I wrapped myself in a robe, plucked the envelope from where I'd discarded it on the bed, and stormed into the hallway. "Hugo!"

A second passed before his door opened, auburn head peeking out. He saw the letter in my hand—impressive since his eyes were still drooped in sleep—and sighed. "Why are you shouting at me?"

I ignored the attitude. "When did this come?"

"I don't know, sometime yesterday? You could say thank you, you ..." He trailed off at my expression. "What's wrong?"

Everything, I wanted to say. *Everything's wrong, and I'm buying a pack mule and setting off on an adventure to escape it all.*

"Nothing's wrong." I planted myself on the floorboards, my back against the wall, legs spread out in the least ladylike approximation decently possible. "It's just really inconvenient."

Nothing would be inconvenient if it weren't for Ansel.

Ansel lying to me.

Hugo slid down, leaned his head against the door jamb, and just looked at me.

"It's Markus," I said, and he snorted. I fiddled with the envelope. "He's finally in Haycock and wants me to go help him with ... something. I don't know what. I didn't read far enough to see."

"So?" Hugo asked, pulling up the sleeves of his white sleep clothes. "How's that different from any other week?"

"What? Oh, right." He thought I'd been frequenting Haycock this entire time and that this would just be another trip. I fell back on my secondary excuse, feeling manipulative for even bringing it up. "My health. I don't know if it's a good idea to keep going."

Ansel slipping blood into my food.

Hugo nodded slowly. "You should be taking it slow. But —and this is my professional opinion"—I rolled my eyes at that, and he smiled wryly—"Markus is going to be able to help you better than I could. Better than you can help yourself. The trip won't kill you, but your stubbornness might."

I pursed my lips at him for speaking a truth I didn't want to hear. "Thanks," I said, then scrubbed my face. "I don't know. I just don't want to go."

Can't go, I corrected in my head. Ansel and I may not have been on the best of terms, but that didn't mean I could just up and leave. I wouldn't put it past him to do something really uncalled for if he found out.

Was that how I was to dictate the rest of my life, however long that was? Too scared to do anything, bound and chained by the whims of a vampire I was, for better or worse, affectionately fond of loathing?

Don't sugarcoat it, Lena, I thought. *You're so head over heels you've nearly snapped in half.*

It was all kinds of unhealthy, but I'd accepted that.

"You think I should go?" I asked, already knowing the answer.

He shrugged and hugged himself. "If you think you can handle it." He looked cold, like he wanted nothing more than to finish this conversation and head back under his blankets. My purple toes could empathise.

"Okay," I said. "And thanks for slipping me the letter. It would have sat there a week, otherwise."

"Yeah, you've been distracted lately. Not that you don't have good reason to be."

Ansel making me dependent on him.

"I'll take the morning shift," I said, wanting to go back to sleep but knowing from the buzz beneath my skin that it would never happen.

"Really?" Hugo blinked a couple of times. "Are you sure you're well enough?"

"Yeah, you go back to bed. Trudi will be over later, and you don't want to look like you do now, trust me. Your blushing bride-to-be will run away screaming."

Hugo smiled, but the curve of his mouth held a sour kind of edge. "You've changed, Lena."

I drew my knees up to my chest, wrapped my arms around them. "I hope that's a compliment."

"It's not a criticism, at least. You just seem different since a while ago. Harder and kind of mean sometimes. And I understand why," he said when I opened my mouth to retort. "I know we haven't talked much, but I want you to know I'm here. I'm here, Trudi's here, all the villagers are here for you."

True. My patience had been spread thin of late.

As for the sweet words he was spouting, they were window dressings in a coffin shop. I appreciated the sentiment but was in no hurry to buy what was inside.

"Thanks, Hugo," I said and stood, stretching my hands over my head and popping my sore joints. They were always sore these days. Ansel's blood wasn't a cure-all.

Hugo gripped my skirt, hiking it to my knees. "What are these?"

I slapped his hand, the sound cracking through the air.

“Ow,” he wailed and then flushed, staring horrified at the hem of my nightgown. “Sorry—I didn’t mean to. I mean, I would never—”

“None of your business, that’s what,” I snapped, angrier at myself than him. Ansel’s bites had scabbed over, leaving a trail of purple up one leg. I’d be curious too if I were Hugo.

His gaze darted anywhere but me. “Yes, sorry, I shouldn’t have done that. Sorry.”

I nearly rolled my eyes again. He didn’t have to act quite so mortified.

“It’s fine,” I said, and he ducked his head, escaping to his bedroom with a final muttered apology.

The morning was uneventful. I spent a few hours preparing tonics and cleaning the surgical instruments before giving in and lugging a chair to a patch of sunshine near the herb garden. I’d hear if a patient came a-knocking.

Knitting kept my hands busy, but not my mind. My needles clacked together as I missed a stitch at the base of the sock, my clumsy fingers belying even clumsier thoughts.

Go to Haycock, don’t go to Haycock. Go, don’t go.

Ansel wouldn’t actually kill the villagers anymore if I left. Probably. Maybe.

Ansel smiling to himself when I drank my tea. When I drank his blood.

My eyes pricked with tears, and I closed them, tipping my head back to feel the warmth of the sun on my face. I understood why Ansel did it. I understood he thought he was helping.

But I wouldn't forgive him. At least, not until he understood how wrong he'd been.

Distantly, I felt repulsed by myself. The betrayal sunk into me deeper, like the stick I'd once embedded in Ansel's stomach, but it warred with the desire to see him. To make sure he was okay.

I stayed outside until midday. Hugo was up by then, sipping a cup of tea at the kitchen table and scratching a pattern into the wood with the knife Markus had given me. I'd taken to leaving the knife in the kitchen, knowing that metal would do little to Ansel and not wanting to give myself the temptation of stabbing someone else. Someone like Hugo.

"You know Markus hates it when you do that," I said, pulling the knife from his hand and wiping it on my skirt. "And you're blunting the blade."

Hugo slurped his tea, obviously over his embarrassment from earlier. The noise hurt my ears and irritated me in a way only younger brother-like figures were capable of doing.

"I'm making it look better," he said.

Someone knocked on the door for the first time all morning, the insistent sound irritating me further. Hugo leapt up from his chair and hurried to the entry, greeting whoever it was and ushering them into the clinic. I was still in the kitchen minutes later, finishing Hugo's tea, when another patient arrived.

"One for you, Lena," Hugo called.

I met Angela inside, her twin sisters sitting either side of her on the surgical table, their legs swinging back and forth. Their father stood behind them with his arms crossed, steely gaze following me across the room as I greeted them.

Angela did look worse for wear, sallow-faced and exhausted, but a quick round of questions and a routine check-up—pulse: normal; breathing: clear; fever: none—made it evident she was battling nothing more than exhaustion. She was a strong and healthy girl, and winter was more than a month off. She would be fine.

"Seems like you had a bit too much fun at the festival. I can make up something that will help you sleep," I said, meeting four sets of impatient eyes, "but otherwise, I'd recommend rest and a whole lot of spoiling." I winked at one of Angela's sisters, the larger, shyer one, and she gave me a tentative smile.

"Thanks, Lena," Angela said tiredly, and with what I thought was a little embarrassment. Her father put a hand on her shoulder.

"Maybe a second opinion would be better." His fingers tightened, turning his knuckles white, and Angela winced. "Is Hugo around?"

He knew Hugo was around. He'd let them in.

"A second opinion?" I asked.

"Yes."

"Why?"

His eyes narrowed. "Because I want his opinion."

I bit the inside of my cheek so hard I tasted blood. For once that morning, I wasn't reminded of Ansel.

"You want his opinion," I said levelly. "I'm sorry. He's busy. So, you can either wait here while your daughter gets even more exhausted, or you can do what I told you and let her get some rest."

His face, ruddy in complexion, reddened even further. "Don't speak to me like that."

"Like what?"

"Like you know better than me."

I tried to be nice for Angela's sake, and for the twins, who were looking as though a volcano was about to erupt and they wanted to be as far away as possible when the lava started to spew forth.

I tried, but I didn't succeed.

"But I do know better than you. In fact, I'm willing to bet that a toad would be more caring of its offspring than you, you ignorant piece of—"

Angela squeaked, interrupting me.

Her father stepped into my personal space, and I finally realised the splotchy red of his face was the lava his daughters were all trying to avoid.

Too late. I'd forced an eruption.

He waved a finger in my face and snarled, "You are a curse on the village, the worst kind of loose woman. Not coming to worship, planting yourself on a strange man's lap in front of the entire village like a common whore. We all know why you were the one to find Father Snow, and the only reason we still allow you to be here is because of the few who seem to see something in you the rest of us can't."

"Father, stop!" Angela grabbed his arm, but he pushed her off.

And that, the fact that he physically rebuffed her, compared to his repulsive words, was what truly upset me.

"You need to leave." My breathing was erratic, but I managed to stay calm. "Now."

He looked like he wanted to say more—do more, even, hit me or spit at me—but Angela tugged on his arm again. He wheeled around to stare at his daughters before clearing his throat and telling them to follow him out.

Angela snuck me an apologetic look as she turned behind her sisters, but I barely noticed it.

I was done.

Markus wanted me at Haycock?

I'd leave at dawn.

I was in luck.

A group of traders were returning to Haycock the next morning and were happy for me to ride along. Trudi had come to see me before I left, but I'd kept my door shut. It was childish and immature, but I didn't want to be kind at that point. I wanted to be left alone.

More than that, I wanted Ansel.

I'd left him a note on the servants' door saying I'd be back in time to bring him blood. The tone was short and unfeeling. Impersonal.

It would upset him.

I wanted to upset him, make him ask for forgiveness. I wanted him to be worthy of forgiveness. I shifted on the back of the cart, trying to keep my stomach immune to the constant bounce of the wheels on the dirt road beneath. My mother's necklace was a weight in my pocket, and I eventually stuffed it to the bottom of my bag, pulling the drawstrings closed.

I didn't want to feel weepy. Not when I was surrounded by such beauty.

The wall of trees that bracketed us from either side withered in the sun, growing thinner the farther we went until the twisted, ancient trunks dissolved into fields of grass and farmland. The village was hours behind, the castle nothing more than a smudge against the hilltops. Fallen leaves the colour of honey crunched beneath the wagon.

The trader driving the cart smoked his pipe, muttering encouragements to his geriatric horse every few minutes. It reminded me of Markus.

The city of Haycock was well and truly awake by the time we got there, black smoke rising in great plumes from the chimneys as if trying to mask the stench of unwashed bodies, food, and livestock. Women strolled through the streets linking arms, while their male counterparts haggled with shopkeepers in booming voices. A boy pulled a sheep down the road, having to stop every few steps to keep the animal from brushing up against the ladies' petticoats. Past all the shops was a girl about my age spreading grain for her chickens.

I'd forgotten what it was like to live somewhere bigger than an anthill. It was a good reminder that Myrtle Gully and its problems weren't the centre of the world.

The traders dropped me off next to a scum-lined fountain, its spout trickling a sad line of water. The ground was slick with muck, and I pulled my hem a little higher than usual as I made my way into the middle of town, keeping an eye out for the Black Bottle Inn.

I wandered for a while, basking in the chaos of it all until midday came and went, and I grew sick of walking. Sick of walking but not tired of walking. There was a distinct difference, for which I was both annoyed and reluctantly grateful to Ansel.

I ate the small amount of food I'd brought, knowing I'd need a full stomach for the afternoon ahead, before stopping a couple of well-to-do young men to ask for directions.

They shot me puzzled looks, but after unsuccessful attempts at flirtation—*have we met before? We feel like we know you*—they seemed happy enough to direct me—*right, left, right, are you sure you want that inn, another right*—and it wasn't long before I was standing in the middle of a quiet street, facing a weathered two-storey building.

It wasn't very promising.

The windows were boarded, and the paint was peeling. The blackened sign above the door squeaked back and forth in the wind.

I sighed and walked inside.

The smell hit me first, a lingering stench that was both sweet and bitter, like cat urine mixed with rotting meat.

I squinted, trying to adjust to the darkness of the room. "Hello?"

"Hello," a voice, glossy and male, echoed. The hair on the back of my neck stood up.

"Hi," I said slowly, trying to find whoever had spoken. The ground was littered with broken chairs, the bar with smashed glass. "I'm looking for a man named Markus, but something tells me he's not here."

"Markus, Markus," he said. I spotted movement across the room at the staircase. A flickering shadow. "Now, why is that name familiar?"

"Older man, kind of gruff. He was meant to be staying here."

A beat passed as the person considered.

If this is a ghost, I thought, *and it wants to make a deal with me, I'm going to have to explain my quota's already full.*

"Oh, yes, I remember," he said finally, and it struck me that I knew his voice from somewhere.

The door slammed shut behind me.

I flinched and groped blindly for the handle. The splinters of the doorframe dug into my palms.

It wouldn't open.

There was movement to my side, the soft fall of footsteps leading away. I opened my mouth to scream, but the hiss of a flame being sparked stole the sound from me.

The boy from the well—René, I remembered—stood opposite me with his back to the fireplace, holding a candle. He smiled, and I flinched.

Where his teeth were once blunt, he now had fangs long enough to rival Ansel's, the white points pushing into his full bottom lip. He'd accompanied me in the village. Chatted and laughed.

I guess now I got the joke.

A tapered green coat followed the lines of his body, a matching ribbon pulling the blond hair from his face. He came towards me, moving with a kind of waifish grace he hadn't possessed in the village. Each step had his buckled shoes clicking against the wood.

A deep calm spread through me, quiet waves lapping at a shore. It saturated my limbs, turning them heavy, slowing my heartbeat.

I should have seen this coming. Maybe I had.

René set the candle on the mantlepiece.

"Well," I said. "You're looking different since the last time we met."

He giggled, peering at me from beneath his lashes. "You should be honoured. The last time I filed my teeth down was more than a century ago, and it wasn't for the sake of a village girl."

"Filed your teeth down? Sounds painful."

"A necessary sacrifice." He touched the tips of his fangs. "They've nearly grown back. Finally."

I sat, leaning back against the door and linking my fingers together. "All right, let's hear it. I presume you have a problem with Ansel you drew me out here to talk about?"

His forehead wrinkled. "Are you laughing at me?"

I hesitated. "No."

"I wish you wouldn't," he said as if I hadn't spoken.

"I'm not laughing at you."

He made a high, keening noise in the back of his throat and moved towards me. "I wish you wouldn't laugh like that."

I stared at him, perturbed. "I'm not."

He crouched in front of me, cheeks dimpling. "Yes, you are."

His smile was brilliant, almost too blinding for me to see the elbow he cocked back and the malice glinting in his eyes. Time slowed as his fist struck my stomach, my breath leaving me in one painful, scraping rush. I couldn't breathe, could barely think past the need to gasp in air that wasn't coming. I clawed at the ground with one hand as I held my stomach with the other.

René made a pensive noise. I looked up, shuddering, to glare at him.

"Oh, forgive me," he said, covering his mouth. "I couldn't resist. You seemed to be asking for it. But what, no coughing? I thought for sure that would get you going."

That comment broke through even my need for air.

How much did he know about me?

In a gesture that reminded me very much of Ansel, he clapped his hands. "Oh, I understand. It's the *blood.* Dietrich has been so very generous with you. It's no wonder you smell like his shadow."

"Who?"

"You don't know?" René blinked owlishly. "Dietrich Ansel. You mean he hasn't even told you his name?"

I ignored that detail. "What am I doing here? And where's Markus?"

"The old man is wherever he's meant to be. Forget about him. Now, I have a small story for you to listen to, and then an even smaller task for you to complete, you understand?"

"I'm not going to—"

René smacked his hand over my mouth, hard enough to bang my head back against the door.

"Shh," he whispered. "I said to *listen*." With his other hand, he tapped a finger against my neck, in time with my pulse. "But where to start? Ah, I know the place. Yes, right there shall do nicely."

And he told me a story.

Once upon a time, there was a big, loving family, full of brothers and sisters, all wasting away in the vicious cycle of eternity.

Their leader, the wisest brother, was a being of unparalleled power, and the family worshipped him in place of the god they'd long since abandoned. The family ruled the darkness, growing larger with each passing year until, finally, their feeding ground became too small. They set their sights on new land.

New blood.

But as they took to their new hunting ground, a vast, bustling city, a certain group of younglings decided to enjoy their spoils to the fullest. In a single night, they slew the entire city. In a single night, they alerted the church to their existence.

Their leader's retribution was cold and swift, and by sunrise, the only sign vampires had ever been there was a deafening silence and fresh piles of ash blowing in the wind.

For a time, all was as it had been. The family continued to expand, but more vampires meant more hunger, and the leader grew tired of his mantel. He grew tired of his family and their unending cycle. The more his brothers and sisters tried to make him stay, with blood and death and finery, the more he desired to abandon them.

And he did abandon them, eventually. Secluded himself away where no one would find him. Some vampires, those that would take his place, even whispered rumours of his death. Baseless rumours. Those that loved him knew he would never leave this existence quietly. So, they waited.

For the signs, for the black despair of his return, they waited.

Until one summer night, when a foolish village girl found a trapdoor in the chapel of an abandoned castle.

"What?" I said, the word muffled beneath René's hand. "Is that it? He killed some wayward vampires, got bored, and left?" I'd been expecting much worse.

René wiped his hand on his trousers and hissed, "He wallowed in guilt because they were mine."

I found that unlikely. Perhaps Ansel felt a little bad, but I'd never seen him wallow in anything but his own opinion of himself.

You only think that because you're hurt, a voice whispered mutinously.

I asked, "You were close?"

"We were brethren. Beings of the same ilk, the *finest* ilk, and incomprehensible to a mortal like you." He stood, smirking. "Have you heard of the Legion Plague? The church would have you think it was a blood sickness, but I remember the truth. The screams of those my children and I feasted on were almost as delicious as their blood."

"The Legion Plague," I repeated. The back of my head stung from where I'd hit the wall, and I rubbed it as I got to my knees. "Ansel said he was there."

"Isn't he cruel? They were mine. My children, only a handful of years old, barely coming into themselves, and he crushed their existence into dust without a second thought of what it would do to me.

"And then he leaves us? He disappears like a ghost in the night, deprives the entire family of his presence for what reason? Because he does not want us anymore? Instead, he seeks fulfilment in the life of a village girl. How many years have you lived? Eighteen? No different from a larva, repulsive and pathetic, guaranteed nothing but the life of an insect."

"You're jealous." The words were a revelation. "Of me. You're jealous that I'm with Ansel."

He caught my hair, wrenching me back. "You are not with him, you miserable mortal. Not unless you count yourself as a parasite that feeds off his grace."

He was throwing a tantrum, trying to get Ansel's attention.

The saturating calm was quickly diminishing. Cautiously, I said, "If I'm not with Ansel, then why am I here?"

"I told you. We have a task for you to complete."

The ceiling creaked above us, like the yowl of a dying animal.

We, René had said.

He wasn't alone.

"Is someone up there?" I asked, grunting when he pulled me up by my hair.

"Would you like to go take a look?" René pushed me in front of him.

I climbed the creaky wooden stairs, clutching the balustrade with shaking hands as he followed at my heels. I hesitated at the top, at the shadows beyond, knowing I was deep in the viper's nest and that every step further would make leaving more difficult.

A shove propelled me forward. I stumbled, hitting my shin on the last step.

"Ouch," I gritted through my teeth.

A quick glare behind my shoulder showed René looking particularly proud of himself. He led me down the corridor, stepping over scattered debris from the smashed-in walls on either side of us. Through the jagged bits of panelling, I could see figures crouching in the dark, twitching and moaning.

"Who are they?" I asked. One of them snapped its head to the side, unnaturally angled, at the sound of my voice.

René looked at the figures with pride. "My new children."

Horror should have struck me, and it did to some degree—being ambushed by a horde of the undead was not ideal—but instead I found myself blurting, "What's wrong with them?"

He stepped close enough for his cloying breath to wash over my face. "You think I made them *wrong*? I know centuries-old vampires that are no closer to creating perfection than when they had their first taste of living blood. I've sired more vampires than there are hairs on your foolish head, and each one has become more glorious than the last."

I laughed nervously. "That's a lot of vampires. They're not all here, are they?"

He growled. "You will show me respect, you wretch, or I will tear off your head and place it in a box like I did that squealing pig."

"Pig?" I parroted. "The pig was you? No, it couldn't have been. I didn't invite you in until ..."

"You think that's the first time I visited? Your friend was happy to help me with a headache one night you were away. You should be grateful, you know. I thought about leaving *his* head in your cupboard, but then you would have run off and cried to Dietrich, and Dawn Lord knows it didn't warrant that type of fuss.

"But, *darling*," he continued, tainting Ansel's name for me, "I just want you to know, I was with you the whole time, there for you. Kneeling by your bed when you found my gift. Following you afterwards as you wandered into the forest. My favourite was your obvious horror at your friends' engagement. Would it have been easier, had they let you just die when you were choking on your own vomit?"

"You stalked me?"

"Watched you. Hunted. Played with the food before it turned cold."

I felt violated. A thought occurred to me, equally as awful. "Did Ansel know what you were doing? Does he know you're here?"

"Ah, Dietrich." His features softened, turned angelic. "He killed all the vampires I let wander too near—didn't know it was me directing them, of course, but I'm sure he suspects." He cleared his throat, overcome by some twisted emotion. "Anyway, the pig was a cheap, overused tactic, but I so enjoyed the aftermath."

"You made me think the villagers despised me." Anger crushed any survival instincts left within me, ground them to dust as I cocked my elbow back to hit him, punch him, slap him, *hurt him*.

He caught my arm easily.

"And they do," he said, "but you're just too dumb and blind and self-obsessed to realise what's right in front of you." Grabbing me by the collar, he wrenched me forward until we reached a door at the end of the corridor. "We, all of us night children, felt the moment he came back. Felt it like our souls ripping from us a second time. This is what you've done. This is the consequence for *waking him*."

He pushed me inside.

All I could do was stare at them in horror.

At the bodies.

They were piled in the corner of the room but had started sliding down the mound as too many had been added.

Discoloured limbs, swollen and bloated, men, women, eyes open to the ceiling, dried blood on their necks, on their arms and legs—*that girl's dress was so pretty and now it's ruined*—and a young man stared at me from his place atop the pile, not just any young man but Ernst's son who'd run off with the butcher's daughter, but he hadn't run off, he'd been broken and thrown away for his body to rot—

René said, "It's disgusting leaving our food scraps here for so long, but I wanted you to understand what was at stake. So?" He smiled, spreading his arms. "Does it inspire you?"

I could barely breathe, let alone speak.

This was Ansel's fault. This was my fault.

But I didn't kill these people.

That's right, I didn't. René did.

I reached into my bag, not having the mental fortitude to try and be subtle about it, but it wouldn't have mattered anyway. René was watching me too closely to miss anything.

"No need for that," he said, grasping my arm again, more gently this time. "Your holy symbol will keep for a different day, I promise."

I pressed my lips together. Tried not to be sick.

He continued, "Now, I have something I want you to do for me. The whole reason for this little game. Go and tell Dietrich that tomorrow night my children and I are coming for the villagers. And after that, we are coming for him."

It took longer than it should have to comprehend his words. "You're just ... letting me leave?"

"Yes," he said. "As long as you pass on my message."

I couldn't stop staring at the bodies, imagining Trudi, Hugo, Angela, in their place. The world spun a little when I nodded. "Yes. Yes, I can do that."

"Good," he said, suddenly cheerful. "Let me show you out." His hands clamped down on my shoulders, and he steered me back down the hallway to the stairs. From the corner of my eyes, I could see a vampire step through a hole in the wall, then another on the other side. Their footsteps were slow and stilted.

A skeletal hand reached for me.

René deflected it, murmuring something too low for me to hear.

We reached the end of the hall, and René pushed me down the first step. I gripped the balustrade to keep from falling and turned, but he wasn't looking at me. His attention was behind him, on the shadowy spectres I knew were there but couldn't quite make out.

Crease between his brows, slight downturn to the lips, the widening of his eyes. It was only there for a split second, so fast I could barely decipher it. When his gaze met mine, I figured it out.

Wariness.

He said, almost managing to sound casual, “Run, little Lena, or I’ll set my children on you for sport. I’m sure you’ll make the trip just fine with one less limb.”

It wasn’t so much a warning as a way to placate the creatures behind him.

Which meant he wasn’t entirely in control here.

I flew down the stairs without preamble and smacked into the door, my knees going weak with relief when it opened, bathing the room in sunlight. Hissing came from the stairs, and I looked back in time to see a smoking figure scuttle to the upper floor.

René crouched in the shadows. When our eyes met, he said, “I’ll see you tomorrow night.”

An idea occurred to me.

Hang on.

Me, standing in the sunlight.

Wait a second.

René, hiding in the shadows.

Is this real?

He’d let me go—in daytime, no less—and expected me to run his errands? Let him threaten the villagers, all doom and gloom like? I’d already humoured one vampire. I wasn’t about to humour another.

My gaze caught on the candle, still burning on the mantelpiece. Behind the counter were bottles of alcohol.

“You,” René snapped from where he was perched, “what are you doing? Leave.”

I felt a smile inch up my mouth, one that was foreign on my face but I knew I'd seen on Ansel's a number of times.

I was going to enjoy this.

CHAPTER EIGHTEEN

By the time flames had engulfed the inn and the shrieks were growing longer, I was on my merry way back home. The mare I'd paid two silvers to rent was named Bonny Belle Bo—we had bonded well over the trip, discovering a mutual love of apples, carrots, and sugar cubes—and, rusty as my riding skills may have been, I arrived in Myrtle Gully just after dark.

I'd had a lot of time to think. Too much time, actually.

First, I'd enjoyed the rush.

But then, when the cold set in and the day grew overcast, when my legs and back started aching, I acknowledged the truth of it. I'd just burned down an inn full of live, sentient creatures and felt absolutely nothing. Well, that wasn't strictly true.

I felt vindicated. Anger for Ernst's son, the girl he had loved, and everyone else who had suffered at their hands. But guilty? Not in the slightest.

I didn't think that was entirely normal.

There should have been something there, some part of me, no matter how minuscule, that felt bad. I narrowed it down to adrenaline and the fact I did it for René's victims. The flames had been justice for them, for their families.

The village was subdued as it usually was that time of night. The festival decorations had been put away for next year, and the only sign there had been a celebration was the unusual amount of kicked-up gravel on the road. I was leading Bonny Belle Bo to the humble stables beside the inn when Trudi, flushed and dishevelled, barrelled into me.

"Thank the Dawn Lord," she cried. "I was so worried when you left all of a sudden, and I didn't know if you were coming back and—how could you do that to me?"

I pulled away, trying to ask what she was doing out so late, but she spoke over me.

"But that doesn't matter now! One of the men got his leg caught in a trap, and Hugo's doing what he can, but I don't know if he'll make it."

I was already handing her the reins. "Who was it? Did the bone break? When did it happen?"

"I don't, um." She hiccupped. "It hasn't been long, and I don't know if the bone broke. I don't know who he is."

"Take the horse and meet me back at the clinic with fresh water, okay?" I kissed her cheek. "And I'm sorry I left without telling you."

She sniffed. "It's fine. But you need to go."

The clinic was quiet when I arrived. Hugo had lit dozens of candles in the surgical room, but I knew from experience the light wouldn't be the same. We'd be straining our eyes for hours into the night. The smell of tallow permeated the air, mellow and pungent like an animal's underbelly.

Hugo was hunched over the man on the surgical table, holding a bottle of whiskey to his mouth. He slumped in relief at the sight of me. "You're back. Quick, give him the rest of this." He pushed the bottle into my hands. "The bone needs to be set, but it may already be too late. I'll get the saw."

"Wait." I grabbed his arm. "Give me some time. Get the saw just in case, but also the sutures and one of those poppy tinctures." I hesitated. "And go heat the cautery."

He wrenched out of my grasp, muttering, "It's already in the fire."

"What's his name?" I asked, washing my hands in the water basin.

"Thomas. His brother will be here soon, and if he's as mean as this one, we'll want to work quick."

"Mean as ..." I trailed off, getting my first good look at our patient.

His beard had been trimmed and his face was layered with sweat, but it was unmistakably the large man who'd picked a fight with me at the inn. I scoffed, unprofessional as it was, glad Hugo had already left the room.

"Right," I said. "Drink this."

Thomas's head rolled under my grip, eyes sharpening as the burn of the alcohol hit him. I saw the exact moment he recognised me.

"Woman," he mumbled. And then again, louder, "*Woman.*"

I ignored him, setting his head down and putting the bottle to the side. Hugo had lined out a myriad of surgical tools on the table, as well as a basin of water and strips of clean fabric. I took a breath, going deep within myself only to discover I was already feeling disassociated. What was tending to a leg when I'd just burned down a vampire-infested building?

Thomas slurred, "Where's the doctor?"

"We're going to help you, Thomas. Just relax."

"You?" He blinked up at me. "You try and touch me, I ain't paying you nothing."

"That's nice." I wouldn't bother arguing with a man who would rather hold on to his pride than his limb.

He coughed wetly and then groaned.

"Here," I said, giving him more whiskey, which he guzzled down.

Someone knocked on the back door. Their shout was muffled. "Thomas?"

I picked up the scissors.

"Thomas?" Another man—oh hell, it was the brother—appeared in the doorway, sober this time and looking murderous.

"Sir, you can't come in here," I said, tightening my grip on the scissors and hoping he wouldn't recognise me. I moved to block his entrance.

"I damn well can. That's my brother lying in there."

Thomas said, "Peter? S'that you? They ... moved the traps ..."

Peter shoved me, and I stumbled back. "Where's the doctor?" he shouted, spittle hitting the floor. "Why isn't he here?"

"You're talking to her," I said. "And you need to calm down before she removes you."

"You?"

"That's what *I* said." Thomas's head lolled around as if pushed by a breeze. He chuckled. "Don't worry, I told 'em we wouldn't pay if she touched me." He was currently higher than a kite in the midday sun.

"Yes, and you'll lose that leg if we wait any longer." I turned to Peter. "There's a man gathering supplies out back if that makes you feel any better. He'll be back soon. Now, I need you to either leave or be quiet so I can do my job, you understand?"

I didn't wait for his reply as I cut away Thomas's trouser leg. Blood had soaked through completely, the dark brown material now slippery. Peter said something hateful opposite me, but I tuned him out, concentrating on the placement of my fingers, the most efficient line to cut.

"I told you to *stop*." Meaty hands ripped the bloody scissors away and threw them to the ground. Peter shouted, "Are you deaf as well as dumb?"

"Look at his leg, you stupid man," I shouted right back. "I don't have time to argue with you."

He did so, blanching. With the trouser leg gone, Thomas's calf was a mash of torn muscle and snapped bone, speckled with fatty flesh. My fingers shook. I had to tell myself, once, twice, not to think of the corpses at the inn.

Peter swallowed. A quick glance at Thomas's face told me the man had passed out. About time, too.

I said to Peter, "Pick those scissors back up and go wash them. Don't come back until we're finished."

He swallowed again and met my gaze. Blinked a couple of times.

Then he promptly fainted.

"Hugo," I called, turning my attention back to Thomas's leg. "You better get in here soon. I think we just got ourselves another patient."

It was pushing midnight when I collapsed at the kitchen table.

The surgery had gone well. Thomas remained unconscious throughout, and Peter, once roused from his faint, stood to the side silently, trying not to empty his guts upon the floor as the smell of his brother's burning flesh saturated the room.

We managed to save the leg, but Thomas would never walk the same again.

Hugo was mad at me, I could tell. He hadn't spoken a word to me after the procedure unless strictly necessary and had all but stormed to the back room under the pretence of cleaning the tools.

Against my instructions and to the surprise of no one, Peter insisted Thomas be moved. I didn't protest when

Father Pentaghast arrived, sporting an impressive head of bed hair, to help wheel the unconscious man out. They didn't act friendly, but I took the shared, furtive conversation to mean they knew each other. A priest's place, I supposed, was with the sinners.

"Lena?"

I opened my eyes.

Trudi was standing in the open doorway, wringing her hands. "I just talked to Hugo. He said everything went okay."

"Is he very upset with me?"

"I think worried is a better word." She sat opposite me at the table. "We both are."

I nodded. My head was heavy, my eyes sore, my thighs chafed from riding. Even more than that, my stomach ached from where René had hit me. I wondered if the next time I drank Ansel's blood it would be to heal an internal wound.

"Was Markus good?" she asked. "You came back so fast. He mustn't have needed much."

"Mm. Turns out he didn't need me, after all."

Trudi started tapping her foot on the table leg. I ground my teeth and tried not to snap at her to stop. The air was so thick between us it might have felt awkward if I weren't so tired.

She picked at her sleeve and said, "I didn't see you after the festival."

"I left early."

"With him?"

"Yes."

"Did you have fun?"

I didn't like what her tone implied. Sighing, I said, "Just spit it out."

"Just—" she spluttered. "What do you mean just spit it out? Do you know how worried I've been? A vampire comes to the festival after he's threatened to kill everyone if you don't bring him blood, and then you just disappear for the night! And *then* you leave the village without saying anything to me. Frankly, I didn't know whether you were actually going to Haycock or just back to the castle.

"And Hugo keeps asking me all these questions, trying to figure out what you're up to, and I end up having to lie to him. The man I'm going to marry, Lena, I *lie* to him. But the worst thing," she said, voice on the cusp of cracking, "is that on festival night, someone you barely know had to tell me—your best friend—that you were embracing the beautiful and mysterious trader. Embracing the vampire. Do you even remember the bruises he left on your neck? Or all the weight you lost or the nightmares you had?"

I was numb. With guilt, sadness, anger, I didn't know.

"I remember," I said.

"Then why him? Do you think the Dawn Lord will forgive you for this? You could have anyone, Lena, if that's what you wanted, so why does it have to be *him*?"

I wanted to say that she didn't know him, that she didn't know what she was talking about. That there was nothing wrong with choosing Ansel. But the first two would have been unfair and the last an outright lie. She deserved so much more than a lie.

"Because," I said quietly, "he makes me feel invincible."

"That's ironic, seeing as though he once tried to kill you."

"My own body is trying to kill me. There'll never be anything as ironic as that."

Trudi recoiled, hugging herself. Her eyes turned watery. "Talk to me, Lena," she said. "Tell me when it hurts, when you need help, and how I can help you."

We weren't talking about Ansel anymore.

I shook my head. "You know I can't."

"Why can't you?" she demanded, tears escaping to run down her cheeks and drip from her chin.

My voice remained level. "Because then it's real. It's real, and I'm going to die before my twenty-first birthday. And the bodies, Trudi, all those people, all dead because of something I did. I don't know if I can face that."

"What bodies?" she whispered.

I stood. "Never mind. It's too late now."

She didn't try to stop me as I left.

In my bedroom, I washed my face. Changed my dress. Packed my bag. Painfully normal actions I'd done over and over, day in, day out, as a mountain of bodies rotted within a vampire den. The pansies on my windowsill had withered. I picked at the leaf of one, crushing it beneath my fingers.

René was ash. I had killed him. And yet, why did I feel like this was only the beginning?

What am I going to tell Ansel? I thought.

I was gathering my knitting when the girl in the mirror caught my eye. I didn't recognise my own reflection, though she blinked when I did. She even copied the fake smile I attempted. The skin of her cheeks looked paper-thin, like it would crinkle and tear when she let go of that smile.

I bit into my cheek, just to make sure my face wouldn't really tear away. Blood leached from the skin. The result was inconclusive.

How was it possible I looked more undead than Ansel? The girl in the mirror shrugged in time with me, blonde hair bouncing.

Tiredness weighed my eyelids down, nearly sewed them shut, but I didn't let it pull me under. I'd gone longer than this without sleep in the last few months. I could handle hours yet.

"But I wouldn't advise you to do so," I said to my reflection, only prolonging the inevitable.

The wind rattled the windows as I headed back downstairs, passing Markus's room as I returned to the kitchen. There was pressure in the air and a musty smell. The rain was coming.

"Trudi?" I called, hitching my bag high on my shoulder.

No answer. Had she left?

"Trudi? Are you there?"

"Lena?" Her voice came from far down the hall. From the surgery.

"What are you doing down there?"

"Lena, would you please come here?" Her voice wobbled on the last word.

"Sure," I said slowly. "Are you looking for something?"

Trudi was curled against the wall, gripping one of the medical saws in her shaking hands. I followed her gaze to the back of the room.

The bag fell from my shoulder.

"My darling, there you are. What *have* you been up to that's kept you so busy?" Ansel stood next to the surgical table, pinning Hugo against his chest in a mockery of an embrace. For one bizarre, chilling moment, I was back in my bedroom, back at our first meeting, as Ansel held an unconscious Hugo, ready to snap his neck.

A fresh wash of despair bore down on me at the memory.

Ansel's usually pristine shirt was skewed, open at the collar, and his cape hung haphazardly across his shoulders. His eyes were bloodshot, the emotion in them something akin to anguish. He looked insane.

"What are you doing here?" I rasped.

He sucked his bottom lip, as though confused by the question. "You left me two nights ago, teary-eyed and distressed, with very little explanation. I tried to give you time"—he sighed—"but I didn't expect you to disappear with it."

"It was necessary, trust me." I considered telling him about René but decided it wasn't the best course of action while he held Hugo's life in his hands. "Ansel? Can you put Hugo down, please?"

"Oh dear, it was necessary? Then I've made a dreadful mistake." Ansel spread his fingers in a bashful flourish as if to say, *silly me*. "You should have said so in your little note. You certainly had the space for it, brief as it was."

"Lena, is he—is he a—" Hugo's voice trembled almost as much as his body.

"Do not speak her name," Ansel said darkly, still looking at me. His grip tightened, and Hugo made a pained sound.

I raised my hands in front of me, palms up. "Please, let go of him."

"Hm? Oh, the *boy*. No. No, I don't think I will."

From behind me came a muffled, "Please." Trudi was crying. "Please let him go."

"Ask me once more, and I'll rip his head off and feed you his entrails."

"*Ansel*," I snapped, hardly believing my ears. But then, I knew he would be upset and let me know in the loudest of ways. I was a fool to think he wouldn't drag anyone else into it.

"Yes, dear?"

"Stop it."

"Stop what?"

"Threatening us." As if it weren't already obvious.

"Us?" he repeated softly. "You would cast your lot in with them? Even when I've come to collect you?"

Just get him out of here, I told myself, *away from them.*

I exhaled, tried to soften my tone. "You know that's not what I meant. And you also know that if you continue threatening my friends, I'll sooner die with them than forgive you for it."

His icy look was calculating. I thought I saw his fingers spasm on Hugo's throat.

"C'mon, Ansel," I murmured, knowing what he wanted to hear. "Let's go home. I have my bag packed, see? I was already coming to see you."

His gaze dipped down to my bag. "You were?"

"Of course I was."

One second passed, then another. They blurred together with bated breath until a minute had come and gone, and only then, reluctantly and achingly slowly, did Ansel loosen his grip. Hugo fell hard to his knees.

Ansel extended his arm to me.

An invitation. An acceptance.

Movement caught the corner of my eye, and I cried, "Hugo, no!"

Hugo leapt for the surgical scissors on the table and scrambled to his feet. With a strength born out of sheer terror, he drove them deep into Ansel's chest, right through his heart.

For one agonising moment, I thought that would be the end of it. The end of our deal, our strange friendship turned stranger romance.

The end of *him*.

A weight came off my chest, but where there would have once been relief, there was nothing. I was a husk. Utterly empty. But then I remembered who Ansel was and that if he hadn't stopped Hugo, it was because he didn't want to. Very slowly, Ansel tilted his chin down, a muscle twitching in his jaw.

Hugo let go of the scissors like they'd burned him.

"Ansel," I breathed. I had an inkling of what was to come.

Ansel inhaled—long-suffering, dramatic—and the scissors moved up and down with his chest, quickening the dark flow of blood beginning to dampen his shirt. A vaguely familiar craving curled within me at the sight, demanding the hot, metallic bitterness I knew to be his blood.

"This," he said, "was my favourite shirt."

Faster than I could possibly follow, Ansel backhanded Hugo across the face, hard enough to send him to the ground. Hard enough that Hugo didn't get up.

Trudi threw the saw down, running to his prone form and crying out at the gash across his cheekbone. Above them, Ansel sighed and pulled the scissors from his chest, a wet, sucking sound accompanying the action. He dropped them to the ground, the harsh clatter breaking through my shock.

I slid beside Trudi, prying her hands away from Hugo's face as she sobbed his name, telling him to wake up, to be okay. Hugo's pulse hammered strong beneath my fingers, and I thanked the Dawn Lord under my breath for the first time in years.

Ansel made a sound of amusement, bringing his fingers to his face. I think he intended to lick them—his tongue teased along the seam of his lips—but he frowned and sniffed.

His eyes met mine. "You clever, clever girl," he said.

I glared at him, clenching my hands so tight I thought my knuckles would split through the skin.

Ansel held his hand out to me expectantly, the one smeared with Hugo's blood, and I hated how familiar the sight was. How accustomed I had become to his petition.

I wished I could take his hand.

I wished I could take it from his body and smack him with it.

"Shall we?" he asked.

"No," I seethed as my ears started ringing. My gaze flicked to the bloody scissors, and I clenched my teeth, forcing my attention back to Ansel. "Now move. You're in my way."

"Chop-chop. He—oh, I'm sorry, *we* don't have time to waste."

He took half a step back, one arm spread out.

I urged Trudi out of the way, prodding Hugo's skull, temple, and jaw. The skin around his brow was turning red—he would have a nasty black eye—and the blood tracking down his neck was starting to dry. The gash was long but not particularly deep; Ansel's ring had caught him at a bad angle.

"Nothing feels broken, but I can't be sure yet if there's a fracture," I said to Trudi, feeling the seconds tick by. "Get a cloth to wipe the blood. He should be waking up very soon, but if it's been too long, there are some smelling salts in the left cupboard, knee-level."

Trudi shook her head. "How long is too long? Should I move him?"

"No, just make sure to tilt his head back so his airways are clear."

A hand landed on my shoulder. "Time's up, darling," Ansel said.

I shook him off. "You've got eternity in front of you, so you can wait five more minutes for me to finish explaining."

"Oh, I don't mind." He peered down at Trudi, baring his teeth. "But do you—Trudi, was it?—really want us here when your beloved boy awakens? I wouldn't want to upset the poor thing any further."

She looked between the two of us. "Go."

"But—"

"Leave." The anger in her voice cracked through me like a whip. If words could cut, I'd be an open wound.

Nodding, I backed away. The ringing in my head had grown ear-splitting.

Ansel and I were almost to the door when Trudi said, "You know she's sick, don't you?"

It was only Ansel's sudden grip on my arm that kept me from stumbling.

"She shouldn't be straining herself so much," she continued, a raw layer of fury simmering beneath the words. "It's getting worse. She thinks we don't notice, but how could we not when she's coughing up blood between meals at the kitchen table?"

Ansel's shoes scraped as he turned. "I beg your pardon? Lena's not sick, she's sickly. There's a difference."

"Ansel, let's go," I tried, but Trudi spoke over me.

"She is sick, has been for years. Why do you think she lives here at the clinic when she could have a place of her own? Why do you think her father left her?"

"Stop it," I whispered.

"It was because she was too unwell to travel. By the time her father arrived back home to the Holy City, Montgomery Mercantile was bankrupt and he had no money to hire the healers he'd intended or even make the return trip. And her mother died from the same symptoms, so Hugo and I are starting to—" Trudi gasped as Hugo's eyelashes fluttered.

"So Hugo and I are starting to *what*?" Ansel asked, and I shuddered. His voice, full of loathing, promised pain.

"Um," Trudi stuttered, blanching. Unlike me, she had a clear view of his face. "We're worried she won't make the winter."

Trudi couldn't have said anything worse. Ansel was shaking, the tremors wracking through my body from where he clutched my arm. I had the feeling that if ripping out Trudi's tongue could take back her words, she would already be choking on her own blood.

Moving in front of him to block his view of Trudi, I took his face in my hands, kept my gaze from wandering to the blood on his shirt.

Ansel's eyes were pure black.

Miraculously, my touch seemed to inject some rationality into him. He caught me by the waist, whisking me outside into the rain. The door slammed shut behind us. I think the wood may have even cracked.

"Ansel," I said as he strode us past the herb garden and into the forest. The fat raindrops sank into my skin. "Ansel, stop." I struggled against his hold, trying to keep up, but it was like he hadn't heard me.

I stomped my heel down on his cape.

Vindication surged through me as his head snapped back. With a snarl, he ripped the clasp clean off.

"I'm cold and sore," I snapped, "and you're walking too fast."

He wrenched the cape from his shoulders in answer, wrapping it around me with pointed, jerky movements. I threw it to the ground and matched his glare. The gauntness of his face, the bruises beneath his eyes, made me wonder what exactly had transpired in the previous days for him. How my absence could have wrecked him so thoroughly.

Ansel lifted the cape from the ground and pulled it even tighter around me, forcing my hands down when I tried to remove it. His fingers were colder than the rain.

"It's too heavy," I said.

"You are cold." His voice was flinty. "And acting like a child."

"Maybe you shouldn't have acted like one first."

He took me by the shoulders. "And you should have told me *you are dying*."

"This isn't about you! Those people are my friends, Ansel. I might have expected you to act like that once, but not anymore."

His fangs flashed. "They would feed you to the wolves if it benefitted them. Do you know what they were speaking of when I arrived? How the boy referred to you? He is lucky I did not rip his spine from his body."

He almost got me. I almost asked.

Instead, I said, "Don't speak about them as if you're any better, because they haven't hurt me half as much as you have."

Ansel flinched. His hair fell over his face in dark swathes, water dripping from the ends. The betrayal on his face was ineffectual. I wasn't the one in the wrong.

He covered his face with a hand, slicking his hair back. "I've upset you."

"Yes."

"Those children mean something to you."

"Obviously." I coughed once, then twice, catching the third time in my elbow.

"You would choose ..." He shook his head. "No. *No.*"

I wiped my mouth, then hugged myself, trying to generate warmth. "No, what?"

He looked to the heavens as if in petition. The trees blackened the sky, turned it into a collage of sickly brown branches. "I would not leave you for a thousand friends."

"Well, that's good," I said acerbically and moved to kick over a dead pile of leaves in frustration. They flew into the air, scattering. My chest tightened painfully, but I managed to say, "Because I may have just set some of them on fire."

He went to speak, certain that whatever was to come out of my mouth wouldn't be *that*, before levelling me with a blank gaze. "You ... Pardon?"

Did I need to be more explicit?

He said, "I don't think I heard you correctly."

"Oh, you did," I muttered, clearing my throat. When that didn't help, I thumped the heel of my hand against my sternum.

He said something then, or maybe he didn't, but I wasn't listening. Shivers wracked through me. My skin was slick with rain, and my mood had plummeted lower than ever.

That, and I'd started coughing. The kind of coughing that had no end in sight, except pain and breathlessness and a possible fainting spell. The kind I had grown to associate with blood.

I shouldn't have been surprised. It had been a long and exhausting day, and now that I was in the cold—shouting, thirsty, and overworked—sickness had crept up on me.

Ansel stiffened at the sound.

He's petrified, I thought, almost amused.

I dropped to my knees, expelling blood and phlegm onto the soil. Mud stuck to my palms as I dug my fingernails into the earth, looking for anything that would ground me.

I couldn't suck in enough air. Everything hurt.

Eventually, I collapsed to my side, uncaring of the dirt in my hair or the twigs jabbing my hip. Pressure had started running up and down my back at some point, gentle but insistent, and I swatted Ansel away with what little strength I had left.

"You go," I said. "I'll just sleep here tonight."

"You will not."

I lied to myself that it was the glow of the moon that turned his eyes glassy.

"Are you able to move?" he whispered, and my answer was a yawn.

Without warning, Ansel pulled me up and brought one arm beneath my knees, the other behind my back. My forehead smacked into his chest as he lifted me. The weight of his cape ached across my shoulders.

"Ansel," I said, not for any real reason. "Ansel, you shouldn't have done that."

He shut his eyes, inhaling deeply at the sound of my voice. "Come," he rasped. "There is still a way to go, and you must rest."

CHAPTER NINETEEN

I didn't fall asleep as Ansel walked us home. In fact, the rocking of his arms made me nauseous, like he was a rickety old boat, and I was the unseasoned sailor that'd bitten off more than she could chew. The rain thundered upon us until his cape was drenched through and the only thing offering me protection was his body bent over mine.

The rain didn't seem to bother him. He was too lost in his thoughts.

It took both forever and no time at all to arrive at the castle. Ansel lit the fireplace in the library against my wishes, depositing me close enough that my hair would smell like smoke for the next few washes.

I shimmied out of my dress and laid it out on the hearth. My shift wasn't in much better shape, the damp fabric itchy against my skin.

Ansel watched, a furrow between his brows. He said, "I will get something to warm you."

It was only then, in his absence, that I noticed the state of the room. Furniture had been overturned, and glass shards were littered across the desk. Crinkled sheets of parchment were scattered across the floor.

His drawings.

I sighed, bending down to gather them.

That was how Ansel found me minutes later: staring blankly at my likeness. He paused in the doorway, holding a blanket, before striding forward and pulling the parchment from my limp hands.

"Stand up, please," he said. I did so, and he wrapped the blanket around me, tucking one corner into another. "What else should I get you?"

A stake? I almost said but bit it back. Hugo was right in saying I'd become meaner. The crackling fire spat its laughter at us when I didn't answer.

After a tense moment, he reached out and whispered, "You should rest."

I slapped his hand away, and he blinked at the sudden rejection. "Really?" I asked. "You think so?"

"Yes." The word was subdued. "Sit."

"I am not a dog."

"Of course you're not."

"Then why do I feel like I've just been punished by my master?"

"You are not a dog," he said. "And you have no master."

I smirked, an ugly expression, and shook my head. "You came to the clinic. You came to *collect* me."

He moved closer, close enough to blend his shadow with mine. “I was upset.”

“Why?”

“Because you—”

“You’re blaming me?”

His fingers jerked like he wanted to touch me. “No.”

“Then why were you upset?”

A heavy pause. “Why don’t you tell me?”

“That’s not how this works.”

“Then tell me how, and I will fix it.” His throat bobbed. His skin looked warm and inviting, bathed in the fire’s glow.

He would fix it? Hugo’s bones weren’t tile pieces he could glue together. Trudi’s tears weren’t his to conjure, and my body wasn’t a canvas to paint with his blood.

I had wanted him to be upset. But I hadn't wanted *this*.

“There is no easy fix, Ansel, not for any of it.”

“But there is. All our troubles gone, there is a way.”

The blanket was suddenly suffocating. I shrugged it off, ignoring Ansel’s protests, and let the air prick my skin. “I have feelings, you know. It’s more complicated than you just snapping your fingers.”

He was agitated, moving his hands to his hips, then up to his forehead. I took another step back, coming level with the rocking chair.

Ansel said, “I was not jesting when I said vampirism cures any ailment. I could turn you now and we would be gone by morning.”

I pressed my fingers against my eyelids. "No. Not right now."

"Not right—" he spluttered. "I'm not offering you a farm contract, girl, I am offering eternity. If not now, then when, on your deathbed?"

"Ansel, I know what I'm doing," I started, but he spoke over me.

"Do you expect me to watch you waste away and not do all in my power to prevent it? Are you so cruel as to ask me to enjoy what little time I have left with you, instead of doing all I can to prolong it?"

"You're not listening."

"And yet you would choose to live a half-life, seeped in infirmity and death, all for what? Those villagers?"

"Ansel—"

"Do you think I have lived for centuries, fought against the flow of time, ruined myself over and over, just to watch you pass on without me?"

"*Listen to me*," I shouted. "Do you think I'm not angry? That I'm content with the cards I've been dealt in life? If I wasn't here, if I wasn't *sick*, then none of this would have happened, but it *has* happened, and it can't just be fixed. I can't just wish away death.

"But how do I tell them, Ansel? How do I tell my friends I lie to them for you, or explain to the patients whose blood I take that bloodletting is useless and I only do it for the sake of a vampire—the very same vampire whose existence has made it impossible to seek the healing I've longed for.

"And then," I continued, the words a fever I needed to flush out of me, "you had to go and do *that.* You fed me your blood, you threatened my friends, and you can't just do that whenever you need something to go your way. That may have worked for you once, but not anymore."

Ansel reached for me, desperate, but I stumbled away, my back hitting the wall. His outstretched hand, gripping the empty air, was like a door slamming shut between us. He turned to the fire, leaning against the mantelpiece as if I'd landed a fatal blow.

Voice strained, he asked, "What were you speaking of in the forest? About my friends?"

I sat down, feeling like I'd float away if I stood any longer. The outburst had been a cathartic and welcome relief. It gave me the clarity to go on.

So, I told Ansel my story, starting from when I met René at the well, then about the letter, until I'd divulged every nasty detail about Haycock I could stomach verbalising. Ansel listened attentively at first, still as stone, but as I spoke of the inn and what René had said, he grasped an iron poker from beside the fireplace.

"Ansel?" I said. "What are you doing?"

The poker bent in his grip. The base turned to powder beneath his hands. "René," he muttered, staring at the dust on his palms. His fangs grew longer, sharper.

"What is happening?" I asked, pushing back against the wall.

"No, no, no," he chanted and twisted the poker into an unrecognisable shape. "She's fine. Can't do that here, not now. She's fine."

I nodded. "Yes. But you're not."

He looked at me. Something fierce and visceral flashed across his face before he fell to his knees and dove his hand into the crackling fire.

It took me several stunned seconds to react. By the time his laboured breathing reached my ears, I was throwing myself against him, trying to pull him free from the flames. He came easily, melding to my side as though the heat had seared away his resolve.

"What possessed you—why did you—" I made a distressed sound in the back of my throat. "Are you all right?"

His shirt had set alight and was curling up his arm. I covered it with the blanket, spreading ash across his blistered skin.

"Quite all right." The gritted words didn't convince me. "Forgive me. I needed a distraction from the bloodlust, and pain was the quickest solution." His skin was already healing, angry blisters smoothing.

It didn't matter that he was healing. Pain still marred his features, the skin pulling tense around his brows.

"I did not mean to make it about me," he said, clutching my arm. "That was not my intention, only ..." He swallowed.

"Only what?" I asked, brushing his hair behind his ear so I could see him properly.

That single touch undid him. Unravelled any thread of control he possessed.

He broke.

Scattered into fragments at my feet and begged me to put him back together as he buried his face in my neck, wrapped his arms around my waist. Trembling, he held me like I was a deity to bring salvation.

He was the devil come to worship.

I slid my fingers to the base of his scalp and tugged gently. He obliged, craning his neck back. His eyes were red-rimmed.

"Oh, Ansel." I sighed, letting my anger melt away. "What a pair we make."

"I love you," he said, frantic. "I did not know I was capable of it, but I am. For you, I am."

I had once thought him devoid of any warmth. The presence that prowled beneath his skin, the one he had granted a hairsbreadth of freedom at the clinic tonight, was a bleak and frigid existence. It was like an emptiness that couldn't be filled, and he subsequently welcomed whatever darkness desired to take up residence there. Not even René, evil as his actions had been, held the same type of hollowness I'd sensed in Ansel.

Now, though, something was different.

The demon was still present. I could see it, simmering in the depths of his eyes, waiting for the opportune moment to rip free from its leash. And I knew Ansel enjoyed letting it happen. Would loosen the leash on purpose.

But a change had been wrought.

I was holding the leash. And the way he stared at me, shattered, beseeching, left no doubt he wanted me to tighten it. Until I was strangling him if that was what I wished. He'd always said as much, hadn't he? Not in so many words, perhaps, but in the way he strove to please, his unrestrained enthusiasm.

He must have taken my silence for reprimand because he was apologising profusely, almost gagging on the words. He was sorry, he said, sorry for the danger he'd brought, sorry for driving me to such despair, sorry for not understanding. And it wasn't that he hadn't tried to understand, I recognised now. It was that he hadn't known how.

The door that had slammed shut between us opened just a crack. Enough for me to see him on the other side.

Four hundred years was a long time to dismiss the merits of humans. I'd had to spell it out for him, place each letter down slowly, one by one, as he tried to relearn the meaning of mortality.

It was miraculous he'd made it as far as he had.

I groaned, knowing I'd have to forgive him eventually.

I never should have woken him. I was still glad that I had.

"Lena," he prompted.

"Yes?" I said quickly, coming back to myself. Ansel straightened and cocked his head. He was wearing silver earrings, and the dim light twisted shapes across their pale surface, like dancers in the night. I could have gotten a gold coin for them at the market. "I like your earrings," I said. "Are they new?"

He looked truly worried now. "Lena?"

"Yes?" And then I realised what he was waiting for. "Oh! Yes, I love you, too." Even if I shouldn't.

His mouth popped open, eyes going wide in disbelief.

What a strange reaction. Had I been wrong?

His tears were long gone, apologies forgotten, when he said, "'Oh, I love you, too'—is that it? Where is the passion, darling? Do you know how long I've waited for this? Quickly, say it again."

"I love you."

"Louder."

"*I love you,*" I yelled, baffled.

There was relief on his face and a poorly disguised upward slant to his lips. "That was adequate. I intend to have you singing it from the battlements by tomorrow."

"I've never been very good at singing."

"Your audience will not complain."

I cracked a tired smile.

His fingertips were soft as they dragged down my cheek. "I am sorry. I did not understand. I probably still don't. But I shall relish trying."

I shrugged, pulling the blanket from where it had fallen behind him on the floor and curling into it. "Me too."

Ansel watched me quizzically before chuckling. "Will you give me your attention for just a little longer before you make a nest for yourself on the floor?"

"Mm. I'm listening," I said, lying down to rest my temple against the cool stone. My cheek itched, and when I went to scratch it, bits of dried dirt fell away. I was filthy.

Ansel smoothed his hand across my shoulder blades, saying, "I know you are tired, my darling, but it is important."

I turned so I was on my back. Looking at him, I raised my eyebrows.

His voice, when he finally spoke, was quiet. "You won't take my blood, and you won't become a vampire. What, then, do you suggest?"

I mulled over the question, fiddling with the little bow on the front of my shift. "I've been planning a trip for a while now. To the Holy City."

"The Holy City? Ah, but of course. Divine healings, professed blessings on the sick."

"And," I cut in before he could get too far ahead, "the best healers in the continent."

He pursed his lips. "That trip would cost at least forty gold coins. More, if you wanted to travel in any type of luxury. If you were to add healing services on to that ..." There was a calculating look in his eyes. "That was what you were doing in my crypt, pilfering things of value. You needed the money for this trip."

I nodded, throwing my arms above my head and stretching. "The traders stayed quiet about it, and I gave them a good deal."

"And I took all access away from you." He rearranged the blanket, pulling it up to my chin.

"You woke up, killed a man, attacked me, and then to top it all off, took my hard-earned stolen goods."

He winced.

I sighed. "The irony is, I'd be living there if I'd gone with my father when I was younger. I may have been unwell, but I really insisted on staying for my mother. And it's not like her corpse ever needed me here."

If Ansel had an opinion on that subject, he did not voice it. Instead, he leaned over me to stoke the fire, adding another piece of wood. As he pulled back, I grabbed hold of his hand.

He paused, and I smiled up at him, distantly aware of the fact that overtiredness was making me act like a happy drunk.

Ansel's features softened. He cupped my neck, saying, "It would be painless. A shallow bite and a few mouthfuls of blood. You wouldn't even feel it when I snapped your neck."

My eyes slipped shut. "Are you trying to scare me?"

"You should be scared. Death is no respecter of persons. But I would make even Death fear to touch you if you'd let me." His fingers tightened, and I wondered if there would be a bruise there in the morning. "Think, Lena. I would be your maker, your beloved, your saviour. You would live forever. All you would have to do is stay with me, and I would be yours to command."

"An eternity is a long time to be chained to someone," I said.

"And yet, with you, it would not be enough."

I hummed, thinking. He was always so dramatic, but for the first time, I acknowledged it may have been the lens of my mortality colouring him as such.

My eyes fluttered open at the thought and stuck on the bloodstained hole in Ansel's shirt. A small burst of energy hit me. Like an addict, I was twitchy, craving something I now knew the name of.

I said, "Don't ever threaten my friends again."

Ansel watched me swallow, following my gaze to his chest. With a playful smirk, he pulled the shirt over his head, and I resisted the urge to roll my eyes.

"I won't. But speaking of which," he said, throwing the material in the fire and making himself comfortable next to me. I knew what was coming. His comment in the clinic—*you clever, clever girl*—had been ringing in my ears ever since. "Have you been canoodling with my mortal enemy again?"

I twisted my mouth to the side. "Maybe. I do love a good canoodle."

I had thought using garlic to protect the villagers was an exercise in futility; asking Trudi to gather all the garlic she could find had been more for her peace of mind than mine.

I moved Ansel's arm to cushion my head, then explained, "It was a simple plan. Trudi infused water with all the garlic she could find and then put that water in the wells. Likewise, where it was harmless, I put remnants in the medicines I made, in the tonics and poultices. I would have shovelled myself full of the stuff if not for obvious reasons."

Ansel had once made a comment about the effect of garlic in a person's bloodstream, and I was counting on the fact it hadn't just been a glib piece of nonsense he'd bandied about to throw me off the scent.

He said, "Luckily for me. I wouldn't have had a chance of smelling it with all the foreign blood in your system."

I shot him a surly look. "René did make a point of mentioning how pungent your blood is."

Ansel laughed. "And he's dead now, is he not? Anyway, the scent of garlic was so subtle in your friend I would have burnt a layer off my tongue before I even realised."

"How did you know, then?"

"I saw the anticipation on your face. Such endearing curiosity while your friend lay bleeding by your side." The words were fond but made me wince all the same.

"So, about René," I said, and Ansel raised his arm with enough force that I was flung onto my side, splayed over him. He pressed an exaggerated kiss to my forehead, and I grumbled into his chest that he should be careful. I almost regretted omitting René's degree of violence towards me.

"A tale for a different night, my darling. Pick a different bedtime story."

I glared at him, and he winked.

I was glad to see he'd recovered his usual good mood.

Squirming to get more comfortable—I may have brought my elbow down on his stomach a little harder than necessary—I said, "Go ahead, *darling*. You're obviously busting to tell me something."

I felt him nod. "Just that your priest came by to trespass the day after the festival with two hunters. They were inept. Didn't make it past the front gates, which I thought was less effort than I deserved."

Another piece added to the puzzle. They were all connecting, a clear picture forming.

"Did these hunters look like brothers? Unkempt and—you dumped that stall owner by them at the festival, remember?"

"Oh, yes! That's them, exactly. You're well acquainted?"

"No, although they have given me a bit of trouble in the past."

Ansel's voice, somewhat exasperated, thrummed through me. "I do wish you'd tell me these things."

I snorted and slid my fingers across his bare skin, smiling when he shuddered beneath me. "We don't need any more dead bodies around here."

"Very well," he said.

We spoke for another hour, about him, about me, about our plans, and decided to leave for the Holy City the following night. I dozed after that to the sound of his sporadic heartbeat, dreaming of a simple life where each new day was full of joy and possibilities. In the quiet, early hours of the morning, when the sun had yet to rise, Ansel offered me the blood-filled pendant again, a solemn question in his eyes.

This time, I took it.

CHAPTER TWENTY

When I wandered into Myrtle Gully late the following afternoon to check on Hugo, apologise, and say goodbye, I was expecting a fight. Whether it was with Trudi over my leaving or Hugo over my audacity, I knew conflict was inevitable.

What I wasn't expecting was a mob.

There was a crowd gathered in the village square, outside the church. Their faces were pinched, their voices low.

I slowed to a stop, the gravel crunching beneath my boots.

"She's here!" someone called, and the words cleaved through the crowd like a fissure wracking the earth.

Father Pentaghast made his way through the villagers. His black tunic was wrinkled, his face unshaven. I scanned the square for any sign of Trudi or Hugo but came up empty.

"Miss Lena," Father Pentaghast said when he reached me.

"I didn't know the village had an event planned," I said, trying to smile. I glanced around the familiar, wary faces and spotted Ernst towards the middle. His expression was murderous. "I'll have to hurry past, I'm afraid. Work has been very busy of late."

"Would that I could let you." The words were quiet, for my ears only. "Something has happened."

"What is it?"

"There was another attack last night."

That drew me up short. Hugo had told them. But then I realised, why wouldn't he? I was delusional to presume he would do otherwise. "An attack. You mean like ..." Silence fell. Not one shuffle from the villagers. Not a single noise. "Who?" I asked.

"Angela."

I felt the blood drain from my face. That didn't make any sense.

"Is she—" I couldn't say the word.

"She's alive. Your friends are treating her as we speak." Father Pentaghast fiddled with the beads around his wrist, the cross at their base swinging back and forth.

I looked back out to the crowd and blinked.

Everyone wore a symbol of the Dawn Lord. Battered family heirlooms, splintered crosses or plain pieces of wood nailed together. Ice clunked in my belly.

They knew.

Play your part, Lena, Ansel's voice whispered in my head. *Be the witless heroine.*

I swallowed. "What happened?"

"We were hoping you could tell us."

Peter emerged from the crowd, looking no better than when he'd passed out the previous night. He dropped his rucksack to the ground, where it landed with a metallic crunch.

"Got it," he said to no one in particular. Before I could react, he took hold of my shoulder and pushed me to my knees.

"That is not necessary," Father Pentaghast began, but someone in the crowd roared their approval. There was a smattering of applause. "Savages," he muttered.

Pain sang through my legs, but I was too disorientated to really feel it. Did the villagers demand this public show? I saw the evidence in front of me, but I couldn't bring myself to believe it.

"A sickly-looking woman came to the village early this morning," Father Pentaghast explained, squatting by my side as if the villagers hadn't started shouting abuse and Peter's thumbs weren't digging painfully into my back. "From what I've gathered, Angela was up early doing her morning chores and tried to talk to the stranger. Fortunately, I was close by when the woman attacked."

Peter interjected, "The thing screamed your name as its head came off."

Not Ansel, but others? I tried not to panic, but I knew what this meant. René's vampires were coming. One had already been, sent ahead to induce terror and punish me. They hadn't all burned like they were meant to. I'd been sloppy, drunk on a victory.

"Peter." Father Pentaghast's voice was flinty. "Do not speak out of turn."

Peter pushed down on my shoulders, as if it were my fault he was being reprimanded.

"I would not have allowed the horde to gather for only that," Father Pentaghast continued, close to my ear, "but if you look behind me and to the right, I think you'll understand why I had such little control over the matter."

Some detached part of my being, the part that had always suspected it would come to this, registered the two boys I'd stopped in Haycock for directions. Behind them were three other young men. My gaze lingered on the frog-eyed one.

I didn't realise I was swaying until Father Pentaghast pulled Peter away and steadied me. He explained, "They arrived not long after the incident this morning. They had a great deal to tell me about you. Unfortunately, the rest of the village happened to hear as well."

"Speak up!" someone in the crowd shouted.

Father Pentaghast ignored it. "They spoke of a black-haired devil, bathing in moonlight and lusting for their blood. Apparently, a human girl was with him."

My mind conjured the image of Ansel waiting for me at the castle, arrayed in all the glory of the night. It was an apt description.

Father Pentaghast must have seen the thought cross my face because his expression fell. Shaking his head, he asked, "What did that creature offer you that we could not?"

"A little bit of happiness," I whispered, echoing his words from our conversation in the graveyard.

For a moment, he looked chagrined. "That's not quite what I meant."

"I know."

"Then I am truly sorry for what is about to happen."

What? I wanted to ask. *What's going to happen?*

"Empty it," he said, standing.

A salacious smile crossed Peter's face as he tipped his rucksack upside down. Hundreds of coins, copper, silver, and gold clunked at his feet. A linen sack was the last thing to fall out.

My linen sack, from beneath my bed.

"Bribes she took from the devil spawn," Peter called, taking the Father's order as permission to speak. "Blood money. Whoring money."

"*No*," I shouted. "I've saved that money for years. I've earnt it."

"Earnt this much? On healing wages? Do you take us for fools?" Peter kicked the pile, and the coins scattered, rolling at the villagers' feet.

"Stop," I said as the first villager, Old Man Kenny of all people, picked up a silver coin. Smirking, he slipped it into his pocket.

The money I'd saved so I could be healed. He smirked as he stole it.

"I didn't get it from the vampires," I said, but it came out weak. "I'm not with them, I swear."

I looked to Father Pentaghast for help, but he turned away. It hurt far more than it should have.

"Lies," Peter said, and the villagers muttered back and forth.

I stumbled to my feet. "Your brother would have lost his leg if not for me."

"It never would have happened if not for you," he spat back.

"I had nothing to do with it!"

"Enough," Father Pentaghast cut in. "We have no proof of that. What we do have is a witness. Marie, come and tell us what you saw that day in the inn."

Marie stepped out from the crowd, clutching little Elain with trembling hands. Her eldest daughter was at the clinic, suffering from a vampire attack, and yet whatever she had to say was important enough for her to be here.

Tremulously, she said, "This man and his brother stay at my inn. One day, after the Festival of Providence, she"—Marie jerked her chin towards me—"came for some supplies. I left the three of them alone downstairs to gather the order, and in the next minute, I hear screaming. I run back, and she's waving a tankard at them, saying they threatened her. She must have known who they were then and wanted them to leave town."

"Marie, no," I whispered. "It wasn't like that."

"Angela was paired with her when Father Snow disappeared, and my girl came home long before he was found. How, then, did this—this *liar* find the Father when she was meant to have left? She probably did it."

The villagers argued amongst themselves, a great wave of anger that was about to crest over my head and sweep me away. I itched to scream but curbed my temper. Raving like a madwoman would only prove their case.

"Thank you, Marie," Father Pentaghast said. "Angela will be well cared for, I promise you."

The crowd stared at me like I was a heathen, a traitor.

Like I was less than human.

"Whore," a man shouted.

"Lock her up."

"Bathe her in holy water."

"Burn her."

My head snapped up. Surely, they wouldn't.

Father Pentaghast raised his arm. "Quiet," he called, and if I hadn't seen it, I wouldn't have believed the way everyone shrivelled beneath his glower. "We will have no talk of that here. This is not an execution."

"Not yet," Peter said, sidling up to me. "Shall we see what's under that skirt of yours?"

At first, I thought he was being crude. His gaze wandered to my waist, following the lines of my hips and thighs. Anticipation distorted his features as he stopped at my calf. Ansel's teeth marks throbbed as if in indignation.

It dawned on me then.

There was no point in fighting anymore. I could scream myself hoarse and these people wouldn't listen. No amount of pleading or common sense could dispute the fact that I had vampire bites on my leg. Hugo must have figured it out and told them. That, more than anything, broke my heart.

"No," I said, feeling the fight leave me. Numbness filled my limbs like lead.

I gazed across the village, at the familiar buildings and trees, the gravel road that stretched on, seeing them bloodstained and abandoned. Myrtle Gully would become a burial ground.

I didn't know how the vampires managed to escape the burning inn in broad daylight, but it didn't matter. It was too late. My guilt wouldn't save the villagers, but it would at least give them a chance to prepare.

I said, "You can't win. When they come—because they *will* come—everyone will die. You have to leave now, all of you."

The warning fell on deaf ears, the villagers' cries more frenzied than scared. I turned to the Haycock boys. The frog-eyed boy's expression bordered on regret.

I looked to Father Pentaghast and whispered, "I'm done for, aren't I?"

He didn't answer. He didn't need to.

They locked me in the inn.

Beneath it, to be exact, in a cold, dark cellar where Marie kept her salted meats and wine barrels. Mismatched crates were stacked at the back of the room, and shelves littered with cheese wheels and old tankards took up the adjacent wall. The villagers' voices bled through from the next room. It sounded like an argument.

The sun was setting earlier as winter approached, and evening fell as I stared out the single grimy window, high above me on ground level. The air was dry, catching in my throat until I'd have to cough. Eventually, when sitting uselessly and expelling what felt like death from my lungs became too much, I started pacing.

Ansel would be wondering where I was, and if he wasn't, then he was occupied with uninvited guests. Ansel was confident in his abilities. René had spoken of him in tones of reverence.

The thought of René made me laugh darkly, for it reminded me where I was and that as unsavoury as the cellar seemed, at least mine wasn't on fire. He and others must have hidden, waited, and climbed out during the night.

I scrubbed at my face, coming to a stop. There was nothing in the cellar I could use to defend myself if the villagers decided they wanted to make an example of me. No axe or hammer, not even a single wine bottle. Just barrels and crates.

And if I continued walking around like this, I would tire myself out, probably trip over something and split my head open—

Barrels and crates.

I stopped, glanced up at the window.

That was a Lena-sized window if ever I saw one. I grabbed a cracked wooden tankard and wedged it beneath my arm.

As quickly as I could, I stacked two crates atop a barrel, climbing up and balancing until I was level with the window. The crates teetered beneath me, and I resisted the urge to look down, knowing a fall from this height would result in a broken limb.

On the other side of the dirt-speckled window were the stables. A few yards beyond that, the forest.

I smashed the tankard against the window. The impact reverberated up my arm to rattle my teeth. A crack webbed through the glass. I hit it again, and the crates trembled beneath me.

The window shattered on the third hit.

A quick wipe across the frame with the tankard to dispose of the shards, and then I was pushing myself through, hoping desperately that no one had heard the window break. I had just gotten to my feet when the footsteps sounded.

"Lena?" Trudi was at the corner of the inn, looking gobsmacked. She clapped a hand over her mouth. We waited for the shouts of villagers on the alert.

They never came.

I skirted the wall and wrapped my arms around her. "Trudi," I rasped, "what are you doing? You should be long gone."

She held me tightly. "Those Haycock boys said something and—well, it sounds like the villagers are going to storm the castle tonight. Oh, and we came to rescue you! I should have known you wouldn't need us though. Hugo said as much, and I should have believed him. He's distracting the men who are meant to be on guard."

"They are?" I asked. "He is?"

Trudi untangled my arms to reach into a bag, pulling out the knife from Markus and a vial of my herbal infusion. "It took some cajoling, but Hugo seems okay. I told him I wouldn't marry him if he did anything stupid."

"You *what?*"

"Shh." She passed me the items. "These should be helpful, right?"

I held the knife and vial close to my chest. They were imbued with a lingering warmth.

"Thank you," I said. "How is Angela?"

"Better than you're going to be if they catch you. Stop standing there and run!"

This could be the last time I ever saw her.

"I love you," I said, pulling my mother's necklace from my pocket. I'd intended to give it to Trudi as a keepsake for when I had left. "Be safe and lock yourself inside. They can't enter without an invitation."

"I love you, too. And don't be silly"—she settled the cord around my neck—"you'll need this far more than I."

I opened my mouth to refuse, but a shout came from the inn. Through the shattered window, I heard the cellar door bang open.

Trudi paled. "Go."

"I'll be back in the morning," I said, memorising one last glimpse of her.

We both knew I was lying.

CHAPTER TWENTY-ONE

The castle was lit from within, a beacon for miles.

Running through the forest had been taxing on my failing body, the terrain slick and unforgiving beneath the curtain of night. I'd glanced over my shoulder constantly, ensuring no one was following. As I made it safely to the servants' quarters, I admitted it was no longer the villagers I should have feared.

There was still a handful of rice left in the larder—I cursed at the small amount, wishing I had saved it all—and I scattered the grains across the stairs that led to the great hall. It would buy me some time, at least, if I needed an escape route.

Conversation floated down from the great hall, and I paused, reminding myself why I was plunging headfirst into danger.

The villagers deciding to storm the castle was a death wish spurred by ignorance. It meant I had a time limit. In this situation, where life and death hung on the line with a precarious balance, my presence alone wouldn't make much of a difference. Except, when the villagers came, perhaps I could stop Ansel from slaughtering them all. He may have made some very pretty promises and declarations last night, but I knew that if a villager shoved a pitchfork in his face, there would be blood.

And if René and his group were still alive when the villagers arrived ...

It didn't bear thinking about.

"Why are you still standing there, little pig?" René's voice was sweet, like summer fruit on the verge of decay. "We're all waiting for you to join us."

I inhaled deeply, taking the stairs one by one to the beat of my heart.

René was the first vampire I saw.

He stood opposite me, his back to the wall. His green coat was ragged, burnt through in some places, hanging on by a thread in others. A gleaming smile distorted his features. That smile stayed in place as he raised an arm to shield himself from my necklace.

In the centre of the curving staircase was Ansel. At his feet, grasping at his clothes, his hands, were a dozen vampires.

I had only caught a glimpse of them in the darkness at Haycock, but here in the candlelight, they were made all the more grotesque with their milky eyes and bony frames. Their lips were drawn back from their gums like their teeth had outgrown their mouths. Each tooth was stained black between the crevices.

Sickly-looking, Father Pentaghast had described. That was an understatement.

They were muttering garbled praise, bowing their heads. One of them licked the ground beside Ansel's shoes.

"Lena," Ansel said in greeting. His face was marble. He didn't even flinch at the holy symbol. "As I understand it, no introductions are necessary."

René laughed. The back of his arm was blistering, yellow pustules beginning to form. "There is no need to act, brother. You can be happy to see both of us. I am not so petty as to deny you that."

Ansel rubbed his forehead as if to stave off a headache before batting away a vampire that strayed too close to his chest.

Meanwhile, I felt like I had walked onstage to a play I had never rehearsed. There was history between these two, emotions to be expertly acted out, and I wanted nothing to do with it.

"Do not speak, René," Ansel said. "Your voice still rankles after all these years. And you"—Ansel looked down his nose at the vampires—"let go."

As though they were one consciousness split across many, the vampires snatched their hands away.

René made a sound of annoyance. "Do not worry, children. Dietrich has never been one for showing kindness —"

"Did you know, Lena," Ansel said over René as he descended the stairs, "that this here is what vampires look like when they're neglected by their sire? This is how they turn out when their creator is selfish and inept and fails to provide good blood for them in their infancy. Such a waste of potential." Ansel's gaze met mine, and he tilted his chin imperceptibly towards René.

Judging by how he'd been trying to rile the other vampire, I decided he intended for me to follow suit.

Dryly, I said, "They're certainly not the glorious creations he made them out to be."

René growled through his teeth, and I was intensely grateful for Trudi's common sense in making me bring the necklace.

Ansel's smile was small, teasing, and absolutely terrifying. "How many of your children have I freed from their miserable existence now, René? Including those you've sent here in recent weeks—and of course those from a century ago, I could never forget them—the count must be climbing very high."

"Recent weeks?" I asked. René had mentioned something similar at Haycock.

"Oh, yes, darling, I forgot to tell you. They came here, I killed them, and they're finally being put to good use fertilising the garden. Did you know that ash prevents common diseases in plants? I read it in a book once."

René's shoulders were heaving. He made to stalk towards Ansel, but Ansel tilted his head, smile widening, and René froze. The other vampires crept down behind Ansel as if hoping he wouldn't notice them lapping at his boots.

Ansel said, "They had their other uses, though, for which I thank you. Perfect bait to lead the vampire hunters off my scent and away from the castle. They'd run into each other sometimes and, well"—he laughed—"your abominations made the most delightful squeals. They didn't know what was happening until it was too late."

René said stiffly, "You confess your sins so easily in front of your pet. Shall I tell her every other depraved and atrocious act you have ever committed?"

Ansel gave an elegant half shrug. "If you must. But at least wait to do so until after I am finished."

"What do you mean?"

"I mean that as easily as you sacrifice these pitiful creatures, I know they are all you have left."

I moved closer to René, unwilling to be at any more of a disadvantage than I already was. The vampires hissed at me, crouching behind Ansel's cape. Ansel himself had an unnaturally red sheen to his skin. He was good at pretending it didn't burn.

René's gaze scoured his children from across the room. "They mean nothing to me."

"Do not lie to me, *little brother*. They mean everything to you. But they're not them. You can dress them up, call them their names and pretend all you like, but they'll never be them." Ansel sighed and addressed a vampire at the edge of the group. "You. Kneel."

The malformed being scrambled to its knees, fisting its moth-chewed surcoat in anticipation.

Why is it doing what you say? I wanted to ask. *Why are they treating you like their ruler?*

René had said they'd all felt when Ansel awoke; like their souls were ripped from them again. I had severely underestimated how highly Ansel was regarded within the vampire hierarchy. The behaviour of these vampires was more veneration than simple respect.

"Stop," René said suddenly. Fear streaked across his face.

Ansel rolled his sleeve up to his elbow. "You have brought this on yourself, René. What did you think would happen when you came here? Did you think I would welcome you? Did you think I would thank you, as if you had been missed?" He flexed his hand. "Come, now. You know me too well for that."

"Dietrich, not in front of me. Not again." It was a plea.

Ansel rubbed his thumb across the kneeling vampire's brow and glanced at me. "You should never have touched her, René. You should never have thought yourself worthy to lay eyes on her."

"Dietrich," René rasped.

"Ansel, if you could hurry this up, I would really appreciate that," I said, not entirely sure of what was transpiring but feeling the time slip through my fingers. "We're going to have more company soon."

Ansel nodded. "Of course, darling." He leaned down to kiss the vampire's forehead, and the creature's eyes fluttered shut. "I am sorry he did not care for you better, young one."

Ansel plunged his hand into the vampire's chest and ripped out its heart.

I covered my mouth, swallowing a yelp as the vampire convulsed, veins bulging like tapeworms. Blood exuded from its mouth and nose. Ansel dropped its heart to the floor. The vampire collapsed, and coarse, black ash scattered across the room, some of it landing in the openings of my shoes. I could feel it there, itching.

I stood there, staring at nothing. The sight of Ansel's hand through its chest was branded behind my eyelids.

The other vampires, still circled around Ansel, nattered to themselves. They pointed to the ash curiously, as if it were a specimen on display. One of them reached out to touch it, rubbing the grains between its fingers.

Ansel said, "I understand, René, my dear, that you want acknowledgement. Approval. So, why don't you cease acting like a petulant child, take responsibility for your actions, and do something that would *really* impress me." He seemed more concerned with checking his sleeve for damage than with the conversation.

The Ansel before me was all charm and control, cruel and regal. I didn't know this Ansel. I didn't want to know him. He was too distracting, too much, and I was reeling from shock.

I was wholly unprepared when René lunged at me.

He grabbed me from behind, one hand encircling my throat. The smell of burning flesh permeated the air.

"Cover it," he grated.

I struggled, trying to loosen his grip so I could breathe, but the more I fought, the tighter he clenched.

"Cover it *now*."

I managed to shove the cross beneath my collar, feeling it settle next to the other pendant I hid there. The tension melted out of René, and I breathed in painfully.

"René." Ansel's voice was guttural, wrenched up from the depths of his throat. It raised the hair on my arms. The vampires shuddered and averted their eyes.

At my back, René started shaking.

Why did you taunt him, you arrogant man? I wanted to screech at Ansel. *What did you think he was going to do, give up?*

Ansel stepped over the mound of ash, savagery lining his features. His teeth were clenched, and a pinprick of white shone in his pupils, a feral kind of maliciousness that belied the part within him that would always revel in bloodshed.

"René," he said again. An order.

René dug his nails into my collarbone. "Why were we never enough for you?" he asked, breath hitching. A tear dripped onto my shoulder. "We've been waiting for you to return, all of us. Why do you take pleasure in hurting what's mine? How can we mean so little to you, and yet you willingly dirty yourself with this withering blood sack?"

Ansel's gaze darkened, and I felt mine do the same. I hadn't come to be a burden or a bargaining chip.

And although I knew it was a possibility, I didn't come to die, either.

We were at an impasse. Whether Ansel or René moved first, the ending wouldn't change. It would be a slaughter, starting with mine.

This great hall with its chandelier and towering staircase was the perfect setting for a finale. The vampires were the nameless cast. And while neither would believe it of themselves, both René and Ansel were the villains.

I needed to take responsibility for what I had awoken the night of the festival. For being the bringer of fear and suspicion. The climax was coming. The curtain was about to close.

It was time for me to take centre stage.

René's words trailed off as I reached into my pocket and pulled out the knife from Markus.

I teased the tip with my finger. It would be sharp enough.

"Lena?" Ansel said slowly. "What are you doing?"

René's fingers tapped impatiently against my throat. "Hoping to kill yourself before I can?"

"Something like that," I muttered. Before I could talk myself out of it, I dug the knife into the soft part of my forearm. Blood welled and stuck to the blade, running down the handle to stain my hand red. I hissed through my teeth.

As Ansel took a measured step towards us, René spun me to face him.

"You," he said, licking his lips. His gaze was riveted on the blood. "You think you can tempt me with this? With flowing blood that smells of Dietrich and whatever foul sickness you carry?"

"Not quite," I said, grasping his coat with my injured arm.

He knew what I was planning before I'd even raised my elbow. I saw it light across his face, disbelieving. It didn't matter, though. If anything, it worked to my advantage.

After all, anyone familiar with the legends knew an ordinary knife couldn't harm a vampire.

René opened his mouth impossibly wide, saliva dripping down his chin as he bent over me.

Then he sunk his teeth into my neck.

Agony tore through me.

At the first taste of my blood, he choked and spasmed. Everything happened almost too fast for me to react.

Almost.

My face pushing into René's hair, my limbs shuddering in desperation, I drove the bloodied knife into his heart. Heard the splitting of his skin, felt the crunch of his bones.

'*It didn't touch my heart.*' Ansel's words from long ago rang in my head, their meaning the judge of my fate. *'I wouldn't have had a chance of smelling it with all the foreign blood in your system.'*

The infusion Trudi gave me had been full of garlic, and I'd downed the entire vial on the way to the castle. I only hoped it was enough to make a difference.

I heard the rip of my own skin when René tore his fangs out to clutch at the knife in his chest.

"You," he started, but it was garbled. His body spasmed like he was combusting from the inside out.

Then Ansel was between us, fingers crushing René's throat. With an effortless twist of the hand, Ansel ripped René's head from his body.

Ash spilt to the floor, some of it floating through the air.

A deafening silence enveloped the room.

It had worked. Easily, fluidly, miraculously, it had worked, and both Ansel and I were alive. Except—the blood, my blood, running tracks down my back, pooling into the hollow of my collarbone and teasing my arm with its warmth.

My vision blurred.

I needed to stop the bleeding, needed to find something to staunch it with. My hands, maybe. But my hands were also covered in blood.

My knees buckled.

Ansel caught me, holding me upright and staring wide-eyed at the gaping wound René had left. The vampires stared ahead at nothing and no one, their gazes empty.

"Lena," Ansel whispered.

Ansel.

I took a gurgling breath and extricated myself, managing to stay on my feet.

A scream broke the silence.

The vampire scratched at its breast as sobs wracked its frame. Another voice joined in the anguish, then another and another until the great hall was filled with the violent symphony that was the mourning of the undead. The vampires crawled, scraping across the ground to their master's remains. No, not to their master, I realised, as one moved past the first littering of ash.

They were crawling to me.

Ansel said something, but it was lost to the screams. I took in the panicked set of his features, watched as his mouth moved.

"Can you run?"

The first vampire reached out to grasp my ankle.

As fast as I could, I ran.

I made it across the room, down the stairs, and to the servants' quarters. In the corner of my eye, I saw a shadow crouch at the stairs and start to count the rice grains.

I was a stone's throw from the opening in the gate when I collapsed, blood swiftly dampening the grass beneath me. My entire side was dyed crimson.

Stay awake, I told myself. Blood gurgled up my throat. *You have to stay awake.*

Ansel would come soon. The depth of his rage had been enough to slaughter a legion of healthy vampires, let alone a hall full of René's abominations. He would be washing off the ash for days.

I groped for the pendant beneath my collar. Inside it, Ansel's blood appeared black. I pulled at the fastener, but my fingers were brittle and slippery. A whine escaped me when it wouldn't open, and eventually, the pendant fell from my limp hands.

My heartbeat pulsed through me. I could feel it in my forehead, my neck. It was slow and shallow, the beat of a drum about to tear. I didn't know if he was real when he arrived. By then I was shaking uncontrollably, hearing sibilant whispers rise from the soil.

"The stars are bright," I said to him. Or I attempted to say. My tongue was heavy. I blinked, and the stars melded together to form a silver sky.

Ansel leaned over me. His hands were on my neck.

What was he doing? I couldn't feel it.

I watched him for what could have been seconds or an eternity. The tears on his cheeks were the colour of moonlight, and I couldn't help but think it was the prettiest colour I'd ever seen.

A bit of red by his jaw marred that colour. I decided to tell him so.

"There's something on your cheek," I slurred, bringing my hand up to wipe away the red flecks, but they melded together. I wiped again. It was a giant smudge and—and how was there more red now than when I'd started?

"Ansel," I tried, but he hushed me, forcing his wrist into my mouth.

I gagged at the taste of his blood. It seeped over my lips and up my nose until I couldn't hold my breath anymore. I coughed it up, my own blood mingling with it.

I'm dying. I'm going to die.

I didn't say goodbye properly, not to anyone. Markus would come back, and I wouldn't be here. Trudi and Hugo would get married without me. My own father would probably never hear of my death.

Ansel would leave me behind, would have no choice but to live on without me, immortal as he was.

"Swallow it." Ansel pushed his wrist deeper into my mouth. "Quickly, you need more. Drink it, Lena, *drink*."

I swallowed as much as I could, but it was difficult. My throat wasn't working properly. The pain was seeping away, leaving the temptation to shut my eyes and rest. My eyelids fluttered.

The sound of shouting in the distance broke through my exhaustion.

I bit down on the inside of my cheeks and focussed on Ansel. Dread pounded through me, despair rank on my tongue. After such a long time fighting tooth and nail, trying to hide the pain from everyone, trying to fool myself that I could be like them, it would be this moment that inevitably shattered me. The moment I lost.

But I would not shut my eyes.

I would not rest. Not for the peace it might bring, not for the Dawn Lord, not even to see my mother again. I would not die tonight. Not for anything.

I made a decision, one that'd been rooted in the back of my mind since I first met Ansel. It was why I'd clung to him. His existence was beyond death. He was everything I wanted, not only in a person, but in life: strength, vitality, and hope for something *more*.

I loved him. I wanted to stay with him. I wanted to live forever.

"Do not die," he begged, holding my face between his hands, "for I cannot follow to where you will go."

He looked ashen. Broken again. Distantly, I wondered if I was the only one to ever see him beg.

"Do it," I said through chattering teeth. The night air was ice against my skin. "Do it, Ansel."

I met his desperate gaze. Gave him permission.

Somewhere close by, a bell chimed.

I thought Ansel would ask me if I was sure. That he would hesitate and ask if I really wanted to lose my soul. I should have known better.

Both of us would have traded my soul for an eternity together.

Ansel did not hesitate. He bit down where René had, claiming the spot for himself. It didn't hurt—or maybe it did, but everything else just hurt more—and when he started to drink, I almost laughed at the way it tickled, except I had no energy left to muster.

I blinked slowly.

About twenty feet from us, Father Snow stood by an apple tree. Ernst's son was there, and the butcher's daughter, and all the other people from the inn at Haycock.

Come with us, their haunted eyes seemed to say. *Come.*

Oddly enough, Father Pentaghast was also there, away from the crowd. By his side was a blond man I didn't recognise. He held a silver bell.

Come with us.

Ansel pulled out, cradled my neck, and the people disappeared.

Everything disappeared.

CHAPTER TWENTY-TWO

Burning. Aching. Torment.

There was no outside world anymore, only my broken body and the vicious, insistent pain.

The passage of time was relentless. Without end.

All that I knew was stripped from me, the darkness feasting on my mind. My blood boiled my organs until they became dense. My bones clicked, cracked, and regrew. My gums buzzed, and I thought I was going to have to pull my teeth out one by one. Excruciating as the pain may have been, it reminded me that there was something more than the obsidian void that surrounded me.

Smell was the first sense that came back to me—rotting leaf litter and something metallic—then sound and touch.

A breath here, a caress there. The pain began to fade.

I felt as though I'd been dug out of hell, but not all of me had made it. Like I'd walked through a refiner's fire and lost the useless parts of me.

I felt ... reborn.

I opened my eyes. A demon held me in his arms.

For a moment, I wondered if he had been summoned to take me back to that scorching place, but he didn't seem inclined to move. He rocked me gently, humming. We were in a wide grassy area, at the foot of a towering castle.

"Am I dead?" I asked. My voice was a wisp of sound, weaving itself through the air and into oblivion.

The demon lowered his gaze, and my breath caught.

"Oh dear," he said, "you are a bit muddled, aren't you? Don't worry. That will pass."

Dark as the sky was, I could see with perfect clarity the tear stains on his cheeks and the blood that marred his jaw and throat. That same blood saturated my dress, crinkled it, and turned the fabric a rusty brown.

Saliva filled my mouth.

"Who am I?"

The demon smiled. Nothing good could ever come from that smile. "You will be a *queen*."

"Queen?" I considered. "That's not my name."

"No. You are Lena."

"Lena." The word was familiar, and I slipped into it, images and flashes of memory awakening. "Lena," I said again. "And you're Ansel. You're a vampire."

The demon's—Ansel's—gaze was heated as he whispered conspiratorially, "Now you are, too."

I nodded, knowing I had been something earlier, something weak and sick and searching, and that I was entirely different now. It occurred to me that where there should have been a wound on my arm, there was now only smooth skin. Where there should have been a scar on my palm, there was only a thin silver line.

I blinked. The action was disjointed. Unnecessary. I did it again.

The scar on my palm.

Ansel.

Now you are, too.

I inhaled shakily. "I'm alive. I'm alive."

"You are." His pleasure was almost greater than mine.

I could hear screams and primal, inhuman noises coming from the castle. They hurt my head. "People are in our castle," I noted, still reeling from the realisation that I felt *good*.

Ansel lifted a shoulder. "A few of René's creations were still alive when the villagers arrived. I did not linger any longer than necessary."

I pretended I understood. Names, words, and faces were vaguely familiar but were overcome by an ache in the pit of my stomach, made worse by the sight of my bloodied dress.

Ansel helped me to my feet, and I tensed instinctually, waiting for something. Dizziness or fatigue.

I need not have worried.

"Lena?" Ansel asked, wearing that same unsettling smile. My attention caught on his fangs, and I brought a hand to my own mouth, feeling the sharp points there. I cut my thumb on them, then watched as I healed.

No wonder my gums had hurt so fiercely.

Ansel chuckled. "They suit you. I knew they would."

The rushing of footsteps from the castle interrupted us.

A priest paused in the open doorway, his black vestments shredded across the torso. The man next to him was filthy, ash littered throughout his beard. I grimaced at the way it bounced between the hairs.

I could see all he was and all he would ever be with perfect clarity. Did people always look so bland?

"There you are," the filthy man said, stalking towards us.

"Do not be a fool, Peter," the priest called. His gaze met mine, and his expression fell. "Now that *is* a sad story." The words were quiet, said to himself, yet I could still hear them.

Hesitantly, I waved.

"What a tease you are," Ansel said to me as the man named Peter reached us, wooden stake in hand.

"Filthy vampire whore," he spat. He cocked his elbow back.

Ansel caught his arm. "Go on," he said, tightening his hold until Peter's bones started to crack. "I want to look you in the eye as you abase my beloved."

Peter's scream of pain was animalistic.

"So you're the runt brother, hmm? The elder one was done in by his own stupidity with those traps."

"It was you!"

"Of course it was me." Ansel bent his head, so they were nose to nose. "But really, bear traps with a compartment of holy water? I've been keeping my eye on you both, and I can't even begin to describe my disappointment."

I exhaled through my nose, frustrated that I couldn't understand the conversation and just who this Peter and the priest were. A surgical room came to mind, with shouting and the rank smell of infection, but the specifics eluded me.

Ansel's eyes narrowed. "You were the one who put those marks on her, weren't you? You are the reason she came to me grazed and hollow. I could fill a river with the blood I've spilt in my lifetime, but yours is the blood I will enjoy spilling most of all."

Peter was screaming curses at us in between calling for help from the priest, but the other man had disappeared.

Strange. I hadn't heard him leave.

"Wait," I said. Ansel looked to me, attentive. "I'm hungry."

"That may be so, but you do not want this one, my darling."

"Do not tell me what I want," I hissed. The ache had spread from my stomach to my head.

Ansel raised his eyebrows. "All right. I overstepped." He tapped the back of Peter's wrist, and the stake fell from his hand.

Peter's face was flushed and damp with sweat. His nose was running.

"Are you sure?" Ansel asked. "He is unappealing."

I wanted blood—*needed* it to sate the ache. I caressed my fingertips down Peter's neck, following the arch of his throat. The thrum of his pulse beat into my skin until I could feel it throughout my entire body.

Ansel placed a hand on his hip and sighed. "I'd prefer it wasn't a man, but do what you must."

I pulled Peter's jaw to the side and bit down hard. His skin gave like butter beneath my fangs. The blood was hot and syrupy, and I swallowed mouthful after mouthful, heaving gulps I could barely control. My body sang at the warmth that entered it, at the sheer relief. At the life that ran through me.

Peter's struggle grew less until he was limp in my arms and his breath was a faint wheeze. My mouth tingled as I drew away. I licked my lips, trying to pick out the flavour.

"Have you been drinking honey mead?" I asked.

Peter fell to the ground.

Ansel nudged his prone form with a foot. "I don't think he's quite able to answer you at the moment, darling."

"I guess not. I didn't drink that much, did I?"

Ansel's answer was to wipe my bottom lip. "You missed a spot."

"So did you."

"Hm?" He prodded his chin. "Ah, yes, but this is your blood. I'd prefer to keep it on me a little longer."

I sniffed, curious, and stood on my toes to lick the dried blood from his neck—before spitting it out on the grass. "That *burns*." Not only that, it tasted disgusting. "Was that really my blood?"

"It's the garlic."

"You drank that?"

His fingers fluttered across my collarbone. "Hurting for you was my pleasure."

The words made me shiver.

I was about to ask him who the priest was and why the inside of the castle had gone eerily quiet when, out of the corner of my eyes, I spotted a four-legged form on a log in the forest.

"A lizard!" I rushed past Ansel, manoeuvring through the hole in the gate with ease. My feet moved swiftly and exactly as I wished them to; there were no misplaced steps. I cleared the distance with unnatural speed and examined the log. The lizard was nowhere to be seen.

"Lena." Ansel was laughing. "Where are you going?"

I spun to face him, beaming. "There was a lizard here. You didn't see?"

"I did not."

"Oh. It must have run away from me. I don't think that used to happen."

He looked me up and down, bemused, but happy to oblige. "I am not sure. I do not think lizards frequent the night."

I listened for the scamper of feet, the slithering of a tail. Had I only imagined it? The thought left me irrationally crestfallen.

Ansel stilled, scanning the sky. "But look," he whispered, "isn't this even better?"

A large, black bat sailed down from the sky and landed on my arm. She climbed over my shoulder to dig her claws into my back, chittering as if in welcome.

"You are a night creature now," Ansel said. "Forget about the day keepers. They are not worthy of you."

I hummed, twisting my arm back to rub between the bat's ears. She peered at me from her upside-down perch. "You are very sweet, aren't you," I said, trying to ignore the way she smelled like a damp hairball.

Grains of dirt blew across the tree roots. The sound of the river, far away as it was, rushed through me.

"What is it?" Ansel asked when I pulled a face.

"The sounds and smells are very distracting."

"Aren't they just? They like to niggle at you from the background, even at my age."

I craned my neck and studied him, trying to place the emotion tangled within his voice. "You're happy," I concluded.

His expression was coy, on the verge of laughter again, and I wondered if I was missing something. "An understatement if ever I heard one."

"I like you being happy, but I don't think it's always a good sign."

"I cannot deny that."

The bat's claws tightened on my back abruptly before she took flight and disappeared amidst the treetops. I made to follow her through the forest but caught a new scent in the air. "Is someone coming?"

"Oh, Dawn Lord save me," Ansel muttered as two people emerged at the tree line.

The girl was about my height, and the boy had a shock of auburn hair that complemented the deep bruise across his cheek. They were both panting—arguing about something.

The boy pulled the girl's hand, but she pushed him away and picked up her skirts, intent on her path.

"Hello," I said when they were about to pass by us unawares.

The boy screamed.

"Lena!" The girl rushed to embrace me. "What happened to you? Are you okay? This isn't your blood, is it?"

I patted her gingerly on the back. Was it my blood? Most likely. I didn't think I should tell her that, though.

Ansel was watching the boy's indecision about where to look with a sardonic twist to his mouth. I was going to ask what amused him, but the girl was still talking.

"I know you said to stay inside, but I just couldn't, not when you were out here by yourself. What was I thinking, giving you a knife?" She stepped back, gesturing wildly with her hands. "And then I remembered what you said about the servants' quarters, so we went to see if we could find you—that horrid man from the clinic had collapsed there—and when we found this in the bushes, I just didn't know what to think." She pulled a necklace from beneath her collar, holding it out to me.

I screamed and hunched into myself as what felt like pure, unfiltered sunlight stripped the skin from my bones.

"Lena?" The girl sounded unsure.

"Cover it," Ansel bit out, shielding me with his cape. I could sense the source of pain in her hand, unmistakable now that I'd experienced it.

There was a shuffling noise, and the pain slowly disappeared.

I peeked around the fabric. The girl had hidden the necklace behind her back. I felt it pulsing, trying to reach me.

Ansel lowered his cape, and I inspected my body. Whatever that was, it had burnt through the fabric. My undergarments were visible in some places, the skin of my torso in others.

The boy looked like he was about to be sick.

“That hurt more than the garlic,” I said, breaking the silence. “What was that?”

“Something I should have buried.” Ansel glared at the girl, and annoyance flared through me.

He shouldn’t be looking at her like that. I had once … I had once told him not to.

I said to the girl, “I know you. We like each other.”

“I’m so sorry,” she whispered as tears streamed down her cheeks. I liked the way they smelled, slightly spicy.

I smiled at her.

The boy *was* sick this time. He doubled over, leaning against a tree trunk. Ansel made a sound of sympathy next to me, and I hid my mirth. I remembered throwing up like that. The memory prompted the couple’s name.

“Are you okay, Hugo?” I asked. He didn’t answer, retching as he was, but hope flittered on Trudi’s face.

“Yes, it’s us! Lena, we’re your—we’re your family.”

Ansel rolled his eyes.

“My family.” I cocked my head. “But you’re not like me.”

“Well, no, but …”

But that was okay. I could fix that.

As if he knew what I was thinking, could sense I was about to move, Ansel clasped my hand. "Ah-ah-ah. Not these ones."

"But I like these ones. They should be like me. Night creatures."

"Yes, but then they would follow you around, and we'd never have a moment's peace."

I found myself nodding along with him. "And they wouldn't like it."

"Yes, that as well." His thumb brushed the back of my hand. "Are you full? Do you need more?"

"No, I'm full," I said, watching as Trudi wiped her tears and Hugo wavered on his feet. Something had changed in Trudi's expression.

Hope had been overshadowed by devastation. It occurred to me why.

"You love the Dawn Lord. You think I'm evil." I ran my tongue along the bottom of my teeth, and she flinched. "But I'm still me, Trudi, and I'm not sick anymore. You don't have to be sad."

Hugo grabbed Trudi's shoulder when she went to touch me again.

It irritated me.

She smells good. Let her come back, just a little closer.

"I'm so sorry," she said again. "I should have done more. I should have noticed sooner."

"Noticed what?" I looked to the sky, growing bored with the conversation. Maybe the bat would return once they left?

She didn't answer.

"Hm? Trudi?" I clasped my hands behind my back and rocked on the balls of my feet. "Noticed what?"

"Nothing," she said eventually. "It doesn't matter anymore. You look happy, Lena."

"That *thing* is not—" Hugo started, but Ansel spoke over him.

"She does, doesn't she?"

Hugo's face was pallid as he glanced between us all.

"I am happy," I said. "You should go lie down, Hugo. Your colouring's all funny."

Trudi swallowed. "You want us to leave?"

"We'll go." Hugo's voice was firm, but he couldn't hide the stench of his terror.

Ansel huffed, and it reminded me of a bird ruffling its feathers. I was surprised by how quiet he'd been throughout the whole exchange. He was probably bored too, by now.

Ansel said, "As entertaining as it would be, and as much as I would like to see it, she is not going to tear you limb from limb. Go, and leave us in peace."

I thought about that and decided I'd allow it. He could have the illusion of control for a little while. Too much too soon and he might feel unloved.

And I did love him. I remembered that much, at least.

"Bye." I blew a kiss. "Make sure you both get some rest."

Trudi was sobbing, emitting little squeaks. "I love you," she said. "I love you."

I shook my head and laughed. “There’s no need to cry about it.”

“Trudi,” Hugo whispered, urging her to leave.

She met my eyes once more, a wobbly smile forming at the corner of her lips. She turned and started stumbling through the undergrowth, Hugo at her heels.

I watched them go. “Do you really think they’d hate being like me? I think they’d be pretty.”

Ansel watched them as well, a strange look on his face. Finally, he answered, “I think you would regret it. Once you remembered, you would grow to hate yourself. And me.”

I accepted that answer. Besides, if Ansel turned out to be wrong, I would simply come back for them later.

Grinning, I stretched my arms over my head. “So? Where to next? The Holy City? We could make stops on the way—be proper tourists!”

Ansel caught my hand mid-air, twirling me around as though we were dancers.

And I could be one if I wanted.

I could be anything.

Anyone.

He pulled me to him, running a hand down my back, and saying, “We will stop wherever you wish. Do and be whatever you wish.”

My heart thudded in my chest, propelled by excitement and a desire for what was to come. My limbs were strong, my skin icy to the touch. I wanted to look in a mirror, even if it was void of reflection, because then I’d know for certain.

This wasn’t a dream. No more hiding, no more fear.

No more sickness.

My mind was still hazy, but if I was certain of one thing, it was that I felt more alive in death than I ever had in life.

I kissed Ansel then, laughing as my fangs clicked against his and drew blood from his bottom lip.

"Come," he said, breathing heavily. "Let us leave now. We do not want to run into any more of those pesky villagers."

"They could be dessert." I was only half-joking. The mention of the villagers spurred contradicting emotions within me: affection yet betrayal. Strangely enough, I was more inclined to act on the latter.

Ansel shook his head fondly. "You are *magnificent*."

I shrugged because it was true. Power wrapped around me. The shadows of the forest strained to touch me, wanted a piece of me.

Anything in this world was mine for the taking. Complete and utter freedom at my fingertips.

Ansel kissed my palm, lips lingering on the silver scar. "Come, my darling. Eternity awaits you."

Together, we walked into the night.

EIGHTEEN MONTHS LATER

The parade reminded him of the night they first met. When the village had been dressed up, grotesque and gaudy and blood stricken. It was one of his favourite memories, if only because of what had eventuated the following months. He thought to say something to her, went to whisper in her ear as they walked through the throngs of spectators, but decided against it at the last moment.

She hated mention of that village. Said it made her feel ill.

They walked together, arm in arm. He could feel the mortals' gazes on them, lapping up their presence. They had been in the Holy City for nearly six months and had inadvertently become trendsetters amongst the middle class. Women lightened their hair and men pierced their ears. It would be amusing if it wasn't so repulsive.

He'd never liked a copycat.

Lena stopped at a street corner, in the shade of a hat boutique. She was wearing her modest green dress, the one he'd commissioned a year ago at a town they'd briefly stopped by on the way. She wore it in an effort to not stand out, he knew.

It amused him. She stood out wherever she went. She always had.

She had settled into her second life quickly. Oh, she mourned for a while, but he knew all that was good about eternity, and she quickly grew strong and alive and too wild for grief. She was as she'd always been, but now she was more. She was *everything*. The scorching sun, the singing moon, the smell of ash and blood, honeysuckle and myrtle trees.

"My goodness," she breathed, leaning over the taut white ribbons that acted as a barrier. "The church has really outdone itself."

He nodded in agreement.

The outfits, the decorations, even the horses pulling the gilded carriages, were all of the finest quality. He may have even been impressed, but then, this was the Holy City, known for its golden spires and mosaic floors. What held it all together was the blood of the lower class, and the nobles fed on that blood more eagerly than any vampire.

The nobility had left their hidey-holes to come out and stare with the rest of the city. Even the imperial family watched from the palace balcony, waving and smiling as though they'd actually wanted this day to come to pass. It was no secret they were at odds with the church. Tyrannical organizations vying for dominance never did anyone any good.

The Holy City and its sycophants took any and every opportunity to celebrate, but this was a special occasion, even for them. Something about a high priestess being ordained, the first in decades. He did not particularly care. They could ordain a snail, call it an oracle, and still it would make no difference to him.

He had abandoned any belief of the Dawn Lord as a boy when his house was burning and his mother swayed in the wind.

He had a new deity now.

"She looks a little young to be a high priestess, doesn't she?" Lena said, tilting her head as the priestess's open carriage neared. "And a little bloodthirsty, too."

He did not look; it was of no interest to him. Instead, his gaze caught on her neck. The evil within him—the evil that loved her, fawned over her, for a reason that had never seemed to matter enough to dissect—wanted to pull her collar down and cup the scar he had left when he drew her rancid blood into himself.

He had never told her this, but the night she died, he'd kept his fangs in her for longer than necessary, ensuring he would leave a mark. His tears had soaked into the open wound of her neck. He made sure his blood had, too.

He had hoped, not that she'd get hurt—never that—but that an event would come to pass in which she had to make a choice. But it had been a little too close, and the taste of her death was an oily fear he still couldn't wash from his mouth. He doubted the taste would ever leave.

It was, perhaps, the only time in his immortal life he had ever known true terror.

Death had been there, next to that unholy priest.

Just as Death was there now, trailing behind the new high priestess's carriage like a jungle cat stalking its prey.

Ansel pitied the girl. Death was a handful at the best of times. To be romantically pursued by him would be most unpleasant.

They did not linger once the parade had finished. The crammed buildings may have offered plenty of shade, but the sun was about to rise, and staying out was too great a risk. The peasants watched from the corner of their eyes as he and Lena returned to their apartment. It was a quaint place, three storeys in total with large windows they could look upon the city through.

He did not know how long they would stay. As long as it took for them both to grow bored, he supposed. He doubted that would be anytime soon if Death was here.

Death *had* been the one to make him a vampire, after all. Ansel himself may have offered the deal as he lay dying—his soul for immortality and then a favour for a favour—but Death was the one to accept. Death had needed someone to keep the vampires in check for some vague and contrived reason.

For the good of humanity, was it?

He couldn't really remember. Again, he did not particularly care.

He'd tried to mediate the situation a century ago by killing the vampires who'd exposed their existence in what was now called the Legion Plague. René always had been slow in understanding the bigger picture, that the deaths of his beloved children were nothing personal.

What *was* personal was the conversation Ansel had had with Death not long after the event. Apparently, it hadn't been the time for all those people to die. The vampires were unnatural. The deaths they caused were not meant to be, and the world was now a worse off place because of it, *et cetera, et cetera.*

Death had tried to take him then, in a fit of rage, but there was no soul left in him to take. That didn't mean it hadn't stung.

His century-long slumber had been intended to regain his strength and as a bit of a peace offering to Death—a *'let me get out of your way'* of sorts. Ansel didn't enjoy going back on deals. He understood Death's wrath.

Still, the reaper tended to overreact at times. He was irrational, but Ansel liked that about him. Unpredictable people were either rare flowers to enjoy or thorns to be plucked away, and Death fell into the former category.

René had fallen into the latter. Though, to give credit where it was due, his presence had been useful at first—had given those inept vampire hunters a worthy distraction.

A smile formed on his lips at the memory.

He followed Lena into the bedroom, watching as she untangled her hair from its coronet. She didn't like having it up for long. He speculated it was the village girl in her.

"Do you have anything you want me to include?" she asked, sitting at her writing desk.

Ah, yes, the letters. She and the other village girl still kept in contact. The couple had been recently wed, and the correspondence was therefore more frequent than ever.

He would have happily attended the wedding if Lena had so desired. Would have pretended to grovel and then given a large monetary gift, if only to demonstrate how far Lena had been taken from their grasp. Lena would not see it that way, but he did not intend for her to.

"Tell her that she must get with child within the next season or two if she wants the baby's name day presents to arrive free of mould. Who knows what will become of them in the dank depths of a cargo ship if we wait for next summer?"

She was shaking her head before he finished speaking. "I'll just tell her you say hello."

She wrote her letter, nibbling on the end of the pen subconsciously every few lines. It had been a full day since she'd eaten.

"Hungry?" he asked.

She pulled the pen from her mouth and frowned at the bite marks. "Looks like it."

Lena wasn't overly picky with food—some vampires would rampage if they didn't get their male-butler-in-his-early-twenties-with-high-blood-pressure-and-a-lisp—but she still needed to eat regularly and well if they didn't want her to become like René's most recent creations.

"I'll fetch you something."

"Thank you," she murmured.

He went down to the kitchen, wrinkling his nose at the lingering smell of fear and perspiration. They had been returning from the theatre a few nights ago when they found their latest meal, a middle-aged man harassing a woman in a dark alley. Lena had taken one look at him, with his untucked shirt and open trousers, and pronounced him their blood source for the foreseeable future. Ansel had knocked the man out, hiked him over his shoulder, and locked him in their apartment's larder.

He would have been happy with any person off the street, but it made her happy to search for the rotten ones.

And he was *very* good at making her happy.

He filled a bowl with blood and pulled a soup spoon from the drawer, stirring as he went back upstairs. Lena once admitted to missing food and the way it crunched beneath her teeth. She then laughed and joked she could always gnaw on someone's bones if it bothered her that much.

She said the most adorable things.

She was lying on the canopied bed when he entered, her letter folded and sealed with red wax on the nightstand. Her eyes were shut.

The image was almost identical to the night of their first meeting: her lying on the bed, and him waiting for her eyes to open. He had considered killing her then, for she had seen too much. Never mind how impressed he was with her survival instincts, for not many people had met him in a state of bloodlust and lived to tell the tale. What saved her in the end was her easy access to blood.

And now he was devoting his existence to her.

How very fickle the fates are, he thought, sitting by her side.

"The blood will be cool soon, darling."

She inhaled deeply before sitting up and taking the bowl. "Thank you." She licked the spoon, and he admired the way the blood shone on her tongue. "The dawn is bright. Even in the shade, it burned."

"That it did." He went to the window and drew the curtains back, sighing. It was always this way when the sun ascended: agitating and incomplete. The brightening sky was cloudless and brushed over with hints of pink and grey. He watched in the distance as men carried crates across the harbour. The water spanning into the horizon was black and still.

Even from across that massive body of water, Ansel heard them sometimes. The vampires that would join them. They whispered in his mind, pleading with him.

He would not let them join, not yet.

He would build an empire for Lena to reign over, but these first few years when she was growing, learning to be immortal—these first few years belonged to *him*.

"Ansel?" Her voice was not a balm. If anything, it made him ache. Perhaps because she found amusement when he came to her, begging to be satiated. She always knew when he was about to crack. Only then would she relent. "Ansel." She came to stand beside him. "What are you looking at?"

He smiled down at her. "Nothing of consequence, although it seems time is once more trying to leave us behind."

It was a common feeling. The world moving forward, always progressing, trying to escape those that would cling to it. The mortals would live through their rotting world, day in and day out, celebrating their priestess and moving their crates for no other reason than to find purpose in life. To dive into their fallibilities with the comforting knowledge that Death would one day grant them rest. They despaired in life and surrendered to their fate.

The consequence of being a vampire was the opposite: to outrun fate, only to despair in eternity.

Not for him and Lena, though. They revelled in it.

Lena shut the curtain and grinned. It was an expression she never used to make, self-assured and anticipating, with a wicked edge. "Again? I suppose we'll have to go do something about that."

She took his hand, and it did not matter where she intended to take him. He was so used to leading, but only by her did he want to be led. Because if this was to be their eternity together—her skin against his, the taste of her in his mouth—it would never be long enough.

ACKNOWLEDGMENTS

Firstly, to my parents. Thank you for supporting me, and thank you for being proud. You've always encouraged me to follow my dreams, and I hope I can learn from your kindness and pay it forward to everyone I ever meet.

Thank you to Mads, Ingrid, and Julia for being my guinea pigs (the experimental kind, not the literal kind). Alyce, for your endless generosity and my insanely awesome logo. Mary, for being so excited and believing in me harder than I believe in myself. Grace Zhu, for such beautiful cover art. Yaz, for always being open to talking ideas with me. Nicholas and Aunty Jenny, for your enthusiasm. Campbell, for your hilarious texts. Nellie, Nuada, and Lugh for the snuggles.

To both my Heavenly Father and my Saviour, Jesus Christ, with whom I would be nothing without. I am so unbelievably blessed. Thank you so, so much.

And lastly, to Amy. This book happened because of you. Thank you for your time, support, and wisdom. For those walks by the creek where you take my ideas and untangle them, then make them even better. You are the bee's knees, the ant's pants, and the cat's pajamas all rolled into one. You are the Meleth to my Luthien. Basically, you are the best.

ABOUT THE AUTHOR

Amanda is an avid storyteller who is susceptible to insta-love in the presence of villains. She emerges at the midnight hour to write but is otherwise found serving her cat overlords. Amanda's other loves include Japanese popular culture, Dungeons & Dragons, painting, and music. *Death of the Dawn* is Amanda's debut novel.

Website: www.amandavking.com
Instagram: @amandavkingauthor

www.ingramcontent.com/pod-product-compliance
Lightning Source LLC
Chambersburg PA
CBHW020257120726
47904CB00001B/230